Killer Art

By
C L Thomas

www.DarkInkBooks.com

This story is dedicated to my family who encouraged me to keep writing even when I didn't want to write. They stood by me and beside me when I was at my most unlovable and picked me up when I was down and broken. Without my family there would not have been a story to tell or a life worth living.

Chapter 1

Overhead a cloudless sky looked down upon Bruce Westman, a private investigator from East Hartford Connecticut, as he opened his eyes for the first time that morning. He sat awkwardly in the front seat of his car, an old, worn-down Ford with rust eating away at the rocker panels. Sunlight streamed in through the dirty cracked windshield, causing his eyes to tear and his head to ache as he struggled to right himself and puzzle out the insistent tapping sound invading the interior of his vehicle. Moaning softly, he glanced out his driver's side window and saw Mr. Davis, a fifty something African American neighbor from across the street, standing on the other side of the door looking back at Bruce through the filthy glass that separated them. Through blurry eyes, Bruce watched as one of Mr. Davis's thick white bushy eyebrows rose into a questioning judgmental glare. Bruce grimaced, swallowing hard against the lump in his throat and raised a hand to show he was all right.

"I'm fine, Mr. Davis," Bruce groaned, slapping at the door handle twice before successfully grabbing onto it and opening the door. Mr. Davis stepped back from the door with his lips curled back in a disgusted look that aged his face more ten years.

"You're going to kill someone one day if you don't get help, young man," Mr. Davis said, wagging a crooked arthritic finger at Bruce as he exited his car. Bruce glanced back over his shoulder and saw that his car, an old blue Ford Escort that had seen better years, was parked right up against a telephone pole. Some of the blue paint had even transferred to the pole, leaving a deep scrape and small dent in the passenger's side front quarter panel.

"Gives it character," Bruce grumbled, getting back into the car. He reached for the keys dangling from the ignition and gave them a twist. The car coughed twice and started. He waited for Mr. Davis to take another step back before backing away from the telephone pole and parking the car correctly alongside the curb. "Better," he muttered to Mr. Davis without bothering to look at him as he exited the car and headed for the apartment door. The old man stood on the street watching him go into the building, shaking his head.

Bruce's one-room apartment was on the second floor of a three-family red brick building with gray siding in front and a small dilapidated one-car garage in the back. The apartment was on Garden Street in East Hartford next to an overgrown field. A rusted out pickup truck stood on blocks in the center of the field, left there forgotten among the weeds and stunted trees long before Bruce took up residence in the building. Bruce climbed up the single flight of stairs, stopping in front of the door at the top. The paint on the door was peeling and chipped, showing the age of the building and the several coats of paint that had been applied over the years. There were old pry marks dug into the doorjamb where the door had been forced open at one time. Bruce fumbled with his keys for a moment before releasing the deadbolt.

He heard the raised voices of the couple downstairs as he stepped through the door, trying not to hear what they were arguing about.

The small one-room apartment was almost completely dark. Only a thin line of light managed to penetrate the thick blackout curtains over the two windows that looked out onto the alley and the street below. His unmade bed was close to the apartment door, cocked at a slight angle. He tossed his keys onto the thin mattress without pausing on his way to the bathroom.

Bruce walked out of the bathroom a few minutes later rubbing at his forehead with a closed fist, trying to remember the night before. He checked his pants pockets for any clues and only found a crumpled up five-dollar bill and some loose change.

"Fuck me," he whispered to the dark shadows that surrounded him. Images slowly came to him as he stood there in what passed for a living room/bedroom. What came to him was fuzzy, but somehow, he remembered going out to a bar on the west end of Hartford. The night had started early but what happened at the end was beyond his reach. This loss of time was becoming all too common and scary. *Maybe next time you'll kill someone or maybe yourself,* he thought.

Bruce walked over to the kitchen sink and poured a glass of water from the tap. Even though it was lukewarm, it still felt good going down, washing away the scratchiness left over from the night before. He set the glass on the counter beside the sink and opened the refrigerator. The white light inside the box hurt his eyes and he had to back up a step as he eyed what was on the shelves. It wasn't much to look at. There was a greasy white bag with a half-eaten cheeseburger inside and a handful of fries, an out-of-date milk carton, some moldy cheese, and some long-wilted spinach that had somehow managed to make its way in there, though how he had no idea. A six pack of beer sat on the lower shelf drawing his eye, but he wrinkled his nose at it, and closed the door. After a moment, he opened the freezer compartment and was greeted by a blast of ice-cold air. Thick mounds of white pockmarked ice clung to the sides and top of the icebox looking like ancient glaciers crawling down toward the sea. The only other thing inside the freezer beside the ice was a frosted bottle of vodka leaning against the wall.

"Fuck it," Bruce grumbled, reaching into the icebox and snagging the bottle before closing the door. The ice-cold glass felt amazing in his hand as he walked back across the room to his bed. He fell onto the mattress clutching the bottle tightly to his chest and fell quickly to sleep before he could manage to take a drink.

Bruce woke several hours later, the bottle still clutched to his chest, no longer cold to the touch. After setting the bottle on the floor, he stumbled across the dark room to the bathroom and turned on the shower before peeing in the toilet. The bathroom steamed up quickly and he stepped beneath the hot spray, enjoying the way it loosened his muscles. When the water started to grow cold, he shut it off and dressed in some semi-clean clothes that he had tossed into a small dresser beside his bed. With his shoes on, he searched the floor for his keys and found them sticking out from under the bed beside the forgotten bottle of vodka he'd taken out of the icebox. Scooping up the keys, he eyed the bottle on the floor and decided to grab that too.

Downstairs, he saw Mr. Davis walking his dog, who at the moment was pissing on a tree across the street. Mr. Davis looked over at Bruce as he got in his car and drove off into the late New England summer, where the days were warm, and the nights were just beginning to cool. Bruce drove with his window down, enjoying the breeze on his face. At the stop sign, he reached across the seat and opened the glovebox, nestling the bottle of vodka safely inside. Turning right onto Park Avenue, he drove toward Main Street and the Dunkin' Donuts that awaited him there. His mouth was already watering at the thought of a hot coffee and glazed donuts.

Chapter 2

Matthew Shovinski sat on the front steps of his parents' house looking out at the street as the last few days of summer drifted slowly by. He was thirteen years old and sad to see his free time draining away with school set to start on the following Monday. He wasn't looking forward to returning to school and starting the eighth grade. It wasn't that he was a bad student, he just got bored with what they were trying to teach him sometimes. School had always seemed so slow as he sat there in the classroom listening to teachers drone on about things that had happened hundreds of years ago. None of it was ever challenging and sometimes he found that he knew more about things than most of his fellow students, and even a few of his teachers. School was just something he had to do, not something that he wanted to do.

Matthew's summer hadn't been anything close to normal. In fact, it had been downright traumatic for him and his family. At the beginning of the summer, he had agreed to help a private investigator named Bruce Westman with a case he was working on at the town swimming pool, Globe Hollow. At first it hadn't been anything all that much. He showed Bruce where the older kids hung out behind the Hollow. The Hollow was what the locals called the Manchester Town pool.

Matthew hadn't thought much of his helping Bruce until his sister Mary had been kidnapped by a serial killer stalking young girls in and around Manchester and East Hartford. On the night Mary went missing, Matthew called Bruce, and together they found the serial killer's house and rescued his sister. During the rescue, Matthew picked up Bruce's gun while Bruce was fighting with the killer. He shot and killed the man that had kidnapped Mary before he had a chance to kill Bruce. There hadn't been much thought in the actions took that night, it was like he was on autopilot, but the nightmares afterward still hadn't gone away.

A smile creased Matthew's face as a blue Ford turned onto his street, interrupting his thoughts. It was Bruce coming to take him to his weekly visits with Father Murphy at Saint Christopher's Catholic Church. Matthew and his parents had agreed to the weekly visits after the shooting, and Matthew had come to look forward to those visits with the old priest. The donuts and the basketball games afterward didn't hurt either. For an old guy, Father Murphy was pretty good on the court.

"You ready?" Bruce asked, pulling to a stop at the end of the driveway. Matthew stood and turned around to face the front door.

"Mom, I'm going with Bruce to the church," Matthew shouted through the screen door.

A woman came to the door and stuck her head outside. She smiled at Bruce and waved a hand. Bruce waved back as Matthew sat down in the passenger seat of his car. "I'll have him home by four," Bruce said.

Matthew's mother nodded, slipping back inside the house without saying a word.

"She worries," Matthew said as they pulled away from the house. "She won't let Mary or me out of her sight yet."

"She has every reason to worry with a little shit like you running around," Bruce said, heading down the street.

"Screw you," Matthew said, looking out his window. Bruce smiled and turned left at the stop sign. Matthew reached for the donuts on the seat between them.

"Back off the donuts, buddy," Bruce said, a hand hovering over the bag.

"Nazi," Matthew said and sat back against his seat.

"How's your sister doing?" Bruce asked, crossing back into East Hartford.

"She's as bratty as ever, I guess."

"You know what I mean," Bruce said. "She's missed the last few sessions with Father Murphy."

"I know. She's been real busy getting ready for the start of school and practicing her driving. I don't think Mom will ever let her get her license but there's always hope."

"She needs to keep up the counseling, Matthew," Bruce said, pushing the bag of donuts against Matthew's leg. "One," he said, turning at a light. Matthew opened the bag and selected the one chocolate frosted donut among the glazed donuts. Half the donut was gone in one bite.

"Try to enjoy it, don't inhale it," Bruce said, laughing. Matthew mumbled something around the mouthful of donut before shoving the other half in there. Matthew and Bruce arrived at the church several minutes later, parking at the back of the lot behind the annex building beneath a tall maple tree. Bruce grabbed the donuts from the seat as he exited the car and Matthew carried the two coffees. They walked alongside the large white building to the front of the church, climbing the steps to the thick beige doors. Inside the vestibule, Bruce dipped his fingers into the holy water and crossed himself. Even though he wasn't reared Catholic, Matthew dipped his fingers as well and crossed himself before following Bruce into the sanctuary.

Everything about the church seemed so large to Matthew. The ceilings were peaked high overhead with large beams as thick as trees cutting horizontally over the sanctuary. Massive stained-glass windows depicting religious scenes marched up either side of the sanctuary beside row after row of pews. The walls beneath the windows were lined with hand numbered wood-carved pictures displaying the Stations of the Cross. The altar, dominated by the crucified Christ nailed to a large cross, appeared as if it were a thousand feet away from where Matthew stood just inside the doors.

As Matthew stepped inside the shadow filled sanctuary, he immediately felt an invisible weight settle over him that left him feeling intimidated, and just the tiniest bit scared. He imagined that giants would have felt more at home inside the sanctuary than mere mortals like him. It was as if he were unworthy to be standing there in such a holy place.

"Bruce, Matthew, I am so glad to see the two of you," Father Murphy said, stepping through a doorway at the back of the church. "You caught me doing some organ repairs as you walked in," he said, smiling at the two of them.

Matthew smiled back at Father Murphy as the priest shoved a wrench into a pocket and wiped his hands on the front of his jeans. It seemed kind of unnatural to see a priest wearing jeans and a t-shirt.

"I'll meet you guys in my office in a few minutes after I wash up," Father Murphy said.

"See you there, Father," Bruce said, starting up the center aisle. Matthew followed him.

Father Murphy walked into his office a few minutes later wearing basketball shorts, white sneakers, and a blue t-shirt. He looked nothing like a priest, and he didn't look anything like a sixty-five-year-old man either. In his hand he carried a Coke in a can.

"So how is everyone?" Father Murphy asked, sitting down behind his desk. Bruce set the donuts and coffees on the desk.

"Good," Bruce said, grabbing one of the cups.

"I'm okay, I guess," Matthew answered, taking a sip of his Coke.

"Still having those dreams?" Father Murphy asked, inspecting the donuts as he spoke. He made his selection, pinching the donut between two fingers. Bits of sugared glazed rained down on his desk before he took his first bite.

"Yeah. Maybe not as much but, yeah," Matthew answered, looking down at the tops of his sneakers. He felt uncomfortable speaking even though he liked the priest pretty much.

"Tell me again what they're about," Father Murphy asked. Matthew sighed and shifted in his seat. He hated having to relive everything.

"I see myself shooting him again and again, except it's always in slow motion so I can see the bullets flying through the air. I can see them spinning as they slam into his body, punching holes where there had been no holes. I see his eyes open wide and he points a finger at me even though bullets are entering his body and exploding out the other side. He points that finger at me and screams."

"What is he saying, Matthew?" Father Murphy asked.

"He calls me a killer. He tells me I killed him and that I'm just like him now. Sometimes he says I'm going to join him in hell one day," Matthew explained, studying the can of Coke perched between his legs. He isn't willing to admit it to either of them but he's scared. The dreams terrorized him more than any bully at school ever could.

"Are you a killer, Matthew?" Father Murphy asked, nibbling on his donut. Crumbs continue to tumble down on the desktop like fallen snow.

"I guess not," Matthew answered, frowning.

"What have we talked about all this time, Matthew?" Father Murphy asked.

"You told me to shout back at the man in my dreams and tell him that he's the killer and I am a child of God."

"Do you believe that Matthew? It's important that you do," Father Murphy explained. "The words themselves have no power, it's the faith behind the words that empower them. All you have to do is take control and believe."

"I don't know," Matthew answered, lifting his coke and taking a sip.

"You're the hero, Matthew. If it hadn't been for you, your sister and Bruce might not be here today, and that horrible man might still be out there killing innocent children," Father Murphy explained. "I firmly believe that, and so does Bruce." Bruce nodded. Matthew let out a long slow breath. His hands were fidgeting in his lap, but he appeared just the tiniest bit more relaxed than when the conversation started.

They continued talking for the next thirty minutes about school and how he was going to react when friends and classmates asked about what had happened. Father Murphy assured him that everything was going to be alright and that what he was going through was normal. At the end of the counseling session, they walked out the back door, stepping out onto a basketball court behind the church. The court was situated between the sanctuary and the annex building and hidden from the street. There was only one hoop on the court but that was enough.

They played ball for over an hour, and in the end, Matthew always beat both of them.

Chapter 3

Jeffrey Westman, an investigator with the Manchester Police Department and the older brother of Bruce Westman, sat behind his desk reading an original offense report on a domestic violence assault case. The patrol officer who had written the report had done a good job collecting the facts of the case and Jeffrey had no trouble understanding everything that had happened. According to the report, the husband had come home from a night out at a local bar on Hartford Avenue to find his wife screwing another man on the couch. The husband threw the man out the front door and then proceeded to beat the living shit out of his wife. After she was unconscious, he went on to rape her vaginally and anally. He had beaten her so badly that there was a tube down her throat to help her breathe. Both of her eyes were swollen closed, and her nose was a mashed mess that was never going to look the same. The first officer on scene found the wife unresponsive in a pool of her own blood, piss, and shit. The husband was sitting in a chair drinking a beer in front of the television. He wore a pair of stained white boxers, a white wife-beater t-shirt, and a sad vacant stare on his face. He offered no resistance when the officer cuffed him. The wife was transported to Hartford Hospital by ambulance without ever regaining consciousness.

"Cheaper to divorce her, asshole," Jeffrey mumbled, setting the report down on his desk to answer his cellphone. "Westman," he said into the phone, glancing down at a photo of the wife taken at the hospital. He moved the folder over the photo so he wouldn't have to look at it while he spoke on the cellphone.

"Officer Westman, Special Agent Shelby," the person on the other end of the cellphone said. Agent Shelby was the FBI agent who had been assigned the Hollow case earlier that summer. Jeffrey frowned, wondering what he wanted.

"What can I do for you, Special Agent Shelby?" Jeffrey asked, glancing down at the assault report.

"I'd like to take you out for lunch today, if you have the time," Agent Shelby explained. "My treat, if that helps."

Jeffrey looked at the wall clock across the room and figured why not. "Where you at?" he asked, dropping the folder into a desk drawer, glad to be rid of it for the time being.

"I'm driving over the Charter Oak Bridge right now, so you can pick it and I'll Google my way there."

"You like pizza, Special Agent Shelby?" Jeffrey asked.

"Of course, I do."

"Nick's Pizzeria on Hartford Avenue in thirty minutes," Jeffrey said.

"I'll see you there," Agent Shelby said, disconnecting the call without saying goodbye.

Jeffrey arrived at Nick's twenty minutes later, parking in the back lot. Since his was the only car back there he knew Agent Shelby hadn't arrived yet. He picked up his cellphone from the seat of the car and called his brother.

"What?" Bruce answered on the third ring.

"Wow, you never cease to amaze me with your people skills," Jeffrey said, shaking his head.

"Fuck you, how's that for people skills?" Bruce asked. Matthew broke out laughing in the seat beside him.

"You got the kid with you?"

"Yeah, we just left the church, I'm taking him home," Bruce answered.

"Well, you'll never guess who just called and asked me to go to lunch," Jeffrey said.

"Jennifer Aniston, and she wants to have your baby," Bruce said. Matthew started laughing even harder. Bruce joined him.

"Screw you and the little shit stain sitting beside you," Jeffrey said. "It was Agent Shelby of the *FBI*."

"Maybe *he* wants you to have his baby," Bruce said, laughing even harder. Matthew sounded like he spit out a mouthful of food he was laughing so hard.

"Can you be serious for a fucking second, please?" Jeffrey said.

"Fine, fine. What does Federal Agent Shelby want with you?" Bruce asked, getting himself under control.

"Don't know, but when I do, I'll call you back and fill you in," Jeffrey explained. "We're meeting at Nick's in a few minutes for lunch."

"Okay, I'll talk to you when you're finished," Bruce said, disconnecting the call without saying goodbye to his brother.

"Asshole," Jeffrey mumbled, dropping the phone back on the seat. Agent Shelby pulled into the lot a few minutes later and parked beside Jeffrey. Jeffrey got out of his car and closed the door, watching as the large black man exited his vehicle. He admired the way Shelby scanned the parking lot without making it too obvious that he was looking for danger. He had skills, for sure.

"Westman," Agent Shelby said in a deep voice with just a touch of southern roots.

"Agent," Jeffrey said, shaking his hand. "Come on, the pizza is good here and we should have the place to ourselves." Agent Shelby curled his upper lip a bit and followed Jeffrey into Nick's Pizzeria. They sat down at a table that offered a clear view of the street outside. Agent Shelby sat with his back against the wall, forcing Jeffrey to sit with his back to the door.

Nick Jr, an overweight African American male, stood behind the counter in his customary blue jean overalls and sauce-stained apron. His chef's hat was tipped to one side and eyeglasses dangled against his chest.

"Jeff," Nick grunted, eying Agent Shelby.

"Hey Nick, large pie with three meats and two beers," Jeffrey said. Agent Shelby raised an eyebrow but kept silent. Nick grunted and opened a glass cooler, removing two Bud Lights from the top shelf. He walked the two beers over to the table and set them down, eying Agent Shelby as he did so.

"Problem?" Agent Shelby asked, grabbing his beer.

"Not yet," Nick said, his mustache twitching as he spoke. He walked slowly back behind the counter and began to prepare the pizza.

"He could have gone pro, you know," Jeffrey said. "In high school, he was the best defensive end in the state, maybe in all of New England."

"What happened?" Agent Shelby asked, glancing at the large man moving around in the kitchen.

"Car accident after graduation shattered his femur in his left leg. He was never the same after that."

"Tough break," Agent Shelby said.

Jeffrey took a long pull off his beer and set the bottle down on the table. He looked over at Agent Shelby, studying the man's face for a moment. "So, why the call?" Jeffrey asked as the other man set his beer down. "I'm not aware of any nutjobs running around right now beyond our usual."

"I got a case in the Bronx that I'd like your brother to consult on."

"I don't think my brother likes you enough to consult on a case," Jeffrey said, playing with a napkin on the table.

"I just want to pick his brain. We've got no leads and I thought maybe he could help like he did earlier this summer."

"If you recall, you didn't want his help back then," Jeffrey said.

"And the truth is, I don't want it now, but we're stumped. We've got the beginnings of a task force ramping up but there's very little real evidence to go on. This guy is good. He moves like a ghost. I thought maybe I could show your brother what we have and see if he can come up with something we're missing. Six girls are dead, Westman, and I'm a bit desperate at the moment."

"You must be," Jeffrey said, grinning across the table as Nick set the pizza down. They ate in silence.

Jeffrey polished off the last slice and finished his second beer. Agent Shelby belched and pushed back from the table. He dropped two twenties and a ten and followed Jeffrey to the door.

"Hey, Nick, good as ever," Jeffrey said before walking out. At the cars, Agent Shelby handed Jeffrey a business card.

"Talk to your brother. Have him give me a call and I can be here in two hours."

"I'll talk to him tonight and let you know something in the morning," Jeffrey said.

"Thanks," Agent Shelby said, opening his door and sitting down inside his car. Jeffrey watched the agent pull out of the parking lot and head down the street.

Chapter 4

William Morrison, Billy to his mother, had always been a stranger among people. Even at a young age he thought that only he and his mother were the only real people in the world. Everyone else, from other children to adults, just existed on the outside to entertain him. People were really nothing more than things in the world. They moved around like ghosts or the fragile wisps of dreams. One minute they were here and the next minute they were gone. It had always been like that for Billy, an only child growing up in a single parent household. He had his books and his tiny green plastic Army men to play with, and no one else.

At the age of nine Billy found a kitten in the woods behind the apartments where he grew up in Milford. It was a thin orange tabby with patchy fur and only half a tail. A few battle scars marked its body where other cats had tried to kill it or chase it off from wherever it had wondered into. The cat was thin, looking hungry and pitiful. Its eyes were large round green orbs and it yowled constantly as Billy approached it beneath the tall pines and ranging oaks.

"Hello there, kitty, kitty," Billy said, holding out his hand. Being wary of humans, the young cat backed up, hissing at the intruder. Billy paid it no mind and pounced on it in a flash. After receiving several scratches and a small bite, he managed to capture the cat. As quick as he could, he tied the kitten to a young sapling with one of his shoelaces and sat down to watch. The cat hissed and spit as it paced back and forth pulling on the shoelace but to no avail. Watching it struggle like that somehow made Billy feel powerful and in control.

After a few hours, Billy grew bored watching the cat struggle against the shoelace. He took a small pocketknife from the back pocket of the blue jeans he wore and unfolded it. As if sensing danger, the cat paused, eyeing Billy, who sat just outside its reach.

A thin smile spread across Billy's face as he stared back at the cat, licking his lips. The knife sat balanced in his hand while fractured sunlight glinted off the tiny blade causing sparks to explode in his eyes. Billy's nostrils flared wide, and goosebumps covered his arms. The ground felt unsteady beneath his feet as if the world had suddenly tilted. He had to reach out to a tree to steady himself as all at once the world and everything around him became very real. Maybe for the first time in his life everything around him suddenly felt solid. He looked back at the cat wondering how something so tiny had managed to penetrate his world like an invading force. It scared him and excited him at the same time.

Billy knew what had to be done. The cat hissed and spit at him again in its rage. Billy ignored it as a wonderful charge of electricity raced through his body. The hairs on his arms tingled. More goosebumps covered every inch of exposed skin on his body. He became aware of the dusty musk of the forest floor as it tickled the hairs in his nose. The world around him stood out in bright relief, like an artist's painting with the cat at the center, his own creation. His own piece of art.

"You're not real," Billy whispered at the cat. "You're not even a cat after all, you're just a thing, an object that only exists in my mind to do with as I please."

Billy released his grip on the tree and stood over the cat, unzipping his pants, allowing them to fall down around his ankles. His pissed stained underwear followed. A yellow stream of urine burst from the end of his penis, splashing onto the cat. The animal hissed and spit, arching it's back as the hot yellow fluid soaked its fur. Billy paid it no mind as he continued to empty his bladder until the last dribbles of urine fell at his feet. Reaching down quickly, Billy snatched the orange tabby up by the throat. The cat's eyes bulged out with bright red lines disappearing back into the sockets. Billy giggled and squeezed tighter. The cat looked like something from a Saturday morning cartoon as its eyeballs began to bulge out from the sockets.

"Beep, beep," Billy whispered, laughing into the cat's face as it clawed at his hand. He didn't notice any of this though as he stood there with the cat dangling from one hand, peering into its terrified eyes. He didn't see the thin lines of blood welling up on the back of his hand. None of it made any difference as he brought up his other hand and pressed the tip of the knife's blade against the cat's exposed stomach. The animal hunched up its back legs, claws extended, but these were wasted efforts. The tip of the knife pierced the skin beneath the thin coating of dirty fur between the rows of tiny nipples.

Blood welled up around the tip of the knife and then Billy plunged the blade all the way in until it was buried inside the kitten. Blood squirted out from the wound, running over the handle and over the back of his hand. The cat screamed a thin high-pitched shriek and Billy squeezed its throat even tighter, choking off any further cries. He felt bones cracking and breaking beneath his hand. The feeling sent shivers of pleasure through his body.

The cat's tongue slipped out from its mouth and hung off to one side as it took a final breath. Billy watched the animal die. The stink of urine and shit filled his nostrils. He saw the life leave its eyes and it left him feeling dizzy. Everything around him became brighter, more alive than it had ever been before. He had created something from nothing, and it made him feel more alive than he had ever felt in his entire short life.

Billy held onto the cat for several minutes after it had died, enjoying that feeling of being alive. He looked down and saw that his penis was poking out in the breeze. *I have a hard on,* he thought. Looking at his body, he saw blood splattered on his hands, his arms, his shirt, and his naked legs. Droplets were even sprinkled inside his underwear. The blood on his exposed skin was still warm, comforting. The lifeless body of the cat slipped from his hand, tumbling to the ground as he stepped back, admiring what he had just created. *I made art like those dead painters,* he thought, feeling proud of himself.

Billy cleaned himself off later as best he could with leaves before pulling up his pants. The afterglow of what he had just done was still there, but the world around him was returning back to its unreal focus again. Billy was sorry to see it all go because for the first time in his lonely life, he felt like he was a part of something more. The hardness was still there inside his pants, and it felt so good, though at nine he had no idea why. He continued to stand over the cat's lifeless body for several minutes until he felt his penis finally begin to shrink, and with its limpness, the world returned to its normal state of dull colors. Billy cried real tears for the first time in his life as he stood there. He didn't cry for the cat or because of what he had done, but because he was alone again in the world, and he knew it would always be that way.

Once his tears had dried Billy gazed down at the cat and realized he had to do something with it because even though he knew the world wasn't real, there were things out there in the world that could still hurt him. He knew and understood on some level that the things that populated his waking dreams, the ghosts that created his reality, would look down on what had been an incredibly wonderful experience for him.

Billy buried the cat beside the sapling, pausing to pee on its grave. He washed his hands off in a stream that ran through the trees half a mile from where everything had happened. He cleaned off the knife in the water and made his way back home. He wanted to make sure that he was there before his mother got off of work. He wondered as he walked through the woods if he should tell her about what had happened and how it had made him feel. He decided not to though when he stepped out onto the sidewalk. *My little secret*, he thought as he walked along between the shadows of people who weren't really there.

The next day Billy returned to the sapling and urinated on the spot again where he had buried the cat. He wasn't sure why he felt the need to do this, but the desire was overwhelming, and the longer he put it off, the greater the release when he finally gave in to it. It was like he was marking his territory, claiming that spot as his own special place.

Billy stood there over the unmarked grave for half an hour with his pants and underwear down around his ankles enjoying the feeling of the afternoon breeze as it worked its way through the trees. It felt so good against his exposed skin, and the hardness between his legs. He felt so in control of everything as he stood there. The world existing all around him, just for his pleasure. His stiff cock twitched and tingled as the world caressed it over and over. The feeling was amazing, and it was all his to enjoy.

Over the next two years, Billy returned many times to that spot in the woods to pee on the cat's grave. He didn't understand why it felt so good to do so, but he always felt better afterward. It calmed him down and settled the urges that seemed to flood his body. Over time, he added to the makeshift graveyard as he came upon strays wandering around the city. He always kept a treat of some kind in his pocket so he could catch the creatures and bring them out to his secret spot in the woods. He craved that feeling he got when he took the life of something. It became a need for him. A way to bring the world into focus so he could continue to exist.

Chapter 5

"What?" Bruce said, answering his cellphone on the fourth ring while he drove over the Route 5 bridge into Hartford. The sky overhead was dark, and the river below invisible, but Bruce knew the water was there. He knew it like he knew that oxygen existed. It was always there moving through and around him, calling out his name like some ancient spirit. The Connecticut river was a constant for him in an ever-changing world. It saw him off to the war in the Middle East, and it saw him return home a broken and shattered man, his soul torn by the horrors of war.

"You're such an asshole," Jeffrey said.

"Fuck you too," Bruce replied, shoving his thoughts of Iraq to the back shelves of his mind. "What did the high and mighty Federal Agent want?"

"He wants you to consult on a case he's working in the Bronx," Jeffrey explained.

"Why me? I thought he found me annoying."

"Oh, I'm sure he does. You have that effect on people, but I think he wants you to do that shit that you do, if you know what I mean?" Jeffrey said.

"When do you have to have an answer?" Bruce asked.

"In the morning. I told him I'd talk to you tonight and call him back in the morning. You don't have to say yes, you know. You can always tell him to get fucked."

"Got it," Bruce said, hanging up on his brother without a goodbye. Across the bridge now, he came to a light and turned left onto Wethersfield Avenue. He drove for a short distance before turning left again onto a side street and pulling into a small parking lot behind an alternative club called Chez Est. He locked his car and walked around to the front of the building. The traffic on Wethersfield Avenue was still heavy even though it was well after ten o'clock. Bruce watched several cars drive by on the street wondering where everybody was headed to in such a hurry. A shiver ran down his back and more thoughts of Iraq forced their way off the shelves of his mind. He frowned, closing his eyes and wishing them away.

"Not now," he mumbled, turning and walking down a short flagstone path that ended at a flight of steps. He took the steps and walked through an archway.

The entrance to the club was set back from the sidewalk with a small outdoor seating area on a brightly painted porch. Colored lights sparkled overhead. Several men stood outside enjoying the warm late summer evening, talking and drinking. Bruce ignored the men outside, walking into the club through a pair of dark double doors.

The bar was what some people might call cozy comfortable. The lights were low but bright enough that you could see your way to the bar or the tables that circled around the dance floor. A red brick backsplash accented the wall behind the bar giving it a western feel, like a saloon from the turn of the century. Backlit bottles of alcohol were lined up in front of the brick wall on double wide shelves. Bruce walked up and sat down on a stool.

"Double shot of vodka with just a splash of pineapple juice over ice in a short glass," Bruce said to the bartender that stood in front of him.

"Got it," the bartender replied, walking off to make the drink. He came back a moment later, setting the drink down on a white paper coaster. Bruce handed the bartender his credit card.

"Run the tab," Bruce said, picking up the drink and taking a long sip.

"Sure thing," the bartender said, walking away with the card. Bruce ignored him and spun around on his stool to see what was going on in the club. He cradled his drink in his lap feeling the cold touch of the glass through his pants.

In one corner of the bar was a pool table surrounded by several men. A line of shiny quarters was lined up on the side of the table like soldiers ready for war. A mirrored disco ball hung from the ceiling, spinning slowly around over a small dance floor. Two girls slow danced on the floor making out with each other. The night was still young.

Most of the tables in the club were filled with couples and groups clutching drinks and eating bar food. Soft rock and roll music played from speakers overhead. The music wasn't so loud that you couldn't hear yourself speak but it was loud enough that you could dance to it if you wanted to. Waiters and waitresses roamed the floor, taking orders and collecting money.

Bruce spun back around as he finished his drink, catching the bartender's attention and pointing at his glass. The bartender nodded and brought another vodka and pineapple juice.

"Hey, can I get an order of wings and pizzelles?" Bruce asked as the bartender set the new drink down in front of him.

"Sure," the bartender said, scratching something on a pad of paper and walking off to let the kitchen know it had an order. Bruce took a sip of his drink and spun back around.

"Is that chair taken?" a tall man in a black t-shirt and jeans asked. He had dark hair, blue eyes and a thin mustache. He wore glasses with small lenses that sat high on the bridge of his nose. He was about a hundred eighty pounds of athletic muscle that stretched the limits of his solid black t-shirt.

"No, it's not," Bruce said. The guy sat down and waved for the bartender.

"Mark," the man said, holding out his hand. Bruce took it and gave it a shake.

"Bruce."

"Nice to meet you, Bruce," Mark said, smiling a smile that showed off all his perfectly straight, perfectly white teeth. Bruce swallowed hard and smiled a thin tight-lipped smile back at him. He finished off his drink and ordered another as the bartender set Mark's drink down on the bar. The food came a few minutes later and Bruce shared his wings.

The next morning, Bruce woke up on a couch in a strange living room. A man stood in front of him holding out a cup of coffee wearing boxers and a black t-shirt. The coffee smelled amazing.

"You look like you could use this," the man said. Bruce took the cup and drained half the coffee in one long hot sip. He smacked his lips together before looking up at the man again. "Thanks," he said, setting the coffee cup down on the coffee table in front of the couch. Several magazines littered the table. Most were exercise magazines offering to make a new man out of you in thirty days.

"Mark," the man said, holding out his hand. "Just in case you forgot my name."

"Bruce," Bruce said. "How did I get here?"

"Well, I think the both of us had a bit too much to drink last night and you came home with me, but before anything could happen you passed out on my couch," Mark explained, smiling his perfect smile. Bruce scratched his forehead.

"I see," Bruce said, picking up the coffee again and finishing off the cup. It was very good coffee, not the typical store-bought brand. "I'm sorry about that. I mean I'm not normally like that," Bruce said, wondering why he felt the need to explain himself.

"It's no problem, Bruce, neither am I," Mark said without looking him in the eyes. "So, look, I have to go to work."

"Yeah, yeah I get it," Bruce said, standing up slowly. "Do you remember if I drove here?" Mark shook his head. Bruce nodded. "Could you drop me back off at the club then, so I can get my car?" Bruce asked, feeling his front pocket for his keys. Thankfully they were there.

"I can do that," Mark said.

"Bathroom?" Bruce asked, suddenly needing to pee really bad.

"Second door on the right," Mark said, pointing in the direction of the kitchen. Bruce followed his finger to the bathroom and did what he had to do in there. He splashed a handful of cold water on his face and ran his fingers through his hair, combing it back. He looked in the mirror and grimaced.

"You look like shit," he whispered at his reflection, turning off the light and walking out of the bathroom.

"So, about that ride?" Bruce asked, standing in front of the kitchen. Mark wore pants now and a clean shirt.

"Let me grab my stuff and we can go."

Mark drove a red Toyota Camry that was only a year or two old. The interior was spotless, and the paint was unmarred by scratches or dents or rust. Bruce wasn't sure why, but he felt a little uncomfortable riding in the car. They rode in silence all the way back to the club. Mark pulled into the side street parking lot and stopped behind Bruce's old Ford. It was the only car in the parking lot, and it looked so sad beside Mark's Camry.

"Look," Mark said as Bruce opened the door. "I know we had a rough start last night, but I'd like to get to know you better if you want."

Bruce looked back at Mark, unsure how to respond. He had never been in a relationship with someone, and he wasn't sure he was ready to be in one now. Most of his encounters since he had returned home were simply drunken one-night stands, no fuss no muss, but he was attracted to this man. He sighed and pulled out his wallet, withdrawing a business card.

"That's my cell on the front, call me if you want to get together for a meal and a drink. I'm not saying it'll be anything other than that but it's all I can do right now." Mark took the card and looked down at it.

"You're a private investigator," he said. "I can see that. You're always watching everything, studying everyone." Bruce smiled and got out of the car.

"Thanks for the ride and for not taking advantage of me last night," Bruce said.

"Well, I won't say I wasn't tempted, but if I'm anything, I am a gentleman," Mark said. Bruce laughed and closed the door. He watched Mark drive off and wondered if they would ever see each other again. He was surprised that he wanted to, but he knew in his heart it wasn't a good idea. He was so broken and fractured that a relationship with anyone was probably a bad idea.

Bruce drove out of the parking lot a few minutes later heading for the Route 5 bridge. The sky overhead was full of thick gray clouds that thankfully hid the sun. It wasn't raining, but he didn't think rain was all that far off either. From the passenger side of his car his cellphone rang just as he was driving across the Connecticut River. He glanced down at the water as he answered.

"What?" he asked.

"Ah, as nice as ever. No wonder you're so alone," Jeffrey said from the other end of the phone.

"Prick," Bruce replied, slipping on his sunglasses even though the sun wasn't out.

"That's big prick to you," Jeffrey said, chuckling. "So, look, do you have an answer for Shelby?"

"Tell him I'll hear him out, but no promises. We can meet at the station this afternoon and talk."

"You have breakfast yet?" Jeffrey asked.

"I haven't even gone to bed yet," Bruce said.

"Well shit, did you get her name at least?" Jeffrey asked, laughing.

"No, I didn't," Bruce said, hanging up on his brother while feeling guilty for lying to him.

Chapter 6

While Bruce was busy getting drunk the night before, a blue Ford Ranger pickup was prowling the streets of Hunts Point in the Bronx, New York. The pickup truck was a nondescript, older model Ford that didn't stand out among the other vehicles prowling through that section of the city. It moved slowly up and down the dimly lit streets, its sole occupant scanning the sidewalks for his next target. He felt like a lion stalking the bushes for its next prey. Approaching the next corner, the driver lifted his foot from the accelerator and slowed the vehicle down. He saw someone standing alone beneath the soft yellow glow of a streetlamp. In his eyes, she stood out from all the others. Somehow, for some reason he couldn't explain, she was just more real than all the others. Like a beacon, she called to him.

She stood there on the corner just at the edge of the circle of light beaming down from the overhead streetlamp, driving away the outer darkness. She wore a red tank top with faded white letters on the front, tight blue jeans, and filthy white high-top sneakers. Her lips were painted bright red and her kinky dark hair was pulled back in a severe ponytail. A stick-on faux diamond glinted in the light from the corner of her left eye like a star sparkling in the sky. She had that hungry look about her like someone waiting on their next fix. She kept nervously glancing up and down the street and scratching at her arms.

The driver of the pickup came to a stop at the curb, rolling down his window. The girl glanced behind the pickup once before walking up to the window and leaning down so she could see inside the cab. The pupils of her eyes were tiny black dots. This close to him he could see that she wore a thick coating of makeup, but it couldn't hide the circles beneath the eyes or the teenage acne that still populated the corners of her mouth. This close, she looked street old, but was probably only in her mid to late twenties. The man smiled at her with a smile that failed to touch his eyes.

"Whatcha looking for, baby?" the girl asked, her voice slow and husky. Up close her lipstick was cracked and dry with just a trace of it on her yellowed front teeth.

"I want to party with you," the man answered, his nose flaring, his tongue darting over his lips.

"How much do you want to party?" she asked, dipping down enough that he had a clear shot inside her tank top. She wasn't large breasted, but she knew how to advertise what she had.

"Forty dollars' worth of partying," the man said. The girl licked her lips slowly, again glancing up and down the street before opening the door.

"I think we can work something out," she said, sitting down in the pickup truck. She closed the passenger side door. The man grinned at her and drove off. In the glow of the streetlights his teeth were large and fierce looking, but the girl hardly noticed as she continued working at her arms with her chewed off fingernails.

The man parked his pickup truck behind a boarded up two-story brownstone that had seen much better days, when people wanted to live in and around Hunts Point. Now the brownstone was a dark boarded up building covered in graffiti and occupied by the homeless and the junkies too strung out to care where they got high. The man backed his pickup against a dilapidated rusted out chain-link fence strung up behind the brownstone, separating the building from an overgrown field. He turned his truck off and killed the lights. The interior was dark, but there was enough light inside so they could see each other.

"Take your pants off," the woman said in her husky voice. The man wondered if that was even her real voice or just something she used on the men she picked up. He hesitated at her request, and she reached across the seat and set a hand on his chest, tracing a line down to the top of his pants. She poked the tip of her finger into his pants, and he quickly did as she asked, shoving the pants down so they pooled around his ankles. The woman stroked the tip of his hard dick with two of her fingers as it sprang free of his under shorts. He groaned softly, and she lowered her face into his lap. The man rested his hand on the back of her head, keeping just enough pressure there as she bobbed up and down on him.

The man finished quickly with a loud grunt, keeping his hand on the back of her head and forcing her to take all of him in as he came. He didn't release her head until he felt himself begin to soften inside her mouth. She didn't complain or struggle to get free because she knew her place. His hand fell away as he slipped free, and she sat up wiping her fat red lips with the back of her hand. The lipstick was smearing across her face like congealed blood. The man glanced across the seat at her, thinking that she had the perfect mouth for what she had just done.

"Dick sucking lips," he whispered, his upper lip curling into a snarl. "You sure do have some dick sucking lips, bitch," the man said, pulling his pants up, ignoring the belt.

The woman frowned at the edge in his voice. She felt suddenly uncomfortable sitting there in the pickup behind the boarded-up brownstone. She fumbled for the door handle, thinking she could run up to the street before he had a chance to do anything, but the attack came too quickly. She felt something stab her. A tiny little prick at the back of her neck that felt like liquid fire racing into her body. She laid a hand across the spot as the man pulled back. He held something in his hand but in the dark cab she couldn't make out what it was. She tried to speak but words wouldn't come even though she told her mouth to move. Everything inside her head felt jumbled and twisted, none of it making any sense. Her tongue felt thick and rough like sandpaper. It seemed to be stuck to the roof of her mouth. A sweet, sickening odor flooded her nostrils. The gorge at the back of her throat rose and she thought she might vomit everything she had just swallowed.

The man watched as the prostitute struggled. He smiled at her, the way a teacher might smile at a stupid child who just can't seem to figure out the answer to a question. He enjoyed this part, watching them struggle. Watching them trying to figure out what was happening.

"You're such a fucking cow," he whispered. "You're a fucking whore who sucks cock and swallows cum," the man growled, but she was beyond understanding his words. Her hand fell away from the door handle that she couldn't seem to operate. She slumped back against the seat, her head tilting to one side. She tried to focus her eyes, but they couldn't seem to get anything straight. The world swam back and forth, and for a second, she thought she had scored some awesome shit, but then the world just disappeared, and she knew nothing else.

The man reached across the seat and touched her. He smiled at the softness of her body. He leaned her body forward and slipped his hand inside the back of her shirt, rubbing the smooth skin at her back. *Perfect*, he thought. *So real. She's going to be so much fun.* The man drove away from the alley.

Chapter 7

"Mr. Westman," the girl sitting at the front desk of the Manchester Police Department said cheerfully as Bruce stepped up to the door. She buzzed him through to the hallway on the other side. He nodded at her as the door slid closed. He couldn't remember her name for some reason even though he was familiar with most of the Public Service Officers at the station. She had only been on the job for a month or two.

"You can just call me Bruce," he said, walking past the open door where she sat.

"Have a nice day, Bruce," the girl said, smiling shyly at him.

"Thanks," Bruce said.

"Little Westman," an older man said, walking up the hallway with a cup of coffee in one hand and a diet Coke in the other. A bag of chips was pinched between two of his fingers.

"Hey, Mr. Watson," Bruce replied, stepping away from the door to the desk area.

"Did Angela give you any trouble?" Mr. Watson asked.

"She handled everything like the professional you trained her to be," Bruce answered. Mr. Watson nodded.

"I saw your brother in the back with that FBI guy who chewed you out that one time," Mr. Watson said, setting the drinks down on the front desk.

"Yeah, I know, that's why I'm here."

"Okay then, keep your cool with him, I don't want to hear that they locked you up because you popped him one," Mr. Watson said, sitting down with a grunt. Bruce smiled, nodded at Angela, and walked down the hallway. At the end of the long hallway, he stopped in front of a door with a handmade sign affixed to it that read, "Bullpen." Bruce walked through the door.

The bullpen was where the investigators caught their cases. It was a brightly lit room comprised of eight desks lined up along the walls. The desks were set up in groups of two, so they faced each other front to front. At the far end of the room was a chalkboard that flipped end over end. Written on the board in white chalk were the names of the investigators and the numerous cases they were working. Open cases were noted with red chalk and closed cases were noted with blue chalk and the date they were closed. The bullpen smelled of bad coffee, body odor, and dust. The overhead fluorescent lights gave the room an artificial glow that left everyone looking a sickly yellow color. Jeffrey sat at one of the desks along a wall and Agent Shelby sat beside it. Three other detectives were sitting at other desks in the bullpen talking on the phone or reading over offense reports.

"Hey," Jeffrey said, standing up from his desk. "Let's go talk in one of the interview rooms." Agent Shelby stood and turned around. He held out a hand and Bruce shook it reluctantly.

"I'm glad you came," Agent Shelby said, picking up a thick file from the desk and following Jeffrey to one of the rooms. Bruce walked behind them, feeling out of place. He hated being inside the police department and how it made him feel like an outsider. The fact that they rejected him because of his PTSD and the traumatic brain injury he received while serving in Iraq still pissed him off.

The interview room was a lightly painted green windowless cinderblock space with a gray and black industrial desk in the center. The desk looked like something picked up from a government auction on the cheap. Eyebolts stuck up through the top of the desk on one side, placed there to secure suspects to the desk during interrogations. There were three chairs in the room, two in front of the desk and one behind. A stark white light bulb in cased in a cage glared down from the ceiling, chasing away any shadows. A camera sat high in one corner, the tiny red indicator light, off at the moment.

"Cold enough in here?" Bruce said, watching Shelby and Jeffrey sit down in two of the chairs in front of the desk. Bruce decided to lean against the wall beside the door instead of sitting in the suspect's chair. His arms were folded across his chest while waiting for his brother and Agent Shelby to turn their chairs around so they could face him. Bruce smiled at their effort.

"Look, I know you and I didn't exactly hit it off," Agent Shelby said. "I know I can be an ass sometimes, but I want you to know that I take this job seriously."

"Yes, you're an asshole," Bruce said, remembering the day Agent Shelby tossed him from the station because he had the unmitigated gall to disagree with the supremely educated profilers at the FBI. Jeffrey glared at him. Agent Shelby cleared his throat.

"Anyway, I'd like to talk to you about a serial case in New York," Agent Shelby explained. Bruce glanced down at the file on the desk and nodded. Agent Shelby continued. "I'm not sure how you did what you did to catch that guy earlier this summer, but you have a talent, and I'd like to tap some of that if you're willing to work with me."

"Has my brother told you anything about me?" Bruce asked, glancing down at the file sitting in front of him. "About how I do what I do?"

"Not really, and truthfully, I wanted it that way," he explained. "Look, read through the file and see what you can see. Call me tomorrow and we'll talk. I'm headed back to the city, but I can be here in an hour and a half."

"I can do that," Bruce said, looking at the file again and feeling a little sick to his stomach. He knew what it meant to touch it, to pick it up, and he knew that he had no other choice. Agent Shelby pushed the file across the desk and Bruce leaned forwards and took it. The file felt like it weighed a hundred pounds sitting there in his hands. It felt like holding the stone tablets Moses received from God up on Mount Sinai, though he had a hard time picturing himself as Charleston Heston in *The Ten Commandments*.

"We think this guy has killed six women so far but we're only sure about three of them since June," Shelby said. "He has a taste for it now and it's only going to get worse if we don't figure out how to stop him."

"Your bosses okay with me looking this over?" Bruce asked, holding onto the file tightly in case Shelby changed his mind. Now that he had it in his hands, he didn't want to let it go.

"They don't know about you and they're not going to know about you," Shelby explained. "You're an outsider with only a thin connection to law enforcement. We're going to keep this quiet. I'm sticking my neck out here. I hope you can understand that?"

"Got it," Bruce said, glancing at Jeffrey. There was a part of his brain that was screaming at him to drop the file and walk out of the interview room, but something deeper, more primal, told him to hold on to it. He followed that deeper instinct. "I'll call you," Bruce said, walking out of the interview room.

"He doesn't look so hot," Shelby said several minutes later as Jeffrey walked him out to his car.

"He has his demons," Jeffrey explained. "He's amazing at what he does but it takes a toll on him."

"I can understand that," Shelby replied. "The profilers at the Bureau can only do this shit for so long before they begin to crack up. I'd much rather be the one who chases the bad guys than the one who has to figure out how his brain works." Agent Shelby sat down in his car and started the engine. "This is all between us, no one else." Jeffrey nodded.

"He'll call you," Jeffrey said. Shelby nodded and closed the driver's side door. Jeffrey watched him exit the parking lot and disappear down the street. After he was gone, he slipped his cellphone from his pocket and called his brother, but it went straight to voice mail. "Asshole," Jeffrey sighed, not bothering to leave a message as he walked back inside the police department.

Chapter 8

Bruce drove out to Wickham Park on the border between East Hartford and Manchester. He found a space to park near the top of the hill where he used to sled during the winter as a child. He remembered living for those days when the snow fell, and school was canceled. He would sit in front of the television with a bowl of hot cereal in his lap while the news played, waiting to hear if classes had been canceled because of the weather. Once he had confirmation that school was off, he would run outside and shovel as many driveways as he could for ten dollars a driveway before pestering his mother to take him out to Wickham Park so he could go sledding.

Bruce smiled at those memories as he walked across the small parking area and out beyond the pavilion with its stone fireplace and covered picnic tables. He sat down in the thick grass on the slope of the hill, looking out over the town of East Hartford. From where he sat, he could see clear across the Connecticut River, observing the Hartford skyline. The Travelers Tower stood out above everything, the top reaching for the clouds like a giant's sword held high overhead. The old Colt Armory building sat to the left, closer to the freeway, reflecting the sunlight off its famous blue domed roof with the golden horse rearing up at the top. Uneven bands of sunlight danced back toward the Connecticut River as it cut through the landscape that divided the Connecticut River Valley. It was peaceful and beautiful to see.

Bruce took a deep breath, enjoying the view in front of him for a few minutes before glancing down at the file resting between his feet in the grass. He was reluctant to open the file. He didn't want to have to see the horrors that it held.

"Hunts Point, Bronx New York," was printed in the center of the beige folder in large black block letters. Several numbers followed, most likely the case number assigned to the murders. In the upper righthand corner, a name was printed in smaller red type, "Shelby, Jerrod, Special Agent in Charge." Bruce sighed deeply, closed his eyes, and flipped the file open.

For the next hour, Bruce read copies of offense reports, autopsy reports, and studied crime scene photos. It was the graphic crime scene photos that got to him the most. The victims were all young women. The youngest, a seventeen-year-old runaway from Worcester, Massachusetts, and the oldest, a twenty-eight-year-old African American female with an extensive criminal record for everything from prostitution to minor drug possession charges. All the women were known prostitutes and suffered from neglect and drug abuse. Even the seventeen-year-old had needle marks between the toes of her feet where she shot up. It was all very sad and typical for the streets of New York City. The women were nothing more than the forgotten and discarded cast offs of society. Good enough to blow you or screw you but not for much else.

According to the profile, the killer was a white male in his late twenties to early forties. He was an organized and sadistic person who took his time with his victims. He liked to strip away large patches of skin from their backs. The FBI profilers weren't sure why he did this, though they suspected he was possibly keeping the skin as a trophy, consuming it as a meal, or using it as a sexual object. The profilers also believed that the killer was educated, though he probably worked some kind of menial job well beneath his level of education so he could hide and blend in with everyone else. They don't believe he's married or in a committed relationship. They suspect he lives close to the city but far enough away so he can take his time accomplishing what he needs to accomplish in private.

The medical examiner reported that the killer used a large razor-sharp blade to flay his victims. The blade had to be twelve to eighteen inches long, one to two inches wide, and had to have handles on either side so the killer could draw it down the victims back evenly. Time of death for each victim was approximately eight to ten hours after they had been skinned. Prior to death, the killer liked to bite his victims. Teeth marks covered their breasts and upper thighs. Each victim had traces of urine and semen in the wounds covering their backs and inside their digestive tracts. Several of the victims had DNA from different men inside their bodies making it almost impossible to pinpoint the suspect.

Bruce felt nauseous and set the file down in the grass between his legs. His hands felt hot and itchy, and sweat ran down the back of his shirt. The dark sky overhead felt oppressive as it bore down on him. He closed his eyes and took several deep breaths before opening them again. The world swam back into view. The cityscape drew his eyes. He forced himself to glance down the hillside at a young mother as she played with her child in the grass. A checkered blanket was set out in front of her with a few toys scattered on top of it. Bruce watched the mother and child for several minutes, allowing their ignorance of the world to wash away the horror that he had just read about. This scene before him calmed his soul. It was cleansing to see something so innocent at play in front of him. A smile played across his face as he picked up the file once more, opening it again and reading.

The three women they knew for sure that were victims were all found approximately twelve to twenty-four hours after they had died. Their naked bodies had been displayed for all the world to see. The killer wasn't shy about his crimes. He wanted to share them with the world. He was intelligent, and he wanted to show that intelligence off. The displays were like a giant middle finger aimed at the New York City Police Department and the FBI. The killer was speaking to all of us. It was as if he were saying, "Fuck you."

The twenty-eight-year-old African American female, the last victim found, had been found in Central Park. The killer had arranged her naked body there in front of a tree beside one of the jogging trails. She had been placed in a kneeling position with the fingers of her hands zip-tied together so she appeared to be praying. A rosary was wound around her hands with the cross wedged upside down between her fingers. The upside-down Jesus was positioned in such a way that he faced the woman. Her eyelids were superglued, so they remained open. The body had been found early in the morning by a jogger getting in a run before work.

A twenty-three-year-old white female with cotton candy pink hair had been found in a similar manner, kneeling in front of a tree in the middle of Joyce Kilmer Park in the Bronx. This victim had been listed as missing for the last three years by her parents. Once upon a time she had been a college student in New Haven Connecticut, and then she just up and disappeared one day before her sophomore year finals. Her parents had reported her missing. They had hired a slew of private investigators to search for her, but she hadn't been found until now. She had no arrest record, but like the others, she was believed to have been a prostitute. She showed no signs of drug abuse and appeared to be relatively healthy for the lifestyle she was living.

Bruce closed the file again and stood. He couldn't read about anymore sadness. He needed a drink, and he knew there was a half-spent bottle resting quietly in his glovebox. Looking out over the city once more, he felt worn and used. His eyes again fell on the mother and her child and suddenly he felt sorry for them. *Life is so fragile*, he thought. "Protect her," he whispered, turning away and heading back to his car.

By the time Bruce pulled in front of his apartment building on Garden Street the bottle from his glovebox was empty. He felt better than he had standing there on Wickham Hill. The file and all its horrors contained inside, sat on the seat beside him. Glancing down at it, it seemed to have lost some of its power. Bruce parked his car along the curb, managing to keep the car straight and out of the grass. He opened his door and stood, wobbling just the tiniest bit. The file still sat on the seat. He considered picking it up, but in the end chose to ignore the file.

Across the street, Mr. Davis was walking his dog and studying Bruce. The dog had its ass pressed up against a telephone pole squeezing out a shit. Mr. Davis held a small plastic bag in his hand. Bruce grimaced at the scene of the man and his dog. The idea of picking up a steaming pile of shit made his stomach roll.

"You just worry about yourself there, young man," Mr. Davis said, reaching down with the plastic bag. "I always pick up after my dog."

"Bully for you," Bruce said, waving quickly before heading into his building.

Bruce walked into his apartment and sighed deeply after closing the door. The room was dark. The blackout curtains that covered the windows allowed very little light to penetrate his humble abode, and he liked it that way. Bruce locked the door and tossed his keys onto the bed before heading to the bathroom. His cellphone rang before he managed to walk through the bathroom door.

"Son of a bitch," Bruce grumbled, slipping the cellphone from his pocket. "What?"

"So, did you read the file?" Jeffrey asked.

"Yeah, pretty morbid shit going on there," he answered, continuing into the bathroom.

"Yeah, Shelby let me have a look at it before you arrived," Jeffrey said. Bruce grunted and began to pee. "Are you in the bathroom? Oh man, do I have to listen to you pee?"

"You called, not me," Bruce said, flushing the toilet.

"That's fucking gross, man," Jeffrey said. "I bet you talk on the phone while taking a shit too."

"Whatever," Bruce replied, setting the cellphone down on the sink so he could wash his hands.

"Well, at least you washed your hands," Jeffrey said after Bruce picked the phone back up.

"Not washing your hands is disgusting," Bruce said, walking out of the bathroom. "So, did you have anything useful to add or did you just call to annoy me?" he asked, sitting down at the end of his bed and kicking off his shoes.

"Are you going to help him?"

"I don't know," Bruce answered. "I don't want to get involved in that shit again but at the same time that fuckwad is killing people out there and getting away with it. They have a bunch of evidence, I mean the guy isn't shy about leaving DNA behind mixed together with the DNA of other people, but they have no idea who he is or why he's doing what he's doing. He's trying to make a statement, though I'm not sure what it is yet."

"Look, sleep on it tonight and meet me for breakfast at Ryan's in Vernon, say around ten," Jeffrey said.

"Yeah, okay," Bruce said, disconnecting the call without saying goodbye. He left the cellphone on his bed and walked over to the refrigerator, opening the freezer door. He removed a frosted bottle of vodka from the freezer, twisting off the cap. The cold liquid felt incredible as it lit a fire in his throat before settling in his belly. He brought the bottle back over to his bed and began to drink. An hour later, he passed out. The bottle sat on the floor at the foot of the bed more than two thirds empty.

Around midnight, Bruce began to fall into a state of half-sleep and half wakefulness. He felt his mind drift drunkenly away until he stood unsteadily in the middle of a strange street in a strange city. Old worn buildings, dark and abandoned, lined shadow filled sidewalks between the glow of pale streetlights. Store fronts stood shuttered and padlocked against those with criminal intentions. The homeless lay sleeping curled up tight against the scarred brickwork on top of cardboard boxes or discarded newspapers.

On the corner beneath a streetlight a woman paced back and forth, always remaining within the pool of meager light. She appeared nervous, anxious, frightened. She wore a short black and white skirt that showed off the bottoms of her pale ass cheeks, red knee-high socks, white shoes, and a tight white t-shirt knotted at the bottom. She had big red hair like Julia Roberts in *Pretty Woman*, and a cigarette sticking out from the corner of her mouth. Curls of gray smoke drifted above her head like an evil halo. A man stood off to the side, halfway down the sidewalk beneath a closed storefront. He was an African American male dressed in all black with a New York Yankee's ballcap on his head. The woman on the corner, young, maybe an old nineteen or twenty, kept looking back at the man as cars drove by.

Bruce watched as a small pickup, blue or black, or some dark color, stop at the corner where the girl with the red hair stood. The passenger side window slipped down, and the woman walked up. She spoke with the driver, always keeping an eye on the street. She glanced back at the man beneath the storefront, and he gave her a short quick wave of his hand. She turned back and spoke again to the driver of the pickup. Bruce couldn't make out what was being said. The passenger side door opened, and in the glow of the interior light, Bruce caught a glimpse of the driver. He was a large white male, not fat but not well built either. He wore a gray shirt that fit tight across his chest. His face was obscured and hidden, out of focus compared to everything else he saw. The girl sat down and closed the passenger side door. The interior light winked out.

The pickup drove away from the curb, disappearing around the corner. Bruce took a step in that direction but felt unsteady on his feet. He tried to fight the dizziness, but his world felt out of control. He bent down with his hands on his knees and took a deep breath, shaking his head slowly to clear the fog. He straightened and looked down the street again as a wave of bright light washed over him.

The world exploded in a violent ball of fire and all at once he was back in Iraq sitting in that dirty Iraqi street watching his squad mates die in pools of mingled blood. He saw a child appear in the smoke after the explosion and watched as he shot the child again and again, screaming the whole time as the world tried to suffocate him.

"Fuck!" Bruce screamed, sitting up in bed. He ran his shaking hands along his body making sure he wasn't injured. He searched his apartment in the soft red glow of his alarm clock, making sure he was home and not on the side of that fucking road surrounded by dead soldiers. Standing slowly, he made his way to the bathroom and stood at the sink splashing cold water on his face. In the mirror, he saw a frightened man looking back at him. He flipped his reflection in the mirror the middle finger.

Bruce Westman had once been a Military Police Officer with the 184th Infantry Regiment assigned to Camp Falcon, outside Baghdad, Iraq. It was there while on patrol in the city that a roadside bomb had gone off, killing four members of his squad. Only Bruce and one other had survived the explosion. Bruce sustained a traumatic brain injury from the blast and the lifetime gift of posttraumatic stress disorder. The other soldier put a bullet in his head years later.

Motherfucker," Bruce groaned, rubbing his chin. He walked from the bathroom, knowing he had no other choice but to assist Agent Shelby. The killer was inside his head now and the only way to kick him out was to catch the bastard. Bruce sighed, walking back into the bathroom again and pissing in the toilet. He washed his hands and made his way back to his bed, noting the bottle of vodka on the floor at the foot of his bed. He ignored it, crawling beneath the covers instead. He fell asleep a few minutes later and slept thankfully dreamlessly.

Chapter 9

Bruce woke up, startled by the shrill ring tone of his cellphone. He glared at the light penetrating the darkness of his room from its screen as the cellphone continued to blare annoyingly beside his head. The small screen informed him that it was his brother calling. He groaned and sat up, ignoring the call until the cellphone stopped ringing. A few minutes later, the cellphone started ringing again as he made his way across the room still wearing the same clothes from the day before. He glanced back at the nightstand beside his bed and flipped off the cellphone. The ringing stopped. He did what he needed to do in the bathroom. The cellphone started ringing again while he was washing his hands.

"Fuck. Give me a break," he shouted into the mirror above the sink. The cellphone went silent once again.

Bruce looked out through the bathroom door daring the cellphone to ring again. It didn't. "Fuck it," he mumbled stripping off his clothes. He took a fast hot shower, enjoying the spray on his face. The steam from the hot water filled the bathroom. He stepped out from the shower and toweled off. The phone began to ring again. He walked across his room naked.

"Someone better be fucking dead," he grumbled into the cellphone, water still running through his hair.

"Where the hell are you?" Jeffrey asked. "I said Ryan's at ten."

"What the fuck are you talking about?" Bruce asked, trying to slip his boxers back on.

"Last night when I called, I asked you to meet me for breakfast today," Jeffrey explained.

"Don't remember talking to you, but breakfast sounds good. I'll be there in twenty minutes."

"Fuck you, it's eleven now, meet me at the station. I'll have donuts and coffee waiting," Jeffrey said.

"Real coffee, not that shit you people drink at work."

"Again, fuck you, but okay," Jeffrey replied, hanging up on his brother.

"Asshole," Bruce said, pulling up a pair of jeans. He dropped the cellphone on his bed and scrounged up a t-shirt from the floor. Looking around the room, he found his keys on the floor by the nightstand and picked them up.

Bruce sat in the bullpen beside his brother's desk twenty-five minutes later. The desk butting up against his brother's desk was empty and devoid of the trappings of occupancy. There were no photos or paperwork cluttering the top and the chair was pushed all the way under as if no one had sat there in a long time.

"You ever getting a partner?" Bruce asked, sipping at his coffee. It was still warm and true to his word, Jeffrey had brought real coffee, Dunkin' Donuts coffee, and glazed donut holes to go with it.

"Not anytime soon," Jeffrey said, popping a donut hole in his mouth.

"I doubt anyone could put up with your shit anyway," Bruce said, dropping his empty cup into the trashcan. He felt fully awake now and ready to attack the day.

"So, now that you're fed and caffeinated, what's your answer going to be?" Jeffrey asked, twirling a pen between his fingers. He looked like a cop interrogating a suspect.

"I'll help out, but he's going to have to let me do it my way. I can't just look at a bunch of photos and tell him what he needs to know."

"I know that, but he might not understand just what it is that you do," Jeffrey said.

"You didn't tell him anything, did you?"

"Fuck no, he would have walked out of here faster than a rabbit's ass on fire."

"A what?"

"A rabbit's ass on fire, it's an expression, look it up," Jeffrey explained.

"No, it's not. No one has ever heard that said before."

"Sure, they have, I didn't just make that up." Bruce shook his head and sighed.

"Call him, tell him I said yes. Tell him to meet me here tomorrow morning," Bruce said. "And don't ever say that thing about a rabbit's ass on fire again."

"Fuck you," Jeffrey said, punching in a number on his phone. He spoke for a few minutes and hung up. "He'll be here around ten. Do you think you can manage to wake up and be here by then or do I need to wake you up?" Bruce shot his brother the middle finger and stood.

"I'm out of here. I'll see you in the morning," Bruce said.

"I'll call you to make sure you're awake. I know how delicate you can be," Jeffrey said, laughing.

"Screw you," Bruce said, walking out of the bullpen.

Standing outside the police station Bruce paused and looked up into the afternoon sun. It felt good on his face, its warmth easing the stress he felt as he walked across the parking lot. He wasn't thrilled about taking on another case like the one he had worked at the beginning of the summer. Just the thought of it made his stomach turn and his head hurt, but it wasn't like he had a choice in the matter either.

"Fuck," he mumbled, fishing his keys from his pocket and opening his car. He dropped down in the driver's seat and cranked the engine. "Fuck," he screamed up into the windshield before throwing the car into reverse and backing up out of his spot. Pausing, he thought about where he needed to go and the thought came to him right away. Saint Christopher's Catholic Church so he could talk with Father Murphy about the significance of the Rosary and the upside-down cross, and maybe about his dream from the night before. Father Murphy was someone good to talk to when there was no one else. He knew when to talk and when to remain silent, and he knew about Bruce's abilities. The father called them a gift from God, but Bruce wasn't so sure about that. He felt like they were more of a burden than a gift. They ate away at his soul and tore at the fabric of his mind. They left him feeling dirty and used.

Bruce made his way back into East Hartford from Manchester, avoiding most of the traffic by taking the back roads. The idea of stopping on Main Street and getting donuts for the priest rose in his mind as he drove but he decided against it. Instead, he stopped off at Augie's and Ray's and picked up four-foot longs, two large fries, and Cokes. His mouth watered all the way down Brewer Street as the delicious greasy smell of the dogs and fries filled his car. The food sat on the passenger seat in separate greased-stained paper bags that teased and tempted him with memories of summer afternoons with his mother and brother. She didn't stop at Augie's and Ray's often, but when she did it was a real treat for the two of them.

Bruce parked his car in the church parking lot behind the annex beneath the tall maple at the back of the lot. He walked around to the front of the main building through long shadows beginning to stretch across the street. At the large beige entrance doors, he paused before stepping inside the dark vestibule. There was always a pang of guilt that followed him inside the church that left him feeling unworthy. Sighing, he stepped inside and crossed himself with the holy water before entering the sanctuary.

The dark sanctuary was full of the shadows of forgotten saints as they crawled across the walls between the stained-glass windows under the watchful eyes of silent souls lost for eternity. Bruce shuddered as something cold and scaly crawled across his skin causing goosebumps to rise. He swallowed hard and hurried up the center aisle, climbing the three steps up to the altar, and making his way over to the hidden door off to the left. He knocked on the door once, waiting for a reply as he stood there with his greasy bags of deliciousness clutched tightly in his left hand, and the Cokes balanced in his right. Glancing over his shoulder, he checked to make sure no ghosts were chasing him.

The door opened and a slow breath escaped his mouth. Father Murphy stood on the other side. A sense of relief swept over Bruce as he handed one of the bags and a Coke to the priest. Father Murphy smiled.

"I see you brought sustenance," Father Murphy said, stepping aside so Bruce could enter the hallway.

"Yeah, I come bearing gifts and questions about something I saw in a police file," Bruce said, following the priest back to his office. "I'm hoping you might be able to shed some light on it." Father Murphy led Bruce back to his office, holding the door open so he could step inside.

"Sit, sit," Father Murphy said, walking behind his desk. "We'll eat first and talk of simple things, safe things, before we turn our attention to the horrors of this world." Bruce nodded; glad they were going to eat first. He sat down and opened the paper bag in front of him and slid out the cardboard boat that contained his footlong hot dog wrapped in white paper. He withdrew the fries next, large greasy crinkle cut fries, and set them beside his Coke.

"You know, you don't always have to feed me," Father Murphy said, taking a large bite from his hotdog. A bit of ketchup ran from the corner of his mouth. He chewed with his eyes closed as if the hotdog had transported him straight to Heaven. Bruce totally understood how he felt.

"I figure if I keep you fed, you'll put a good in a word with the boss upstairs when you talk to him," Bruce replied, starting in on his own dog. Father Murphy smiled around a mouthful of food and nodded, shoving a fistful of fries into his mouth. The two of them ate in silence, not bothering with conversation. Just enjoying the food and the company.

"So, now that that's out of the way," Father Murphy said, crinkling up his paper bag and tossing it into the trashcan beside his desk. Bruce wiped his mouth with a napkin and sighed. He felt full and satisfied. *A good meal was good for confession and questions,* he thought.

"I have this new case I'm working on," Bruce said, shifting in his chair. He brushed a lock of hair off his forehead.

"With your brother? How is he?" Father Murphy asked, licking away the bit of ketchup that sat at the corner of his mouth.

"Jeffery is fine, Father, but this case isn't really with him. I mean he set it up and all but it's with the FBI. I'm still trying to work out the details."

"That's interesting," Father Murphy said, nodding. "What's your question?"

"Someone in New York City is killing hookers. They think he's already killed six women so far, three they know for sure, but there could be more. He has a distinctive way of disposing of the bodies. He's not shy. He leaves his victims in a way they'll be found quickly," Bruce explained. "Each one is found naked, kneeling in front of a tree in different parks across the city. They were found with their hands zip-tied together so it looked like they were praying. A cheap plastic Rosary was wound around their hands with the cross wedged between their fingers. The cross is always left the same way, upside down with the crucified Christ facing the victim. He pins the women to the ground by driving the sharpened end of a length of rebar through their backs and out their chests. That way they don't fall over. He wants everyone to see his handiwork."

"Very disturbing," Father Murphy said, scratching his chin. "You know, Saint Peter was crucified upside down by Nero in Rome. Church history says that Peter requested that he be crucified this way because he felt he was unworthy of dying the same way that Jesus died," Father Murphy explained. "The Pope employs the upside-down cross as a symbolic reminder of Peter's humility and martyrdom. So, there is nothing evil about it if that's what you're thinking. Hollywood and writers with twisted minds might want us to look at it that way, but the church doesn't. The cross is a symbol of sacrifice whether upside down or right side up."

"Do you think he's doing this then as a way of saying these women are unworthy?" Bruce asked.

Father Murphy sat there for a moment with a hand on his chin. He took a sip of Coke and set the cup back down on his desk. A wet ring formed around the bottom of the cup, spreading slowly across the desktop. "He could be, but that would mean he was reared with at least an understanding of the Catholic faith. A novice wouldn't know the difference." Bruce nodded.

"Could he be a priest, or a former priest, or someone connected with the church?" Bruce asked.

"Maybe, but I hate to think that someone inside the church could do something like this. It's so unthinkable, so twisted."

"Father, I know you believe in the Catholic Church, but you have to admit that there is a sickness within the church. So many stories of abuse and outright evil perpetrated by so called men of God."

"I know, Bruce, but I still have to hold onto the belief that there is still good to be found as well. We cannot allow the actions of a few lost souls to paint a broad brush of scandal on the whole. Our Father is a loving, forgiving Father but he is also a God of vengeance. I have to believe that those who have hurt the innocent will not go unpunished in this world or the world to come. They will not enter into paradise, but rather into the lake of fire. I believe this down to my very core." Bruce nodded, feeling guilty that he had brought up the scandals plaguing the church today. He could see that Father Murphy was upset so he decided to back off and change the subject.

"I had a dream last night about the killer," Bruce said. "I saw him pick up a girl on a dark street that I imagine was somewhere in New York City. There was another man in the dream, her pimp maybe. I'm sure he got a look at the killer. I started to chase after the pickup but there was an explosion and suddenly, I was back in Iraq."

"What did you see, Bruce?" Father Murphy asked.

"It wasn't much but I saw my squad die again on the side of that dusty road. I saw their blood run into the gutters and soak into that filthy sand."

"Did the child appear again?" Father Murphy asked.

"He did."

"And."

"And I shot him again, and again, and again, before I woke up. Does it ever end, Father?" Bruce asked, throwing his trash into the wastebasket. "Do the nightmares ever go away?"

"It doesn't ever end, Bruce, it only hurts less as time has its way and the mind heals. You're doing much better than when you first came to see me." Bruce smiled a thin smile that failed to touch his eyes. He didn't want to tell the priest about his self-medicating or his thoughts of suicide. He didn't want to tell the priest about waking up in the beds of strange men with no memory of how he had gotten there. He didn't want to tell the priest that he was gay or how much guilt he felt because he was gay. It was all so royally fucked up.

"Thanks, Father," Bruce said, standing up from his chair. "I got to get going."

"Bruce don't be so hard on yourself. You're a good man with a good heart. Lean on God and he will help you," Father Murphy said as they walked to the office door.

"Sometimes I think God has forgotten all about me, Father."

"Never, Bruce. He watches over all his children. You just need to have faith." Bruce smiled and walked out of the office. Guilt chased him from the church. He felt dirty and unforgiven as he stepped outside. Looking up at the blue sky, he wondered if there was even a God up there looking down on him. With so much evil in the world he doubted there was one. With all that he had seen in his short life, it was hard to believe in anything.

I need a drink, he thought, driving out of the parking lot. *I need several drinks.*

Chapter 10

Billy Morrison sat naked in a shadowed filled room in Upstate New York. Dust motes spiraled around his body up toward the ceiling like exploding galaxies in the eye of a telescope. The room where he sat was in an old, forgotten, two story farmhouse. From the outside, the house appeared abandoned. Weeds grew wild around the foundation. Overgrown bushes blocked the front windows and the walkway leading to the door. The exterior was covered in chipped, flaking white paint faded and dulled by weather and time. Shutters hung askew from windows or lay in the weeds and bushes, having fallen there during one storm or another.

The house sat in the middle of thirty-three acres of overrun farmland off Interstate 88 in Maryland, NY. A deeply rutted leaf-covered path, just wide enough for a single car, lay hidden from the roadway leading back to the house. A chain hung across the path an acre into the property. A No Trespassing sign hung secured in the middle of the chain. From there, the path led back along a winding hilly trail that carved its way through the trees until it reached a small clearing. The house sat at the edge of the clearing. There was no electricity or running water and the house was virtually invisible from the roadway. It was the perfect place for Billy to hide and conduct his private business with his pieces of art.

The light of the morning sun filtered softly through a dirt covered window, illuminating the room beyond the glass in a fractured light that sliced the shadows like so many blades. Billy sat in a darkly stained wooden chair in the middle of the room. All around him dirt and dust and discarded trash lay on the floor. Forgotten wrappers and empty water bottles danced among empty packets of ketchup and mustard. In one corner of the room was a green military-issued cot with a tiny pillow and a blanket on top. In the opposite corner, just in front of Billy, was an old wooden wagon wheel. The wagon wheel was gray and faded, the wood old and split. A rusted, pitted, iron band was wrapped around the outside of the wheel. As old and decrepit as the wagon wheel looked, it was one of Billy's prized possessions.

Inside the room, bits of sunlight fell upon the wagon wheel, revealing a naked woman secured face down on top of it. She was strapped down to the wheel, so her arms and legs were spread wide apart. Ropes wound in and out through the spokes and around the calves of her legs and around her arms. Her face was pressed between two of the spokes. She cried softly into the filthy floor, watching her tears splash into the dust beneath her. She was no longer able to scream, her throat too raw and used up from a night of screaming. Billy smiled at the woman, listening to her mew like a cat in heat. It excited him, thrilled him to listen to her plead and beg for her life, her wasted forgotten life.

Billy never spoke to his works of art. He just liked to watch them, study them, until they were ready to be shaped like clay on a potter's wheel. The process took time, and he had nothing but time to watch and wait.

"Hello," the woman moaned into the tear-soaked floor. "Are you there? Is anyone there?" she asked. Billy remained silent. He didn't like to speak to things, filthy things, things that hadn't become his art yet. "I won't tell anyone, I promise. Just let me go, please," she begged. Billy watched his thing as she pissed herself again, the urine puddling beneath her body, the sharp musky stink filling the room. He watched as the urine rolled out from under the wheel, soaking into the filth on the floor.

It's just a disgusting animal, he thought, rocking back in his chair. In his lap he held a two handled blade. The handles were worn round nobs of wood and the blade was long and sharp with a slight curve. He loved his blade even more than he loved his wagon wheel. His blade was like a sculptor's chisel and the thing strapped to his wagon wheel was no more than a block of stone to be worked beneath his hands. He rocked forward, the legs of the chair striking the floor like twin rifle shots. The block of stone before him was finally ready to become art.

Billy smiled, standing just behind the woman now, enjoying the hardness dangling between his legs. His nostrils flared as he literally choked the wooden handles, working the knife back and forth in his hands, feeling the heat of the friction on his palms. The act sent shivers of pleasure through his body. Goosebumps broke out along his arms. He felt like he was on the edge of orgasm. The crying beneath him stopped.

Billy kneeled down behind the thing, the object, his prize, and caressed the soft white skin just beneath her buttock. The touch sent shivers of electricity up his arm. The thing screamed. He laughed hysterically, the sound of his laughter bouncing off the ceiling. Leaning further out over the body, he ran the tips of his fingers down the spine, feeling the nobs of bones just beneath the skin. It was finally ready for creation. He licked his lips before gently pressing the blade of his knife against the skin along the shoulders, just beneath the base of the neck. The sharpened edge of the blade sank into the skin just enough to draw a thin line of blood along the blade. Billy drew in a shuddering breath. A bit of precum dribbled from the end of his dick.

"I'm Debbie," the thing cried at the touch of the blade. "Debbie Anderson from Manchester New Hampshire. My mom's name is Betty and my father's name is Ralph. Please, please, please, stop."

"I don't care who you are," Billy said in a lusty voice, pressing his lips against her ear, licking the lobe with the tip of his tongue. The blade sank slowly beneath the next layer of skin, and Debbie screamed a blood curdling scream that bounced off the walls of the house. The scream grew and grew until her voice cracked. Billy smiled and worked the blade in just the tiniest bit more and the thing that called itself Debbie kept screaming. Billy drew the blade downward along her spine, peeling back its skin all the way to the top of its ass. He stopped it there and carefully withdrew the blade. The screaming had stopped. He set the blade on the hump of the ass and pressed down. The screaming started again with a renewed ferocity. It defecated on itself, the shit plopping on the floor, the stink filling the room. Billy sat up and snarled, pulling the patch of skin away from the body before it managed to contaminate it. Blood ran from the wound, mixing with the piss and shit on the floor. Billy ignored all of it and stood, carrying his prize from the filthy room so he could begin the task of preserving his trophy, his new work of art.

The house was still silent hours later. The only sound was the wind outside the windows. Billy liked it like that, when he worked with his art. He hated distraction during this critical time. He worked quickly now finishing up in another room inside the house. This room was spotless. There was no trash on the floor or dust or dirt. The walls were freshly painted a bright white. The windows were covered with black blankets. A chair, painted the same white as the walls, sat in the middle of the room. Picture frames adorned the walls, lined up in perfect rows spaced perfectly apart. Lanterns hung from hooks in the corners of the room casting a pale yellow light upon the walls. This room was Billy's art gallery. It was where he displayed all of his works of art.

Billy smiled as he approached a blank space on the wall. In his hands, he held a picture frame. Carefully, he held the picture frame up to the wall making sure to measure the distance between the frame above and the one to the left. Everything had to be perfect. He stepped back from the wall and admired his new piece of art. He took two more steps back and sat down in his viewing chair, positioned so he could admire his entire art collection.

The wooden chair was cool beneath his naked skin. It sent chills through his body. Billy ignored all of this, though, as his eyes settled on the oldest frame displayed on the wall. Beneath the glass of that frame was the well-preserved hide of an alley cat. He had caught the creature wandering between two dilapidated apartment buildings in Harlem, two years ago. Beside that frame were more cats beneath glass, a few dogs, and a racoon he had found on the property. There was the skin of a squirrel collected from the side of the road and that of a fox that he had hit with his car one night. All of it was enough to excite him but no more than that. His biggest thrills came from his more recent collections. These newer additions held his most favorite works of art, the flayed skins of the lost and unworthy. Each work of art was signed and dated by the artist, William, Billy the Kid, Morrison.

Debbie woke up in a world of pain. Her back felt like it was on fire, like someone was holding a flaming torch to it, moving it slowly back and forth, up and down. The pain was beyond incredible. Sobs racked her aching body and tears fell from her eyes, mixing with the dried urine and blood on the floor beneath her. She was still tied down to the wagon wheel and unable to move. The room smelled of piss and shit and dirt and blood and of things that had died long ago. She wanted to vomit but fought the urge to do so. She tried to lift her head from between the spokes, but she couldn't. She tried to wiggle her body enough to loosen the ropes that held her, but she couldn't even manage that much. All of her efforts sent wild bolts of flaming pain up and down her back. She didn't even know if she was alone in the room or if that sick bastard who had caused so much pain was there looking down at her. She wanted to scream but her throat felt like broken glass from all the screaming she had already done.

"Fucking whore," a voice whispered from somewhere behind her. She licked her lips and tried to speak but the words wouldn't come. The pain was just too much. It had become her whole world. It surrounded her like an ocean of water threatening to drown her.

The echo of footsteps crossing the room pounded at her eardrums. She couldn't see the feet, but she knew they were close. A hand touched the side of her face and caressed the side of one breast. Fingers that she couldn't see because her face was pushed so firmly between the spokes, reached beneath the breast and painfully squeezed one of her nipples so hard that everything else that hurt momentarily receded. She cried out, forgetting the ground glass in her throat, but the cry was choked off quickly as the wheel she was strapped to was lifted off the floor and leaned against the wall.

She opened her eyes and saw faded wallpaper in front of her face now. The wallpaper was a faded pink color with tiny, yellowed flowers creating some sort of pattern that she couldn't discern. Brown stains marred the wallpaper running down from somewhere above toward the floor. She let out a slow breath that caught in her throat as hot liquid splashed against the open exposed wound that was her back. She discovered she could still scream, and her screams filled the house. They rose and rose in pitch until she just simply passed out.

Debbie woke up again some unknown time later. She was no longer strapped down to the wagon wheel and that was a relief. She looked around and saw that her surroundings had changed as well. She was outside somewhere. It was dark and eerily quiet. A light breeze, cool and gentle, blew against her exposed body, drawing goosebumps along her skin. Everything around her smelled like cut grass and decaying leaves and city pollution all at the same time, though from her vantage point all she could see were trees. There was a hand tangled in the hair at the back of her head holding her up in a kneeling position. Her ankles and thighs were tied tightly together with strips of cloth or rope, she couldn't tell which. She was facing the trunk of a large tree. Her arms and hands were tied together in front of her with plastic zip ties that bit into her skin. A rope was looped around her neck and tossed over a branch.

He's going to hang me, she thought, but didn't really care very much. The idea of death was welcoming. It would release her from all the pain she felt. The hand that held her hair let go as all the slack in the rope was taken up. *Here it comes*, she thought, but nothing happened. She could still breathe. The rope was looped around her arms not around her throat. All it had done was lift her up, so she was in a kneeling position in front of the tree. A cheap plastic necklace with a cross at the end was wrapped around her zip-tied hands. The cross was wedged between two of her fingers with the thorny crown of the crucified Christ resting on the tip of her finger. *He wants me to look like I'm praying*, she thought, looking up into the tree.

"Our Father who art in heaven, holy is thy name, perfect and blameless among all names," a man's voice whispered from just behind her head. She tried to speak but the words wouldn't come. All she could manage was a weak pathetic mumbled whimper. "You are unworthy of my Father's blessing," the man whispered into her ear. "You are something to be condemned as an affront to his perfect holiness."

A tear rolled down Debbie's face. She was so scared, so terrified, and yet she believed every word that this man said. She knew she was unworthy, and she knew that she was about to go to hell for living such a sinful life. *Please forgive me*, she thought as more tears fell. She drew a breath to speak, to say something in her defense, but before she could utter a word, something beyond pain was driven through her body. She felt it rip through her back and explode out through her abdomen. The pain was incredible. It took away the very breath from her body. Her eyes were opened wide, staring uncomprehendingly. A silent scream lashed through her brain as she fought to take a breath that wouldn't come. Her world flared bright white as pain lashed at her very being. The tree disappeared as she lost all sight. Shadows faded away and the world became darkness, and the darkness was good.

Debbie expelled a final shuttering breath of frothy blood and then died. She died with her eyes opened and fixed. She died with a piece of sharpened rebar forced through her body and into the ground, pinning her in front of the tree like a bug in a collection kept under glass.

Billy stood behind his display, watching her as the life left her body. He watched her eyes as her soul fled from one reality and into the next. He enjoyed watching his works of art die. Once he was sure she was gone, he removed an envelope from his pocket and gently laid it on the ground beside his display. Written on the front of the envelope in the cursive writing that he learned in grade school were five words, "To Whom It May Concern."

Billy walked quickly from the small park. It was still dark outside. The world was still a couple of hours away from really waking up. At the exit, he stepped over a gate and began walking through a dimly lit Brooklyn neighborhood. He hurried down the sidewalk for several blocks until he reached his pickup parked on the curb. He opened the door, the dome light did not come on, and he got in the truck. He drove away from the neighborhood, making sure never to exceed the speed limit, even though the street was as empty as any street ever got in the city.

It was four in the morning as Billy drove away from Brooklyn. He took the Lincoln Tunnel out of the city, heading back upstate to his hidden house and his art studio. He was excited and hard and ready to explode.

He told himself to wait the almost four hours it would take to drive back because sometimes the waiting was the best part. It was like looking at that last piece of candy sitting at the bottom of a bowl. The longer you put off eating that candy, the better it tasted once you were able to eat it.

Billy exited the Lincoln Tunnel and continued driving north. Traffic into the city was beginning to pick up but he was headed away from all that. He smiled and drove on, anxious to see how they responded to his note. He wanted them to understand that what he was doing was art and not something to be feared. He wanted them to know that what he did was an act of mercy, not murder. He grinned and squeezed the steering wheel.

Twenty minutes later the pressure became too much. His groin ached and he tried shoving down on himself to let up on the pressure, but it didn't help. A rest stop sign appeared on the freeway, and he exited, parking in the first available space he found.

The rest stop was well lit. Eighteen wheelers were parked in several spaces but few cars. Billy walked quickly up the sidewalk, following the signs pointing toward the restrooms. Lights came on as he stepped through the door. The bathroom was empty. He hurried into the farthest stall from the entrance. It was cold in the bathroom. The overhead lights shone down with a sickly yellow glow. Billy dropped his pants, so they puddled around his ankles. His dick stuck straight out, pointing at the wall behind the toilet. He closed his eyes, spit into the palm of his hand, and began to masturbate.

He finished quickly, emptying himself into the toilet. The restroom door opened with a pained squeak. Someone walked in with heavy footsteps. Billy grunted and yanked up his pants, making sure to flush the toilet before he exited the stall. The other person who had come in was already occupying another stall. He never saw Billy.

Chapter 11

Bruce sat beside Jeffrey's desk waiting for Agent Shelby to show up. It was well past eleven and he was almost an hour late. A cup of bullpen coffee sat in front of him on the desk growing cold. Jeffrey sat reading over a theft report from the night before. The phone on the desk rang and he answered, setting the report down beside the phone so he could pick up where he left off when he finished with the call.

"Westman," Jeffrey said, looking across the desk at Bruce sitting there looking inpatient.

"Oh shit, yeah, I understand. I'll tell him," Jeffrey said into the phone and hung up. "Shelby isn't coming. They picked up another body this morning and he's working that scene."

"Where?" Bruce asked.

"Brooklyn," Jeffrey answered. "He said to have you drive into the city and he'd meet you somewhere for a bite to eat when he has a chance."

"Okay," Bruce said, standing up from his chair. He had his copy of the case file in his hand. He left the half-finished bullpen coffee on the desk.

"Do you want me to tag along?" Jeffrey asked.

"No. I'm not sure I'll make it back tonight."

"Are you going to call Shelby back?" Jeffrey asked.

"I don't know. I might poke around a bit and see what I can find out on my own. You know I work better that way."

"I know, but this is a federal case, and they don't work that way. You're going to have to work within whatever parameters he sets up for you," Jeffery explained, standing up from behind his desk. He stepped around to the front and looked at his brother. "You be careful out there and call if you need anything."

"Yes Dad," Bruce said around a smile.

"Fuck your dad, you just be careful, New York isn't Manchester. If I have to, I'll come out there and kick your ass and then solve this case for you," Jeffrey said, slugging Bruce in the shoulder. Bruce nodded and walked out of the bullpen. Jeffrey watched him go, feeling sorry for his brother as he disappeared through the doorway. He knew what it was that he was about to put himself through to solve this case and that worried him. As much as Bruce would have liked to have been a cop, he wasn't, and he didn't handle the sick shit like a cop either. He let it dig into his head and sleep there. He didn't know how to leave it behind at the end of the day.

Bruce left the parking lot at the Manchester Police Department and drove out to Matthew's house. He parked his old Ford in the street and walked up the driveway. Matthew came out the kitchen door before he could even knock. He had a grin on his face and a sandwich in his hand, sporting a milk mustache.

"Hey Bud," Bruce said, fighting the urge to wipe the mustache away from Matthew's upper lip.

"Hey," Matthew replied. "Are we seeing Father Murphy today?" he asked, his mouth full of mashed sandwich.

"Nope, it's not that," Bruce said. "I'm going to New York today to help the FBI out on a case, and I just wanted to say goodbye before I left."

"Wow, the FBI," Matthew said, making the words sound holy.

"Yeah, but it's that dick from earlier this summer who gave me such a hard time. Anyway, I'm not sure when I'll be back, and I wanted to tell you good luck at school Monday."

"You sure you don't need me to help out?" Matthew asked, shoving the last bit of sandwich into his mouth. It had only been a couple of months ago when Matthew had shot and killed the serial killer that had kidnapped his sister, Mary, and who was about to kill Bruce.

"I'll call you if I need something," Bruce said, smiling.

"Hey Mr. Westman," Mary said, walking up the driveway.

"Hey Mary, how you doing?" Bruce asked.

"I'm okay, I guess. Starting school in two days sucks but it is what it is."

Bruce looked at Mary and saw dark circles under her eyes. The pink hair was gone, and she wore little to no makeup. She was still pretty in that adolescent teenage way but there was something darker there behind her eyes that spoke of things hidden. She was still haunted by what had happened to her at the beginning of summer. He was sure the nightmares hadn't gone away and wondered if they ever would. He knew his hadn't.

"I want you to keep seeing Father Murphy, while I'm gone, Mary," Bruce said. "Keep talking to him, he'll help you sort things out."

"Sure, Mr. Westman," Mary said, reaching out and wiping the milk mustache away from Matthew's lip before walking inside the house. Matthew watched her go. He turned when he was sure she couldn't hear.

"She's still messed up, you know," Matthew explained. "I hear her at night, crying in her bedroom."

"Go with her the next time she sees Father Murphy. Make sure she knows you're there for her. It's very important that she doesn't feel alone." Matthew nodded. "Anyway, I got to get going. If you need anything, anything at all, call me. New York isn't that far away, I'll come back."

"I will," Matthew said. Bruce turned and walked back down the driveway, getting into his car and driving away. Matthew waved until the car was gone. Stepping back inside the house, he saw Mary sitting in the family room. Her phone sat ignored in her lap. There was a sad expression on her face as she gazed through the blank screen on the television. She looked like she was somewhere far away.

"Hey dipshit," Matthew said, walking into the family room. Mary looked up. The expression on her face was blank for a second, and then life flooded back in.

"Fuck you, turd licker," Mary said, sticking up her middle finger. She was his sister again. Matthew smiled.

"Asshole," Matthew said, snatching up the remote from the arm of the couch and turning on the television. He found a movie and sat down beside his sister to watch. Mary didn't say anything, but the sad expression didn't return to her face.

Bruce arrived at his apartment and packed a few clothes in an old, ragged gym bag. He added two bottles of vodka from the freezer, his gun, a box of ammo, the phone charger, and some toiletries. He gave his apartment the onceover, making sure nothing was left on or left out and stepped into the hallway outside his door. The key clicked in lock, and he walked down the stairs. Mr. Davis was outside walking his dog around the telephone pole again. Bruce wondered if the old man just hung out there all day long waiting for him to appear. The dog had its leg up in the air as it pissed on the pole.

"Going somewhere?" Mr. Davis asked as Bruce tossed his bag in the back seat.

"None of your business," Bruce said, dropping down into the driver's seat.

"Well, if you are, the neighborhood will be a whole lot safer," Mr. Davis said. Bruce flipped him off and slammed the door. He left a patch of burnt rubber on the street as he drove off. Mr. Davis watched him go, shaking his head. "God help wherever he's going," he said to his dog as it squatted to poop in the grass. Mr. Davis's lip curled up in a disgusted snarl as he pulled a yellow plastic poop bag from its holder on the leash, waiting for the dog to finish its business.

Chapter 12

Bruce left Hartford on Interstate 91, heading southbound. Even though it was between rush hours the traffic was still heavy getting out of the city. Getting into New York wasn't much better either. Once he entered the Bronx, the streets didn't clear up at all. He followed the commands of his GPS through one light after the other, caught up in bumper-to-bumper traffic. What should have been an hour and a half to two-hour drive to Barretto Point Park on Viele Avenue in the Bronx, took more than three hours to complete.

Barretto Point Park was a small pocket park located along the East River in the Bronx. It was established in 2001 by the city parks department after the landfill that had once been there was filled and capped. In 2008, a floating pool was added, and the location became a popular spot for Bronx residents to hang out, take a swim in the floating pool, or listen to a free concert.

Bruce found a place to park on the east side and stepped out of his car. He held the case file in his hand as he surveyed the trees and tennis courts in front of him. The park was filled with a scattering of people walking along the paths or sitting in the grass enjoying the afternoon sunlight. In the distance he could see the dock and the floating pool anchored in the East River. With the sour smell coming off the water it didn't seem like such a great location for a pool but what did he know.

Bruce set the case file on the trunk of his car and opened it to the first victim. She was a seventeen-year-old runaway from an abusive home in Waterbury Connecticut. Even at such a young age she showed the obvious signs of drug use and street abuse. Her name was Allison Malinowski, Allie to the few friends she left behind before she ran away. There had at one time been a Department of Child Services case opened, investigating possible sexual abuse against her by her stepdad, but nothing had been proved beyond the suspicions of Allie's homeroom teacher, and Allie had run away before anything else could be done to make a case.

Bruce closed the file and followed a black asphalt path out of the parking lot that ran along the east side of the park. He used the photos from the case file to find what he believed was the tree where Allie had spent the last moments of her life. The area around the tree looked normal. The ground might have been a bit neater than what lay beneath some of the other trees in the park, but an outsider would never have known that something horrible had happened there. Bruce sat down in the grass beneath the tree, leaning his head back against the rough bark. His head tipped back enough so he could look up into the branches. The leaves were green still, fluttering in the breeze that blew in from out over the river. Soon enough though, they would turn to bright oranges or reds, but for now, summer still hung on. Shafts of sunlight leaked through the foliage creating dancing shadows on the ground. Birds flew in and out of the branches twittering their songs. It would have all been so very relaxing if not for the horrible death that had occurred here.

Bruce closed his eyes, listening to the sounds of the park as they ran over his body and through his ears. His breathing slowed to where a casual observer might think he had fallen asleep. His right hand settled on the ground, the fingers softly touching the grass. The earth was cool to the touch. It spoke of life and death over and over as the seasons went from one to the other. His breathing slowed even more as he tried focusing his thoughts as he reached out for Allie's life. The drift swept over him slowly as his mind began to travel.

Ever since an IED explosion in Iraq, Bruce had been able to do something that he called drifting. He gave it this name because that's what it felt like when he slipped through realities. It felt like drifting on the open ocean and riding the waves until he crashed ashore. One moment he was firmly planted in reality, and the next, he felt himself drifting sideways, separating from real to the unreal.

Sometimes this drifting caused him to enter the killer's mind, and sometimes it drove him into the victim's mind, and at other times he was forced to simply be a spectator to whatever it was the drift wanted to show him. In many ways it was all very maddening because he couldn't interfere with the events that were happening. It was a torturous experience to have to go through. It left his mind damaged and bruised.

Within the drift, Bruce no longer sat beneath the tree on a late summer afternoon. Though his body physically remained there the rest of him was somewhere completely different. On this occasion the drift swept him away through an ocean of darkness, twisting his body this way and that until it was deposited right back where he started. Though now it was dark outside, and the park was empty of daytime traffic and daytime sounds. He was still in Barretto Point Park; only the when had changed.

Bruce looked around the park as shadows drifted through the trees like forgotten ghosts. Tiny pools of light close to the ground lit the pathways and no more. Crazy shadows of creeping ghouls wound through the trees as distant lights appeared and disappeared. Looking around, Bruce saw that he still stood beneath the same tree where his body sat oblivious to the daytime world. Above, what he could see of the sky was dark. He couldn't see stars or the moon through the gray mass of clouds. The only sounds he heard were the few cars traveling along the streets, but they seemed to be miles away even though he knew they weren't. Beyond the dark shadow of the dock, he saw the faint lights of boats and tugs as they chugged up and down the East River. The park was such a lonely, haunted place to visit at night.

In front of Bruce, facing him, was the body of Allison Malinowski. She was pinned to the ground like so many butterflies in a display case. She was arranged on her knees in front of the tree, so it looked like she was praying. Her hands were pressed tightly together in front of her face. There was a rosary wrapped around her hands. The killer had cut away her eyelids, so it looked like she was awake, staring up into the tree, looking for God or salvation. A rusted length of rebar had been forced through her back and out her stomach. This rebar held her body in front of the tree. An envelope sat on the ground just behind her feet. He could see that something was written on it, but he was unable to read it. He wondered why the killer left an illegible note.

Was he bragging about his crimes? He wondered. *Or trying to make a statement of some kind?*

Bruce felt his body shift and he closed his eyes. When he opened them again, he found that he was the girl now. He felt her flayed back, raw and ugly, burning as if it were on fire. He wanted to scream but before he could the world shifted once more and now, he stood behind the girl, except this time he was the killer. He felt the breeze off the river and realized his pants were down around his ankles. He was peeing on the girl's back. Urine splashed into her wounds, running pink into the dirt beneath her body. He wanted to scream, but somehow only laughter filled his head.

The world shifted once more and he was no longer beneath the tree but walking along a dimly lit path toward what appeared to be a parking lot. The killer cut through lot, emerging out onto the street. He kept walking down a tree-lined sidewalk, watching his steps as he went until he came upon a small pickup truck parked along the curb. For just a second, he caught a glimpse of himself in the glass before the driver's door opened. He wore a hoody that obscured much of the reflection in the window, but he saw a thick mustache and stubble on a cleft chin. The reflection disappeared as the door swung open. No light came on inside the truck.

Bruce lost the drift at the sound of the truck's door closing. His eyes opened and once more he was beneath the tree with sunlight fighting to make its way through the branches. His stomach felt queasy, and he had to take several deep breaths until he felt sure he wasn't about to throw up. Sometimes that happened when he drifted, not all the time, but enough that it was embarrassing when he tossed his lunch all over his shoes or in his lap. He sat there beneath the tree until he was positive that he wasn't going to throw up the bad bullpen coffee he drank earlier. He listened to the birds above singing their songs. He listened to the small children playing somewhere off in the park. Their laughter chased away some of the ugliness he had been forced to witness. Sighing, he slipped the notebook he always carried out of his back pocket, and wrote down his observations from the drift, making sure to underline, "Like insects under glass."

Does he see himself as some kind of collector?

Bruce slipped the notebook back into his pocket and walked out to the path. He followed it down to the river, strolling along the water as if he had no cares in the world. In front of him the East River lapped at the shoreline. Tiny rocks rolled back and forth, growing smaller with each passing wave. A kite drifted in the breeze out over the water. It looked like a giant red bat. He sighed and headed back to the parking lot.

Chapter 13

Billy's first and only arrest was when he was fourteen years old. Back then he liked to go out at night and sneak into people's homes while they were sleeping. He didn't sneak into their homes to steal from them, even though he did take things sometimes. He thought of the things he took as rewards for his efforts, tokens reminding him of his daring exploits.

The real reason he broke into these houses at night was simply because he could, and because he needed to feel something. At the age of fourteen, Billy lacked the words to explain all of it, but deep down in his soul, he felt nothing. He didn't feel love or shame, sadness or joy. He just felt empty inside, except when he broke into a stranger's house and stood there watching them while they slept. That thrill, that control, he felt that. It was like a bolt of electricity rushing through his body. The need for that feeling was so strong that it became something he craved every minute of every day.

Once inside the homes, Billy liked to sneak into the bedrooms and watch the people while they slept. He didn't interact with them or disturb them. All he did was stand there hidden in the shadows and watch. He thought of himself as one of those ninjas dropping down silently from above on an unsuspecting victim.

No one ever knew he was there or had ever caught him up to that point. He could stand still for hours watching, studying, making mental notes, wondering what it was that allowed him to be real when everything around him wasn't. He felt energized standing there in the dark with the power of life and death in his hands. It filled him with that same thrill he felt when he killed one of the cats or dogs, he found roaming the neighborhood. It was intoxicating in a way he had no words to explain.

Billy's nighttime adventures began when he was ten years old, and his mother had an overnight job. She left him at home by himself five nights a week without supervision. During the nights that she worked he would sneak out of the house to prowl the neighborhood. At first, he just walked up and down the streets around his apartment complex. Sometimes these walks brought a tiny little tingle of excitement, but it never lasted. After a while his walks at night expanded, one street over, two streets over, but soon that wasn't enough. He started walking through backyards and peeking into windows, watching what was going on, on the other side of the glass. Then one night, he found one of the windows open with only a thin screen separating him from what was inside the house. He stood at that window, watching television with the family that lived inside the house, pretending he was part of the family. Mom and Dad sat on a loveseat while his brother sat on the floor. The glow of the television lit everyone up with its artificial light. He felt like he was a part of something real, like they existed with him somehow.

The program ended and his brother went off to bed. Mom followed a few minutes later. Dad watched the news with Billy standing only a few feet away, separated by a window screen. The news ended, and dad went upstairs where Mom had disappeared. The lights inside the house eventually winked out. Billy felt a wave of something wash through his body as silence drifted out through the screen. He wanted to be on the other side. He wanted to scream at the unfairness of it all.

One night during his journeys through the backyards, he peeked into a house through one of the windows on the lower floor. There was a light on inside the house that provided just enough illumination that he could see that the window wasn't latched. He stood there at the window, behind that house, hidden from the street, bathed in shadows that crept through the backyard, watching an old lady pass back and forth from view. He thought of her as Grandma and smiled at the idea of this fantasy. He waited for Grandma to turn out the lights and go upstairs. Above his head a light came on, the glow throwing shadows across the backyard. He waited for the light to disappear, and soon it did, bathing the backyard in darkness.

Billy approached the window again and slid it open. It rose silently in its track. He listened to the sounds inside the house. The drip, drip, of water from somewhere. The click of the furnace coming on, sending hot water through the pipes heating the house. It was all so comforting and inviting. The tingle that he normally felt was a bolt of lightning now inside his body. It lit up all of his senses until it felt as if they were on fire. He climbed through the open window, landing silently on the floor. Something warm ran down his leg and he saw that he had peed himself a little. He didn't mind. It felt good, comforting.

Billy crept through the house on silent feet, making his way to Grandma's bedroom. The door was open, just like the window had been. A nightlight in the hallway threw his shadow into the room, urging him to walk forward. He paused at the sound of Grandma snoring. Her snores were muffled little snorts like she was having difficulty breathing. He watched her take each breath, breathing in and out. The fire inside his body was incredible. Flames licked at his senses igniting his brain. He had a hard on.

I could kill her, he thought. *I could take her life and there's nothing she can do about it.*

Beside the bedroom door was a dresser and on top of that dresser was a glass figurine. A Rosary was wrapped around the figurine with the cross hanging down over the edge of the dresser. Billy looked away from Grandma and studied the Rosary. He reached out and touched the cross with the tip of his finger. He felt Jesus, clinging to the cheap plastic. The crucified Christ felt so phony and yet he felt power there too. He slipped the rosary from the figurine, clutching it in his hand. He felt himself pee a little more. He felt the liquid run down his leg.

Grandma grunted from her bed and snorted a little, letting a little fart slip out. Billy studied her, wondering if she somehow knew that he had taken something from the dresser. Stepping back into the hallway, he made his way back down to the window and back outside once more. Staying in the shadows, he snuck through the backyards again until he reached his apartment complex. Silently, he entered through the back door and up the back stairs. Once he was safely inside his bedroom, he removed the rosary from his pocket, enjoying how it glowed green in the dark. A smile creased his face. *My treasure, my reward*, he thought, hiding the rosary inside the depths of his closet. Closing the door, he slipped out of his pants and his pee-stained underwear, tossing the soiled clothing into the basket in front of his bed before slipping under the covers. He slept well that night.

After that night at Grandma's house, Billy lost count of the number of times he had repeated his acts of burglary. He taught himself how to slip window locks with a metal shim. He became really good at breaking into houses. He even practiced on the apartment windows where he lived whenever his mother was out or at work. By the time Billy was fourteen, he was a well-trained, well taught burglar who could slip through almost any window, locked or unlocked.

On the night he was caught Billy had broken into a house not too far from where he lived. He picked the house because he knew who lived there. He went to school with the girl. She was special even though his mother referred to all girls as dirty little things doing dirty little things with all the dirty little boys at school. He didn't know if that was true or not, but he had seen her once behind the baseball diamond in back of the school doing dirty little things with a dirty little boy once.

The day had been overcast, threatening rain. The air was thick and heavy as the last bell rang. Billy had gone into the woods behind the school to check on an orange tabby he had found the other day near his apartment complex. He wanted to see if the cat was ready to become a work of art. It had been out there for over a day tied to a tree. He didn't think it was dead yet, but close. The summer before school started that year, he had learned to skin his catches with a pocketknife so he could display them like pictures on a wall.

On this particular day Billy was walking through the trees that grew close to the schoolyard, following the chain link fence that separated the school from the woods. It was while he was hidden there in the shadows that he heard laughter. The sound was pitched high. It had sounded like one of the girls from his school. He paused and listened, following the twitter of laughter across the empty ballfield just on the other side of the fence. He crept closer to the chain link fence until he could see the shadows from the trees snaking across the ballfield like hungry fingers searching for something to grab.

Billy heard the laughter again and smiled. It sounded so free and real. It sounded happy and excited. He wanted to feel that same excitement. He wanted to know what it felt like to be free. Carefully, he stepped from the safety of the trees through an opening in the fence and crossed the outfield grass. The snaking shadows swallowed him up, but he ignored their hunger and pushed on toward the giggles.

The laughter was coming from behind the visitor's dugout. Billy licked his lips and swallowed hard, wondering if it was something dirty going on back there. He walked across the infield, careful to be silent. Reaching the front of the dugout, he paused, dropping to all fours. Rocks and pebbles bit into his skin but he ignored these as he crawled around the dugout. At the corner, he stopped and carefully peeped around to the side just enough so he could see what was causing the girl to laugh.

Behind the dugout, lying on a blanket with her shirt and bra off, was Robin Young. She was Billy's age. She was even in two of his classes, though he didn't think she knew who he was or that they shared classes. She had long curly blonde hair and large blue eyes. She wasn't fat but she hadn't been skinny either. She had what some people referred to as baby fat, but in Billy's mind, she was just right. Her skin was white and freckled, her breasts large and round with dark pepperoni sized nipples. They looked perfect. There was even a mole on the side of one breast that grew and shrank with each breath she took. Seeing her like that, exposed, made Billy so hard that his pants tented out.

In front of Robin was a boy from the next grade up. Billy didn't know his name, but he had seen him in the hallways at school, and he immediately hated him. The boy had his shirt off and his pants unbuckled. Robin clawed at the boy's pants with hungry fingers. The boy shoved her hands away and pushed his underwear down below his knees for her. His penis popped out, waving back and forth looking like some kind of mushroom on a tiny stalk. Robin reached a hand up and touched it. Billy felt a shiver of pleasure worm through his body. He felt heat building inside his pants as he watched Robin touching that boy's dick with her delicate fingers. He wanted to know how that felt. He needed to feel it, to experience it.

"What the fuck do you think you're doing?" Robin screamed suddenly, her breasts bouncing with each word. All Billy could do was watch as he exploded inside his pants. He was helpless to move because the orgasm was so powerful and because whatever was happening, it was so fucking real he didn't want to let it go.

"Motherfucker," the boy that was with Robin shouted. He stood with his pants pooled around his ankles. He reached down to pull them up and Billy snapped out of it. He ran before the boy could pull his pants up. He ran as fast as he could across the field and back into the woods. He ran through the trees until he came up behind his apartment building. He flew up the stairs to the second floor and crashed through the door, locking it behind him. He was terrified and thrilled at the same time because nothing like that had ever happened before.

Leaning against the door, Billy caught his breath, listening to the other side of the door for several minutes to see if something was going to happen. Once he was sure nothing was going to happen, he stripped out of his clothing and took a shower. If his mother found out that he had had another accident, she would make him wear the rubber pants again, and he hated wearing the rubber pants.

After taking his shower, Billy threw his clothes into the washing machine. He sat on his bed, naked, thinking about Robin Young and her large bouncing breasts as his clothes ran through the wash cycle. He grew hard again as images of Robin danced in his head. He touched himself and imagined it was her touching him. His fingers felt like electricity. He kept touching himself over and over until he had another accident in the palm of his hand. He took another shower so his mother wouldn't know what he had done.

For the next several days and nights thoughts of Robin Young played out over and over in his mind until he couldn't resist the urge, the need to see her again. He hungered for that feeling that he felt watching her behind the dugout that day. If she could just understand how special she was, how real she had become to him, everything would be alright. He could have her then and maybe, just maybe, they could be real together.

Billy snuck into the backyard of Robin's house and waited until every light in the house had turned off. He waited for an hour after the last light had gone out before he crept up to a window and slipped the lock. It was well after midnight and the house was silent. He noticed the odor of cooked fish and baked bread. His stomach growled as he crawled through the window. Crossing the living room, he paused at the stairs and thought about going back. He could still leave the house, but that wasn't really an option.

Billy climbed the stairs. At the top, he peeked into one of the bedrooms and saw a young boy sleeping. He thought about walking inside the bedroom but didn't. The room next to that first room was opened just a crack, and Billy pushed it in enough that he could look inside the bedroom. It was Robin's room, and she slept beneath a pink canopy. A nightlight cast a soft yellow glow over her body. Boy band posters decorated the walls. Clothes littered the floor in tiny pools as if she had just shimmied out them and let them fall.

Billy stood in that hallway outside her bedroom for several minutes. He knew he should turn around leave, but his dick was so hard now, and his body was on fire. Shivers of pleasure ran up and down his spine. He wanted to feel what he had felt that day behind the dugout again. He wanted her to touch him like she had touched that boy. He needed her to become real for him.

Billy stepped into the bedroom and silently closed the door while watching Robin sleep. He matched his breathing to her breathing. He drank her every curve into his body until something leaked into his underpants. Waves of electric pleasure raced through his body lighting up every nerve.

Billy pulled back the blanket that covered her until he could see her. She wore a white t-shirt that pressed tight against her chest. Her nipples showed beneath the fabric, pressing against the cotton underside. She wore dark shorts that showed just the tiniest bit of her pink panties. Below that was milky white skin. Billy wanted to see more. He wanted to see what lay hidden behind those pink panties.

You need to stop this, Billy told himself, but he was so far beyond the point of being able to stop. He felt helpless, powerless to do anything but stand there drinking her into his body the way he wanted to be inside her body. As if his hand had a mind of its own, he caught a glimpse of it moving to the top of his pants. His fingers fumbled with the clasp, managing to undo it. The zipper fell, or he yanked it down. He wasn't sure which. The pants fell to the floor, pooling around his ankles. His underwear had followed. He touched himself. A bolt of pure electricity ran through his body, and he came just like that all over his hand. He came so much that it ran down his leg dribbling into the carpet. It felt hot and thick, and he knew, he knew that it wasn't pee like his mother said. It was sex.

"This is what sex feels like," he whispered, grunting again as more stuff ran over his hand. His eyes rolled up into his head and he felt dizzy. He felt amazing.

Across the room, Robin opened her eyes. At first, she hadn't been sure what it was that she was seeing. Her first thought had been that it was her younger brother standing there after having another nightmare. She sat up in bed and cleared her eyes, realizing right away that it wasn't her brother standing in her room. It was that boy from the other day, the one that had been spying on her, and he wasn't wearing pants. *Oh my God, he's playing with himself,* she thought just before screaming at the top of her lungs. She screamed so loud and so long.

At the sound of Robin's scream, Billy opened his eyes and turned. He tried to run but he tripped over his pants and plowed into the bedroom door. The jolt of smacking into the door sent a wave of pain through his body. He yanked up his pants as quickly as he could and opened the bedroom door. He ran out into the hallway chased by Robin's screams. He ran out into the hallway and right into the arms of Robin's father.

Billy kicked at the much bigger man as hard as he could and tried to flee, but Robin's father had a hold of his shirt, and he threw him to the floor like a rag doll. Billy screamed. Robin's father kicked him several times in the chest and stomach. Billy curled up into a ball and began crying as more blows landed. Through his tears he saw Robin standing in her bedroom door looking shocked and scared.

Billy had been arrested that night for breaking and entering with intent. He was sent straight to juvenile detention where he received six months for his crime. While there in detention on that first night, an older boy raped him. He raped him again the next night, and all the following nights until Billy stabbed him in the balls with a butterknife he snuck out of the kitchen. Billy never told anyone why he had done what he had done. The guards and the counselors weren't real after all, and he didn't have to share with them if he didn't want to. The boy he stabbed never raped another child again. Billy received six more years for that assault, but he didn't care.

Growing up, Billy had never attended church. His mother didn't believe in God. She said that people who did were weak things that needed someone or something to tell them how to live and what to do. The first time he went to a religious service was while he was locked up. He only went to break up the monotony of his day-to-day life in detention, but it turned out to be life changing.

The priest, Father Michael from the Holy Sisters of Christ Church, presented the mass every Sunday. He was a stern man, always dressed in black except for the white collar around his neck. His face was clean shaven, and his dark hair was always combed straight back from his forehead. His skin was marred by pock marks left behind by adolescent acne. He never smiled and if a boy got out of hand, he was quick to strike him with the thick black Bible he carried everywhere. There was always a rosary wrapped around the Bible and sometimes the beads left indentations wherever it struck a child.

The cross dangling at the end of the rosary was the brightest shiniest silver that Billy had ever seen. He always fixated on it as Father Michael stood to read from the Word. The priest would slowly release the pages of the Bible from the rosary, making sure to wrap the beads around his hand until only the cross hung free. Billy found this whole act hypnotizing as he focused on the cross while the priest spoke.

By the time Billy was released from detention, he had most of the New and Old Testaments memorized. Father Michael taught him about sin and hell and damnation. Billy paid attention to it all. He was hungry for knowledge, and he drank in all the priest had to say.

On the day he walked out, his mother wasn't there to pick him up, but Father Michael was there. The priest drove an old black four door Ford Taurus with fake leather seats. It smelled of nicotine and old sweat. Father Michael brought Billy to the apartments where his mother lived and dropped him off. Billy thanked him and went into the building.

At the door to the apartment was an envelope taped to the frame with his name on it. Inside the envelope was fifty dollars and a note saying she had left town and he was on his own. Billy spent that first night of freedom there on the floor outside that door with his note clasped in his hand and the money in his pants pocket. The next day he walked outside and stood on the sidewalk watching cars drive by. He hoped to see his mother in one of the cars, but he hadn't. He grew bored after several hours and began walking with no particular destination in mind. At a convenience store he stopped and used a payphone. He called the priest. Father Michael came and picked him up.

For the next two years Billy lived at the church in the basement, doing odd chores for the sisters and the priests. He didn't have much, but he was never hungry, and he was always allowed to gather clothes from whatever donations were left at the church. He slept on a threadbare mattress on an old iron framed bed with a lightbulb dangling down from the ceiling. It was always cold in the basement, but it was home.

Billy was forced to leave the church after two years. The sisters had become uncomfortable. Two had caught him watching them through an outside window while they were in their rooms. Father Michael questioned Billy about what he had been doing outside the windows and Billy confessed that he had been touching himself. The priest beat him with that Bible he carried. The rosary beads left tracks across his back wherever the Bible struck.

"You are unworthy of our kindness," the priest shouted with each swing of his hand.

"I am unworthy," Billy cried each time he felt the blow land.

The next morning, he left the church. He drove away in an old beat-up Volkswagen Bug that was more rust than yellow. He never saw the priest again, but he didn't hold any grudges. The man had done his best.

Chapter 14

Bruce drove around the Bronx for several hours just taking in the sights and sounds of the neighborhood. Trash littered the streets and the sidewalks, most of it caught up in the gutters or swirling around in mini funnel clouds. The buildings that crowded the sidewalks were rundown and covered in elaborately drawn graffiti that advertised local gangs, local attractions, or simply commented on society at large or who's dick was bigger. Bruce admired the artistic skill that went into the graffiti and wondered how someone found the time necessary to create such drawings. He marveled at how so much skill was wasted on the sides of buildings instead of filling the walls of museums or galleries.

On the sidewalks, people hurried along in thick groups with heads down, eyes focused on the tiny patches of real estate in front of their feet or on the tiny screens of their cellphones. They walked along unconcerned with vehicular or human traffic, solely focused on getting from point A to point B. The homeless watched all of this coming and going from perches against shuttered storefronts and boarded up buildings, smoking bummed cigarettes or drinking from hidden bottles of alcohol. Spent needles and crushed glass pipes mingled with the trash and filth that they sat in every day.

Bruce continued driving around for a few hours until he decided he had witnessed enough poverty and squalor for one day. He drove his car out of Hunts Point into a cleaner, more residential area of the Bronx. The zoo was nearby and there was less trash and graffiti scattered about, though there was still some. The homeless occupied the street corners out here, holding signs declaring themselves hungry, out of work, or veterans. A couple of the more honest ones held up signs that read, "I just want a drink." Whenever a light at an intersection turned red, the homeless hurried out into the streets, walking between the cars taking whatever handouts they could get from kindhearted people, but they had nothing on the Iraqi beggars Bruce encountered in the war.

At a side street near the zoo, Bruce used his cellphone to find a room for a hundred dollars a night on Tremont Avenue. It was in a red brick building close to the road on a street full of similar looking red brick buildings. Trees filled many of the lots in front of the buildings which were fronted by chest-high brick and iron walls with iron gates. Bruce parked his car in the street beneath a large oak tree and walked inside his building. The front desk was just inside the door. A black male sat behind the counter ignoring him for several minutes before taking his money and handing him his room key. Bruce made sure to keep the receipt for Agent Shelby.

Beside the front desk was a wide stairwell, and since there were no elevators, Bruce began to climb. His room was the first door on the third floor. There were six other doors on the third floor beside his own, but he had a feeling that those rooms were empty at the moment. The room was basic but nice. It had a queen-sized bed along one wall and a clean bathroom. Exposed brick on one wall added a touch of class to the room that Bruce found somehow comforting. The one window looked out into the thick branches of a tall oak tree that stood in front of the brownstone. A note card on the nightstand said there was off street parking and fresh coffee in the lobby every morning.

After putting his things away, Bruce walked back outside to look for something to eat. He found an Italian restaurant a few blocks away and ate a decent enough meal. It wasn't homemade but it was well presented, and the staff was friendly. The restaurant had a local feel about it that allowed Bruce to relax and feel like he was at home. There were red and white checkered tablecloths on all the tables and faux leather booths along the walls. Dim lighting from above gave everything a private feel while soft music played from speakers positioned in the corners. Each table had a flickering candle on it that sent dancing shadows on the walls and the tabletops. He had no trouble imagining gangsters from the 20's sitting at these same tables deciding who to kill and who to let live.

The waitress was an older woman with a white apron and a note pad for taking orders. She wore bright red lipstick and had a cigarette firmly planted behind her right ear. She looked like something out of a 60's movie. She could have been Alice from that Arlo Guthrie song, 'Alice's Restaurant.'

Bruce finished his meal, left a nice tip on the table, and walked back outside, strolling slowly down the sidewalk, enjoying the cool evening. He knew fall would be here soon but for now summer was holding on by its fingertips. On the street, traffic rolled by, rushing home at the end of a long workday. Headlights chased away the evening shadows encroaching on the sidewalks. Overhead streetlamps came on, leaving tiny pools of artificial light on the sidewalks.

Bruce found his car still parked along the curb and drove back to the Hunts Point neighborhood to see what the night life was like. The streets weren't as busy as they had been earlier in the day. Fewer people walked the sidewalks. The ones that did though clung to the shadows and dark corners beside the buildings, hiding like sharks in the ocean waiting for unsuspecting prey. A few prostitutes patrolled the edges of sidewalks, close to the streets, trying to stay in the light as much as possible so the men driving by could get a good look at them.

Bruce drove his car along at a slow pace through the neighborhood, studying everything he saw along the way, trying to get a picture of what life was like in this section of the city. A prostitute standing at a random street corner caught his eye and he eased up to the curb, rolling down his window. She approached his car, keeping her eyes moving up and down the street. She seemed nervous, ready to run at the slightest sign of danger. In the light of the streetlamp, she looked clean, but when she leaned into his window she smelled like an ashtray. Her eyes were bloodshot. She had a little meat on her bones still and appeared to have all of her teeth. Except for the cigarette smell, she seemed pretty healthy for a prostitute.

"Whatcha looking for?" the woman asked. She had a thick Southern New England accent that made Bruce smile. She looked to be in her late twenties but could have been younger. She had a poorly done dye job that left her hair looking more orange than red. Black clumps of mascara clung to her eye lashes and she wore too much makeup. Even if Bruce liked girls, he would have had a hard time finding her attractive.

"Company," Bruce said, holding up a twenty.

"You a cop?" she asked, looking up and down the street again. Bruce glanced into his rearview mirror but saw nothing back there that appeared alarming.

"No, I'm just someone looking for a bit of company tonight," he answered. She looked down the street again and then at Bruce. She smiled and he noticed that her lipstick had stained two of her teeth. The sight of it made his stomach roll for some reason. The lipstick, the makeup, it was all kind of gross for some reason.

"It's gonna be a hundred for that company. We can discuss anything else you might be interested in after that."

"What about fifty and a meal?" Bruce asked. The woman looked into the car, her eyes searching for trouble. Bruce wondered if she thought he might be the killer or if she was just paranoid that he was a cop.

"Deal," she said, walking around to the passenger side and getting in. Bruce watched her sit down and close the door. He wondered if she had a weapon. He couldn't see where she would have kept one, but he still wondered. Pulling away from the curb, he kept his window down so her perfume and the odor of her last cigarette could drift out of the car. He hated perfumy smells and he wasn't a big fan of cigarettes either.

"Turn here," she said, hooking her thumb to the right. Bruce turned. "Keep going until you see a food truck parked in a vacant lot. Best truck in the whole damn city." Bruce nodded, keeping an eye out for a food truck. He found the food truck easily enough and pulled up along the curb.

The food truck was an elaborate affair, painted in bright colors. A large face with large eyes and purple hair covered one side of the truck. Food items surrounded the face like a halo. On the opposite side of the truck, people lined up along the sidewalk for food. Bruce handed the woman a twenty and told her to get whatever she thought was best. She returned ten minutes later with four stuffed tacos wrapped in wax paper and drinks.

"Don't think about it, just eat it," she said, handing Bruce two of the tacos. Bruce did as she said, and they were amazing. The two of them ate in silence, standing outside the car. Bruce finished the first taco and started in on the second. It tasted just as amazing as the first. After he was finished, he tossed his trash in a trashcan in front of the food truck.

"So, how long have you been doing what you do?" Bruce asked, watching as she finished off her last bite.

"First off, I do what I do to survive. So, fuck you for asking," she answered.

"I meant no offense," Bruce said, deciding to tell her who he was and why he was out there. "Look, I'm a consultant," he explained. "I'm working the prostitute murders and I just want to talk."

"You got no case on me, asshole," she said. "I never took your fucking money and I never offered anything for any money, so fuck you."

"I told you, I'm not a cop, I'm a private investigator. I've only been hired to assist on the case. My name is Bruce Westman and I'm sorry if I've upset you. I'll take you back to where I picked you up if you want."

She looked at Bruce for a moment, considering what he had just said. Bruce took her trash and tossed it in the trashcan while she sat there thinking. "You can call me Laurie," she said finally. "And you can give me my fucking money. Call it a fee for services." She held out her hand and Bruce paid her. She slipped the money inside her bra before looking back at him. "So, what do you want to know?" she asked, brushing her bangs off her forehead.

Bruce studied Laurie. He wasn't sure if he could trust her or not, but he thought he might be able to, so he went on. "Have you seen a small pickup, maybe an old blue or black Ford Ranger or something small like that, driving around? White guy, maybe my age or a little older behind the wheel picking up girls that don't come back."

"I guess, I mean small pickups are sort of common out here. You know, little Johnny looking to get his dick sucked before going home to the frigid wifey or an empty bed and his right hand."

"Okay, but how about one truck in particular. Big boy, dark hair," Bruce explained. "He wouldn't so much stick out from the other guys that come around here, but he's in shape. There might be a gunrack or something like that behind the front seat."

"Maybe, I guess. I don't pay too much attention if the action doesn't come my way." Bruce nodded, disappointed she wasn't being more helpful.

"If I gave you my cellphone number, would you keep an eye out and call me if you see something?" Bruce asked.

"How much are you going to pay me? I don't do nothing for free," Laurie explained, cracking the window and lighting a cigarette.

"A consulting fee," Bruce said, smiling. He liked her. She was street smart.

"Yeah, a fee like what you get paid. I can kinda be like your assistant on this," Laurie said, smiling back at Bruce. He resisted the urge to tell her to put out the cigarette.

"I'll pay you fifty dollars a day, but you have to earn it, you can't fuck me over."

"You talk to your mother with that mouth?" Laurie asked, blowing smoke out the window.

"Fuck you," Bruce said, smiling.

"A hundred dollars a day, and I'll be your girl on the street," Laurie said, holding out her hand. Bruce let it hang in there for a minute trying to decide if this was a good idea. Sighing deeply, he shook her hand.

"Fine, a hundred, but you better not screw me. I want good information."

"If I screwed you, it would cost you extra," Laurie said, flicking the cigarette out the window. Bruce nodded and started the car, pulling away from the curb. He drove back to the spot where had picked Laurie up and stopped. Laurie exited the car and leaned back into the open window.

"Do you have a phone?" Bruce asked.

"Are you buying me one? I lost my old phone the other day." Bruce sighed again.

"Fine, I'll be back tomorrow with a phone," Bruce said as Laurie took a step back from the window. "And Laurie, be careful out there, don't get caught by this guy, he's a sick fuck."

"Baby, I've been taking care of myself since I was ten, I can handle my shit out here." Bruce nodded.

"Just be careful," Bruce said.

"Sure, Dad," Laurie said, walking away from the car. Bruce watched her go until a beige Mercury pulled up along the curb. He watched in his mirror as she leaned into an open window and began talking with the driver. He wanted to jump out and tell her not to do it, but he resisted. He drove off before he could see the results of her conversation with the driver.

"You can't save everyone," he whispered, turning at the intersection.

Chapter 15

Bruce's cellphone rang early the next morning. He glared at the screen wishing the light would wink out. The cellphone stopped ringing after the fourth ring. He smiled thinly and closed his eyes again, but the cellphone rang again a few minutes later. He snatched it up from the bedside table, squeezing it hard enough to choke the life out of it, if that were possible. The screen displayed a number he didn't recognize.

"What?" he asked, taking in the thin shaft of sunlight slipping through the thick curtain over the lone window.

"Westman, where the fuck are you? I called your brother and he said you had gone into the city yesterday," Agent Shelby asked. He sounded irritated. Bruce couldn't have cared less.

"I'm in the Bronx," Bruce answered, sitting up in bed now, his feet planted on the cool laminate floor.

"Why didn't you call me?" Shelby asked.

"Because I didn't want to," Bruce answered, irritated with him now.

"Well, fuck you too," Shelby said. "You eat yet?"

"I haven't even gotten out of bed yet," Bruce answered.

"Well, get the fuck out of bed and call me back. We'll meet somewhere for breakfast and talk things over. I know this Jewish deli on Arthur near the Bronx Park."

"Fine," Bruce said, hitting the disconnect button without saying goodbye.

Bruce rolled out of bed and took a shower, stepping outside thirty minutes later. There was a slight chill to the air. A stiff breeze blew between the buildings sounding mournful as it crawled through the city landscape. Gray clouds scudded across the sky looking fat and ready to burst. It was a dreary day that seemed to press down on him as he left the protection of the brownstone.

Out on the street, he walked quickly to his car, wanting to get safely inside before the heavens opened up. The driver's side door unlocked with a metallic click that sounded loud in spite of the traffic on the street. Bruce sat down, closed the door, twisting the key in the ignition. The engine coughed once and roared to life. He could still smell the odor of Laurie's cigarette from the night before as the car idled for a few minutes. He grabbed his cellphone and hit the call back button. The phone rang twice. Agent Shelby answered after the second ring.

"Shelby," Agent Shelby answered.

"Westman," Bruce responded, trying to sound as serious as Shelby sounded.

"I'm already here," Shelby said. "Just go to the counter when you get here and order your food. Find me at one of the tables." Bruce disconnected the call and pulled away from the curb. He used his cellphone's GPS to find the deli on the map. It wasn't that far away, and he found it quickly. Finding a parking spot on the street proved to be more difficult than finding the deli.

Bruce walked through the glass doors fronting the sidewalk and stepped up to the counter. A line of New Yorkers was crowded in front of the counter shouting orders and Bruce had to squeeze his way through the crowd to place his order. He ordered a bacon, egg, and cheddar on rye with a cup of black coffee. At the register, his food was waiting, and he paid for his meal.

Agent Shelby sat at a small table by the window. He sat with his back to the wall, facing into the deli so that he had a clear view of the front door. Bruce sat down across from him and took a long sip of coffee before allowing the sandwich to slide free of its paper bag. A smile spread across his face as he took his first bite. The sandwich was perfect. The bread was toasted just right, slathered in butter. The egg was a perfect medium, and the bacon had just the right amount of crispness. He chewed his food around the smile, childishly hoping that Shelby would find it irritating.

"I just want you to know that you're working for me, not the Bureau," Shelby said. Bruce nodded and continued chewing. "I'll pay you under the table. All I ask is you make sure to keep out of everyone's way."

Bruce frowned and set his sandwich down on a napkin. He wiped at his mouth with the back of his hand and took another sip of coffee. "That's not how I work, so fuck you," Bruce said, picking up his sandwich again and taking a large bite.

"It's how you're going to have to work with me," Shelby said, finishing off the last of his coffee and setting the cup down on the tabletop.

"Let me tell you how I work," Bruce said around what he had in his mouth. "I don't play well with others. I don't share. I have to get to the crime scenes as soon as possible or I can't do what I do." Shelby held up a hand.

"Look, your brother told me a little about what it is that you do. I don't buy it, I think it's all a bunch of bullshit, but you got results with that freak in Connecticut earlier this summer. So, I am willing to see what you can do, but you have to understand, I can't let the other investigators know or I'll be laughed out of a job."

"I got your number," Bruce said, chasing his last bite down with a big slurp of coffee. "I'll work things out on my own. You just make sure to tip me off when something happens, and I'll make sure to keep you up to date on what I find out. Oh yeah, I hired someone on the side to assist me, so you'll need to compensate her as well."

"Look, I don't make a hell of a lot of money," Shelby said, holding up his hands.

"She costs a hundred a day and I cost two hundred plus expenses like this breakfast and my room. If you can't handle that I can always go back home."

Shelby studied Bruce for a minute. "I can manage that short term but not for long. Get it done and check in with me every day. I'll call you if our boy hits again."

Bruce smiled and stood up from the table. He reached down for his coffee, swirled the cup, and drank what was left. "By the way, your boy, he drives a small pickup. A Ford or something similar. Its old, ten maybe fifteen years and a dark color. Either blue or black. He's white, late twenties early thirties and he has facial hair. He likes getting his dick sucked but that's not why he does what he does."

Shelby sat up and looked across the table at Bruce. He was amazed and suspicious at what he had just heard. "How?" he asked.

"It's a gift," Bruce explained. "If you ask my priest and therapist that's what he'll tell you anyway." Shelby nodded. "That's all I got so far."

"You didn't answer my question," Shelby said, standing up now and walking around the table so he stood right next to Bruce.

"I went to that park where the first victim was found and sat down where he left her in front of that tree. I call what I do drifting, and I saw what I saw."

"Fucking weird," Shelby said, shaking his head.

"Yeah, it is," Bruce said, before turning and walking out of the deli. On the sidewalk he took several deep breaths, tasting the moisture in the air, and wondered if he had made a mistake agreeing to help Shelby. *Asshole will never understand,* he thought, watching the cars hurrying by on the street.

Chapter 16

Billy was struck by an eighteen-wheeler on the highway when he was just twenty-one years old. The driver of the truck had been at fault in the accident and Billy had spent two months in the hospital recovering from head injuries and a fractured hip. He spent three more months in rehab learning to walk again and to hold a fork. As part of the rehab, he took art classes, discovering he enjoyed creating art. He loved painting and sculpting and writing poems. He enjoyed the feeling of sitting back and looking at what he had created with his hands. It was all such a rush, that feeling he felt whenever he looked at what he had done. It didn't come close to what he felt when he did his secret things, but it was a nice feeling just the same.

A lawyer sued the driver of the truck and the company that he worked for on Billy's behalf, and after paying the lawyer, Billy had three hundred thousand dollars left over to do whatever he wanted. The first thing that he did was buy thirty acres of land in Upstate New York. The property came with an old, dilapidated farmhouse and a small barn. The house was unlivable, but it had something about it that drew Billy. All of the rooms were full of trash and things left behind and forgotten by past owners. The property was set well back from the road, the house virtually invisible to anyone driving by. It was just perfect.

At one time, the property had been farmland but that had been a long time ago. Now it was overgrown and full of wildlife. Squirrels, racoons, and deer roamed everywhere. Northern red oaks, silver maples, and tall pines populated the land, creating a natural barrier between the roadway and the property. It was the most perfect piece of property he could have ever imagined. He hunted on the land, unmolested and undisturbed. The closest neighbor was almost two miles away and showed no interest in his new neighbor. Billy was free to do as he wanted, to come and go whenever he desired. He was free to create art however he liked without others passing judgement.

Billy didn't have much use for most of the farmhouse, except for one of the bedrooms upstairs that faced to the west. He felt drawn to that room as if there was a living presence inside there. The room was real and alive, and whenever he was inside the room, he could feel its energy. It was as if the walls spoke to him.

Billy cleaned the room from top to bottom until there was nothing left. He painted the walls and stained the wood floor. He set trim along the baseboards and the ceiling and down each corner, so it appeared that each wall was a large picture frame. He used a high gloss white paint so in the right light, the walls looked almost like glass. He called this room his art studio, and when it was finished, he brought all of his art to it so he could display it there. In the center of the room was a wooden chair that he had found in the basement of the farmhouse. He spent three days stripping away the layers of old paint, sanding down the wood, and refinishing the chair until it looked like new. Every chance he had, he sat in the chair and gazed upon his art.

Along with the house was an old barn on the property. He found an old wagon wheel that looked like it had come off one of those old stagecoaches from the wild west. The wheel was a faded gray color with a pitted and rusted steel band wrapped around the outside. He brought the wheel into the farmhouse and set it in another room, close to his art studio. He cleaned this room too, but not like he had the other room. He didn't paint the walls or strip the floor. No trim went up. He simply made the room presentable so he could set his wagon wheel inside. Along with the wheel he placed another chair that he found in the basement inside the room. He called this room, his workshop. Over time he placed tools inside his workshop on a child's desk. Along with the tools there were several notebooks and a cracked coffee cup filled with pens and pencils on the desktop. On the wall beside the desk, he hung his blades. They hung from hooks pointing down toward the floor.

An old, tattered Bible sat in one corner of the desk. Its pages yellowed and well thumbed-through. A cheap plastic rosary was wound around the Bible. A candle stood in a brass holder beside the Bible. Wax pooled beneath the holder and down the side of the desk. Scrawled on the wall in black marker facing him was one word. It was written in large block letters, all capitals as if it were shouting back at him. "UNWORTHY," the word shouted. Billy looked at it every time he sat at his desk.

The rest of the house was left as he had found it. He had no desire to clean it or fix it up. The stairs leading up to the second level leaned slightly away from the wall. Nothing looked safe about them, even though Billy had installed anchors so it wouldn't fall over. Billy liked how the house looked. He didn't want trespassers to get the wrong idea. He even allowed trash to build up on the floor of his workshop, so it appeared nasty to the casual observer. The only clean room in the whole house was the art studio, which he kept locked at all times when he wasn't there.

After Billy had finished setting up the farmhouse the way he wanted it, he sold his old Volkswagen VW and bought a used two door Ford Ranger pickup. He could have bought something new, something nicer, because he still had plenty of money, but he wanted something that only he would want to drive and no one else. He paid cash for the truck and twenty dollars more for the old plates. The pickup was a little beat up and showed its age. The windows were hand cranked; the fenders had a tiny bit of rust eating away at them, but he was okay with all that since he wanted something that didn't stand out. The truck did what he wanted. It ran, the wheels rolled, and the best part was, no one ever paid him much attention when he drove around the city.

Billy took a part time job delivering packages for FedEx. He didn't need the work, but needed to do something, and delivering packages around the city allowed him to get out and see things that he might not see otherwise. He drove a white-paneled truck around three days a week. When he was working, he stayed in a small one-room apartment on the upper west side in a rundown neighborhood. No one paid him any attention there either as he came and went. No one missed him when he was up at his land, viewing his art.

During the days that he was delivering packages, Billy was able to view the world as it existed. He saw the wealthy and the poor, the gutter trash and the well-to-do existing side by side without ever really seeing each other. He quickly learned that most people were unconcerned with how they affected the lives of others. The sidewalks were like vast rivers of humanity racing back and forth to countless destinations. The street people, the homeless, the victims and the predators, the drug dealers and the prostitutes shared space with the businessman or woman, never seeing, but always aware of one another.

The whores prowled the streets like jackals, seeking whom they may devour. This unworthy trash bothered Billy the most. They were the most disgusting of all the unworthy things, and they needed to be removed from his world before their disease infected all the other things that populated his world. They only pretended to really see him, when in reality they were ignoring him as he moved between light and dark.

The whores were Robin in her bedroom, screaming when she saw him, disgusted by the sight of him. Oh, she pretended to be something that she wasn't, just like his mother had, but he knew better now, she was like all the rest. He knew they were all the same. Nothing but simple whores only pretending to be real.

Billy hated all of them so much. They deserved to be punished, and he wanted to punish them. He wanted to punish his mother because she left him all alone. He wanted to punish Robin because she was the cause of everything that had happened to him. It was her fault that he was sent to juvenile and attacked, fucked like somebody's bitch. It was her fault that his whore of a mother left him when he was released. It was her fault that the son of a bitching eighteen-wheeler crashed into him leaving him with a limp for the rest of his life. Her fault, her fault, her fucking whore ass fault, and he would make them all pay.

Billy drove around the city while he worked, watching and studying, his hatred always there, always growing, always just existing beneath the surface of everything he did. The world was a simple place after all. Men took whores and did what they did with them. It wasn't until after the accident that he had done anything with a whore. Before that, the boy who had attacked him had been the only one to ever touch him that way. He knew how to touch himself, how to release the sin inside of him, and he knew what an asshole was for, that lesson had been painfully taught to him, but he himself had never been with a woman or a girl.

What Billy knew about sex he learned while locked up. He watched the other boys touching themselves, releasing their filth on the floor or in the toilets, or inside each other. There was one boy in particular who enjoyed helping others release their filth. That boy taught him how to touch and play with his thing. How to please himself. He even showed him what a mouth could be used for that didn't cause pain. Billy always felt guilty afterward, dirty, but the release was always incredible when it happened. It was in that one moment that he felt connected with the rest of the world, like he wasn't the only one who truly existed.

Billy picked up his first whore late one night after work. She wasn't pretty and she wasn't young. She was thick around the middle and in truth, she grossed him out. Her hands were dirty, and her lipstick was cracked and peeling away from her lips. Dark shadows ringed her eyes and she looked sick. The odor of spent cigarettes clung to her body. She seemed just as nervous as he felt. Walking up and down the sidewalk, trying to look everywhere at once while scratching her arms as if ants were crawling over her skin.

Billy stopped along the curb in his pickup, leaning across the seat and rolling down the window. She walked up to the open window and leaned in enough so her shirt opened so he could see her breasts. She wasn't wearing a bra and he had a clear shot of her nipples. He felt himself grow hard. He forgot all about how she looked.

"What are you looking for?" the whore asked, her eyes darting nervously. Billy was speechless. He didn't know what to say or do. The whore smiled a thin sad smile that aged her face even more and drew lines at the corners of her eyes. She knew a virgin when she saw one. "I'll take care of you, baby," she said, opening the door and getting into the pickup. Billy swallowed hard and drove away from the curb, following her directions to a dark vacant alley. She had him park at the rear of the alley and turn off his lights. Slowly, he released the steering wheel and turned to look at the woman sitting across from him. In the darkness of the cab, she didn't seem so bad. His hard on painfully poked at his jeans. He wanted to shift it but was too scared to touch himself.

A hand slipped into Billy's lap, causing him to draw in a deep breath. Thin fingers gripped his dick through the fabric of his jeans. He let the breath out in one long groan. His eyes rolled back, and his head fell against the seat. The whore tugged at his zipper, pulling his dick free of its prison. The coolness of the pickup sent sparks of electricity crawling up and down the shaft as her lips fell on him. She cupped his balls, squeezing and tugging at them while going up and down with her mouth. It was incredible. It was the most incredible thing he had ever felt before. He lasted only a minute or so before exploding inside her mouth. She sat up quickly, wiping at the corner of her mouth with the back of her hand as a little bit of his cum ran out.

"Thirty," she said. "I swallowed so it costs more."

Billy opened his eyes and glared across the seat. He was beyond mad that she had ruined his moment by talking.

"Come on, sweety, pay up," she said, sounding inpatient now.

Before Billy knew what was happening, his hand flashed up and he slammed the whore's head into the passenger side window. The glass exploded. The whore's eyes rolled up into the back of her head until he saw only the whites. More cum dribbled out of the corner of her mouth. He watched it roll down her jaw. The sight caused him to feel more rage and anger toward her. The hand flashed out again, this time punching her in the face several times. She fell back against the seat and the door like a lifeless doll. Blood ran from her mouth. He liked the sight of that much better and the rage started to release its hold over him.

Billy sat in that alley for thirty minutes looking at what he had done. The whore hadn't moved at all while he sat watching her. He wondered if she might be dead, but he wasn't sure. Inside the dark cab of the truck, he couldn't tell if she was breathing. He reached across the seat and lifted her shirt until both of her breasts were free. They sagged a bit, but he was alright with that. With his other hand, he grabbed and twisted one of her breasts. It was firm enough, and pleasant feeling, warm to the touch. He held it in his hand, pinching the nipple between two of his fingers. She didn't move or cry out.

You have to go, a voice shouted inside his head. Billy let go of the breast, looking out the windshield now, expecting to see the police, but the alley was still empty. He looked up into the rearview mirror and saw his scared eyes staring back at him. "Fuck you," he whispered at his reflection, twisting the key and shifting the truck into drive. He drove slowly back up the alley and out onto the street.

Billy left the alley with no direction in mind, but it wasn't long before he realized he was headed out to his property. He parked outside the abandoned farmhouse hours later and carried the whore's lifeless body up to his workshop. He set her down on the floor at first after stripping off her clothes and then laid her across the wagon wheel. She looked like putty there in the dim moonlight filtering in through the dust covered window of his workshop. She looked like something begging to be shaped and molded into something new.

Billy found his blade among his tools and set about carving away a patch of skin from her back. It was messy work, but he kept at it until he had the perfect piece of art for his display. He took the skin away and prepared it before placing it under glass, inside a frame. He hung the skin on the wall among his other collected items inside his art studio. Once the frame hung just right on the wall, he removed his clothing, folding each piece neatly, storing each piece under his viewing chair. He sat down on the chair, the cold wood on his buttock surprising at first, and looked at what he had created. It was wonderful. It was a masterpiece. Billy masturbated several times that night into his lap while looking at his latest addition. He masturbated until it ran down between his legs, turning sticky. He masturbated until he fell asleep with his hand wrapped around his dick.

Billy left his studio hours later, carrying his clothes in one arm as he walked across the hallway to his workshop. The whore was still there tied to the wagon wheel, her filthy ass pointed up into the air. He gazed down at the red raw patch he had left on her back and in spite of everything, found himself hard again. The clothes fell to the floor as if forgotten. He took hold of himself and masturbated once more over the body, allowing himself to spill out into the wound. It felt amazing. After he finished, he lay down beside the wheel among all the filth on the floor and fell asleep.

The next morning, Billy awakened to sunlight streaming into the room. He stared over at the body on the wagon wheel and felt himself stirring. He thought about doing more but he was sore. He stood and peed into the open wound instead. His urine turned a pink color as it ran down over either side of the body, spilling onto the floor. He watched it spread among the trash beneath the wagon wheel. Turning around, he saw his clothing on the floor and gathered up the articles before walking back across the hallway to his art studio.

Billy set to work on the body later that morning. First, he released it from the wagon wheel and dragged it down the stairs. Outside in the yard, he began chopping the body up. He cut off the arms and legs. He sliced away each breast and cut her from asshole to vagina. He split her torso up the middle, making sure to remove the organs as he went. He removed the head with a saw and set it off to the side. Gore covered the grass and weeds, but he ignored everything as he went about his work. Once he was finished, he placed everything in a trunk he had come across in the basement of the house. He stood back and admired his work. It looked incredible.

Billy dropped to his knees and slipped his hands into the mess of dismembered body parts. Some of it resisted, some of it yielded. It felt like slime as he flexed his fingers beneath the gore. It felt like he was touching the primordial essence of life. Withdrawing his hands, he stared at them. They were covered in blood and tissue. Bits and pieces fell from his fingers. He stuck one of those into his mouth, and then another, and another, savoring his work, tasting her spirit. It was so empowering. A jolt of pure energy shot through his body and he orgasmed right there into his pants.

Love, he thought. *This is what love feels like.* Billy finished cleaning off his fingers and stood. He dragged the trunk across the yard to the edge of the forest and dug a hole. He spent that whole afternoon digging until he thought the hole was deep enough to protect his precious from predators. After the trunk rested at the bottom of the hole, he opened the lid once more and placed an old plastic rosary on top of the body parts. He made sure the cross rested upside down since in life, she had been a whore, after all, and was unworthy of God's forgiveness.

Chapter 17

Bruce stood in front of a shuttered storefront, leaning against a red brick wall covered in a thin film of soot. A rust covered, gray metal grate covered the windows so he couldn't see inside the store. Bits of light still managed to leak out from behind the grate, shining thin shafts of illumination onto the sidewalk. It wasn't enough to see much, just a tease really, but Bruce's focus wasn't on the sidewalk. His eyes were focused on the activity on the street in front of the store. He stood silently beneath a tattered awning watching the activity going on at a small strip club across the street from the store. Occasionally, he took a pull from a small pint bottle that he kept secreted in his back pocket, but his gaze never wavered.

The neon lights above the club lit up the sidewalk out front driving the shadows away from the entrance. Men and a few women from all walks of life entered through the front doors of the establishment. Some were young, some were old, and some fell somewhere in-between. Music blared annoyingly from inside the club every time the doors opened. A bouncer the size of the Rock stood just to the side of the entrance, glaring down at everyone entering the strip club.

As the hour grew late, men and women began exiting the club together. Some got into cabs or Ubers, some walked down the sidewalk to wherever they parked, disappearing into the shadows beyond the lights of the club. Several people simply found dark spots in hidden alley alcoves to do whatever they were going to do with whomever they were going to do it with. Bruce paid close attention to these persons, watching the men, studying their faces, and making sure the women they went with returned. Most of the women, strippers, prostitutes, or both, reappeared ten or fifteen minutes later going back inside the club. It was all very steady business, very disgusting and very sad, and Bruce was forced to watch it all.

Around two thirty that morning, Laurie strolled up and took a spot on the wall beside Bruce. She wore a lowcut shirt that showed plenty of cleavage and exposed an inch of stomach at the bottom. A silver chain with a red ruby dangled from her belly button. Her blue shorts were extremely short, riding up the crack of her ass, allowing her cheeks to hang out just the tiniest bit. Her lips were coated with a thick red lipstick. She wore a dirty blonde wig that allowed only a few strands of her natural brunette to escape around her ears. Bruce had to resist the urge to reach up and straighten out the wig. A Virginia Slim cigarette dangled from the corner of her mouth, the smoke curling away above her head.

"Got my money?" Laurie asked, blowing out a gray cloud of smoke. Bruce watched the smoke spread out and disappear into the darkness above them.

"You got any information that I can use or are you just trying to yank my dick?" Bruce asked without looking back at her.

"If I yank your dick it's going to cost you extra, asshole," Laurie said, looking at Bruce while blowing smoke through her nostrils.

"Information, that's what I pay you for and nothing else," Bruce said, looking back at her.

"I asked around about a small dark colored pickup truck. Some of the girls say they've seen it, but they describe different guys driving. There were a couple of them that talked about a creepy dude. He likes for them to blow him, which is an easy twenty, but somehow he's creepier than most."

Bruce looked back across the street and the business in front of the strip club was still steady. "Fine," he said, handing her several bills. "You need to dress better if you're going to work with me. No blow jobs or anything else, you work for me until we catch this asshat."

"Got it, you're my pimp until this guy is caught," Laurie said, dropping the cigarette on the sidewalk. She smashed it with the tip of her shoe.

"No, I'm not your pimp. I'm your employer and you're my employee," Bruce said, stepping away from the wall. Laurie chuckled and stuck another cigarette in her mouth.

"Okay, boss," she muttered, lighting her cigarette with a thin pink bedazzled lighter. Bruce shook his head.

"Come on, show me around the neighborhood. Show me where he's hunting." Laurie paused, giving Bruce a questioning look, through slitted eyes. He frowned. "That's what he's doing out there, you know.

He's hunting these girls and killing them." Laurie nodded, the cigarette jumping a bit between her lips.

Laurie took Bruce's hand as they walked away, leading him down the sidewalk, away from the storefront. Behind them the music from inside the strip club flared louder for a moment before fading away as the door closed again. Dark shadows crawled over the sidewalk like injured soldiers on a forced march. Bruce turned his eyes away from the shadows and thoughts of dead soldiers, noting that even at this late hour the streets and sidewalks held a steady flow of people and cars. New York was proving that it really was a city that never slept.

Over the next two hours, Laurie showed Bruce where she and other girls worked the streets that wound through the Bronx. She pointed out all the men on the prowl for a hook up. She pointed out the pimps hiding in the shadows watching their girls. She took him to the alleyways that were used for sex and drugs. Bruce paid attention to everything, noting how easy it would be for someone to just make one of these girls disappear. It was so easy because the girls were nothing but runaways, addicts, homeless, living on the fringes of society, existing in the shadows. They were all so vulnerable and disposable. He wished he could talk with Father Murphy and get the priest's take on all of this sadness.

Laurie led Bruce down the sidewalk past several girls working the curbs, leaning into cars, huddling beneath the streetlights. The girls all tried to occupy the odd-shaped pools of light that spilled down from overhead like invisible prisons. Bruce listened to the transactions taking place as they walked slowly along the sidewalk. He studied the desperate men offering money for sex and the desperate women, some so young they should still be in school, offering sex for money. It all made him ill, and he wanted to be somewhere else.

Bruce followed Laurie down the dark alleys where the transactions were completed. The alleys were all the same, full of shadows and dark corners. Dumpsters and trash lined the walls. Rats and cats fought with each other over scraps of food. Meager light sometimes filtered down from windows up high, but most of the time the alleys were nothing more than dark caves set between the buildings. It all felt so heavy and depressing. The walls felt like they were closing in and the smell of rotting food and worse clung to everything.

Down one of the alleys a small car was parked, its lights off. Bruce crept up close to the car and saw a man inside through lightly fogged windows. He sat in the driver's seat with his head leaning back against the headrest. Another head, a woman's head, bobbed up and down in the man's lap for several minutes before finally sitting back up. Laurie leaned close and whispered into Bruce's ear. "That's Stacy. She's young, still decent looking. She does maybe ten blow jobs a night for twenty-five dollars a suck. She'll swallow for thirty. She's good. She can get most guys off in three minutes, and even tickles his asshole, if he likes that sort of thing." Bruce nodded. "She's hooked on smack though, spends her money as fast as she makes it. She won't last long out here."

"What about you?" Bruce asked. "Do you use?"

Laurie watched as the car left the alley. She watched Stacy get out at the curb, scratching her arms, dying for that next fix. She looked at Bruce, her face hard in the darkness. "Fuck you," she said. "Not everyone is a pampered white boy from the suburbs with a mommy and daddy who loves them."

"I'm not all that pampered, so fuck you back," Bruce said. "I just need to know who I'm working with. I understand demons, believe me," he said, pulling the bottle from his back pocket and taking a swig. Laurie looked at Bruce and nodded.

"No, I don't use anything other than alcohol and cigarettes to get by," she said, reaching for the bottle. Bruce handed it to her, and she took a long swallow.

"I drink copious amounts of alcohol," Bruce said. Laurie handed the bottle back. Bruce slipped it back into his pocket. "I want to go down there where they were parked," Bruce said, walking further down into the alley. Laurie followed. At the end of the alley trash littered the ground. Bruce took out a penlight and shone it around the concrete. Empty bottles, discarded condoms, spent cigarettes, and tons of paper covered the ground. He ignored most of it and positioned himself in the middle of the alley between the tracks left behind by the tires where the car had parked. "This feels right," he whispered, rolling his shoulders and neck, getting ready to do what he didn't want to do.

"What feels right?" Laurie asked. "It's just a fucking honey hole. There's hundreds of them out here."

Bruce held up a hand to quiet her and closed his eyes, willing the drift to come. The drift came over him quickly. He felt himself slipping away from reality into a world of darkness and slowly moving water. Up and down, he rode the waves until the light returned.

Bruce found that he was still standing in the alleyway as things took shape around him. In front of him was a parked car where none had been a moment ago. Like a voyeur watching a peepshow, he watched a man force a woman's head down into his lap. The act finished quickly, nothing more than a transaction, and then the car pulled away from the alley, only to be replaced by another car. Over and over, he watched women and girls service men inside their cars and trucks. He saw blow jobs, hand jobs, and straight out fucking. He saw abuses of every kind. Rapes and beatings and drug use. Time didn't seem to matter in the alley as he was forced to witness all of this misery. So many cars coming and going. So much pain being dealt out. His heart felt like it was breaking. He wanted to scream at women, to lash out at the men. He understood now why the killer was picking prostitutes for his victims. They were nothing more than objects to the people using them. They didn't exist beyond what they were doing or having done to them. They were nothing more than a means to an end, something to be discarded once its use was finished.

Laurie stood a few feet away from Bruce watching as tears slid down his face. She didn't know what to do. She didn't even know if she should do something. He hadn't prepared her for anything like this. From where she stood, he looked like he was having an epileptic seizure. His body trembled and tears fell from his closed eyes. His head leaned back so far that his Adam's apple stood out from his throat like a clenched fist. Soft moans passed from between his tightly pressed lips. She was terrified. She wanted to run away but her body wouldn't respond. So, much like Bruce, she was forced to simply watch.

The world finally slowed down. The endless parade of vehicles came to a stop as a final set of headlights appeared at the top of the alley. He could tell right away it was a small pickup. Maybe a Ranger or Tacoma. It drove slowly down the alley, turning off its lights, and hiding in the deeply shadowed darkness at the end. Inside the cab of the pickup, he saw two shadowed shapes. For all he could tell they could have been two men or two women, or one of each, but he knew it wasn't. He knew this was him. This was his killer. He had used this very alley.

Bruce drew closer to the pickup and looked into the window. The man was getting a blow job. The hooker's head bobbed up and down in his lap. He had a hand on the back of her head, his fingers tangled in her hair. The windows of the truck fogged up and he heard the man suddenly groan. His hand fell away from the hooker's hair. She sat up wiping at her mouth as a thin line of cum ran from the corner. She had slender fingers with dark painted nails. The man looked across the seat as she wiped the cum away. His lip curled into a snarl, his eyes blazed hatred. All at once he jumped across the seat with a shout of rage. A struggle ensued. The passenger side door flew open. The girl tumbled out of the truck, falling into all the trash surrounding the pickup. The killer reached for her, but she was quick. She gained her feet and ran down the alley. The killer leapt out the driver's side door to chase her, but he was too late. She turned the corner and disappeared into the night. The killer pounded his fists on the side of the pickup, screaming his frustration into the alley. His voice echoed off the walls. A light came on from a window set several floors above.

"Son of a bitch," Bruce whispered, opening his eyes. He looked at Laurie.

"Son of a bitch, motherfucker, what the hell was that?" Laurie asked, concerned and a little bit frightened. Bruce leaned over and vomited. Laurie jumped back to get out of the way. Bruce wiped at his mouth and thought of the girl wiping away the cum from her mouth. He threw up again.

"I'll tell you about it later," Bruce said, looking out at the street. "I think someone got away from him in this alley. We have to find her."

"What the hell are you talking about?"

"Just trust me," Bruce said, reaching for a wall to steady himself. He slipped a notebook from his pocket and began writing on the pages. "Come on," he said, finishing what he was writing. Laurie followed him out of the alley. On the sidewalk, Bruce handed her the notebook. On the page was a description of the prostitute that had run away. Laurie read the description.

"I think that's Betty Two Cups," Laurie said, handing the notebook back to Bruce. "She disappeared for a while, but she's been back for about month now."

"Why do they call her Betty Two Cups?" Bruce asked.

"Because she's always two cups away from being wasted," Laurie explained.

"Well, we have to find her," Bruce said, walking down the sidewalk. Laurie followed just a step behind.

"Why?" she asked once she caught up with him.

"Because she escaped. She's seen him and she can describe him." Laurie nodded, deciding it was better not to ask how he knew that. A shiver raced up her spine as they continued down the sidewalk.

Chapter 18

Bruce and Laurie found Betty Two Cups an hour later sitting off the road in a small patch of withered weeds and trash. She wore piss-soaked shorts and smelled like something left out in the sun way longer than it should have been. Old pee and smoldering vomit were the primary odors Bruce smelled, but there were plenty of other odors competing for supremacy about her person. Looking down at her, Bruce was positive that she was well past two cups away from being wasted. She wore a stained yellow shirt with some kind of floral pattern hidden behind all the filth. The shirt was pulled down just enough that her right breast was left naked and exposed for anyone walking by to see. She wore frayed jean shorts that were all scrunched up in her ass and soaked through with urine. The shorts were undone, and the zipper was down but they still rode above her hips. A forgotten hand clung to one side of the shorts as if it were holding them up or perhaps preventing them from being pulled down. A bit of pink frilly fabric showed in the valley left between the zipper. Streaks of dirt and dried vomit clung to her thighs and tracks of tears lined her face. One eye was swollen and bruised, and scratches lined either side of her neck. Bruce wanted to look away but couldn't seem to make himself.

"Betty," Laurie said, the sound of concern in her voice as she kneeled in front of the woman. Betty opened one eye, the eye that wasn't bruised and swollen shut, and smiled a slow lazy smile. "It's Laurie, Betty," Laurie said, pulling up the shirt so her breast wasn't exposed anymore.

"Laurie," Betty slurred, pushing away the hand that was tugging up the shirt. She fell over from the effort and lay with one side of her face in the dirt. A stream of spit dribbled from the corner of her mouth.

"Is there some place we can clean her up?" Bruce asked, stepping back, disgusted by what he saw.

"There's a twenty-four-hour shop on Southern that lets us use the facilities in the back for a price."

"What's the price?" Bruce asked.

"It depends on who's working," Laurie said without looking back at him. Bruce's face tightened. He wanted to feel sympathy for this woman, but it wouldn't come. What he really wanted to do was look away and forget she existed.

"Fuck it, I'll get my car and we can bring her back to my place and sober her up. I got a blanket in the trunk. We can spread it across the back seat."

"Do you really think that's a good idea?" Laurie asked. "It might be better if you just leave her with me and I'll call you when she's aware of things and can answer a few questions."

"I'm coming with you. We can get her something to eat and fresh clothes, but I'm not leaving you to babysit her alone."

"Okay," Laurie said, looking out at the street as a few cars drove by, slowing down just enough to see what was happening. "Go get your car and we'll take it from there." Bruce nodded, walking back toward the sidewalk.

Betty Two Cups was up and aware two hours later. Laurie and Bruce had brought her back to a small rundown apartment in a three-story faded red brick building close to the warehouse district in Hunts Point. The apartment, if you could call it that, was nothing more than four poorly painted white walls surrounding a small room with a mattress on the floor. Scattered clothing circled the mattress in tiny pools of forgotten filth. A kitchen stood to one side of the room. There was no stove, but an old grease-stained microwave sat on the counter beside a dented toaster. The sink was filled with dirty dishes spilling out onto the countertop and pushing up against the microwave. The only other room in the apartment was a small bathroom. Through the open door, Bruce saw a toilet, a sink, and a shower stall that was just wide enough to fit a very skinny human. A flickering light bulb above the kitchen sink lit the main room and a dull florescent light lit the bathroom. Roaches scurried away into the shadows beyond the flickering glow of the kitchen light. Bruce could hear their spiny little legs scratching on the walls and inside the cabinets.

Laurie took Betty right into the bathroom after they arrived and stuck her in the shower. Bruce stood in the other room looking around, afraid to touch anything. He wanted to sit down but there was simply nowhere to sit and even if there had been, he wasn't sure that he could have made himself sit down. In the end, he went over to the kitchen sink and began washing the dishes while taking pulls from his back pocket bottle. He finished the bottle before he finished the dishes. If it had been a race, it wouldn't have even been close.

Laurie came out of the bathroom thirty minutes later with Betty leaning heavily into her. The woman looked horrible but at least she didn't stink anymore. She wore a white t-shirt now and yellow panties that sat low on her hip. Her dirty blonde hair hung in wet strands over her shoulders and down her back. There were a few strands of silver mixed in with her hair. The black eye stood out in the flickering light above the sink. It was swollen shut and looked ugly and painful, but she hadn't seemed to notice as Laurie guided her over to the mattress. She lay down on top of the sheet beside Laurie and fell asleep. She was the little spoon. Laurie wrapped a protective arm over her shoulder and fell asleep a few minutes later.

Three fitful hours later, Betty Two Cups sat up screaming as if being attacked. Her arms flayed around, one catching Laurie before she could wrap the woman in a hug. A red handprint spread across the left side of her face as she enveloped the woman in her arms. Bruce stood beside the kitchen sink unsure of what he should do to help. Laurie sat on the mattress now, holding tightly to Betty Two Cups and whispering softly into her ear. Betty calmed down after a few minutes and looked around the room in confusion with her one good eye.

"Some water," Laurie said. Bruce turned and selected one of the glasses he cleaned, and filled it with lukewarm water from the sink.

"Here," he said, handing the glass to Laurie.

Betty drank quickly from the glass as if she hadn't had water in days. Bruce filled the glass again, and she emptied that one as well. Drool ran from the corner of her mouth. She wiped it away with the back of her hand and burped. Bruce briefly flashed back to her inside the pickup. He pushed the image away before it became solid.

Betty looked exhausted and beaten. She looked like she was just a step away from death, one foot already in the grave and the other about to slip off the edge. Bruce wondered if she could even recall what had happened that night in the alley. Looking at her, he thought it was very possible that she didn't even know her own name or where she was or how she had gotten here.

"Betty, this is Bruce Westman. He's a friend of mine and he's trying to catch the guy that's been hurting girls," Laurie explained. Betty squeezed the empty glass in both of her hands. She turned her one good eye to Bruce and studied him. The eye was a dull blue with flecks of green. Bruce thought she might shatter the glass in her hands the way she was squeezing it so tightly in her grip.

Betty took a slow shuttering breath and let it out. Her nostrils flared wide. "Girls," she whispered into the mouth of the glass, her breath fogging up the sides. Her eye rolled back to Laurie.

"He thinks you might have had a run-in with this guy in the alley off the Point," Laurie explained. Betty looked back at Bruce. Her eye was wide with fear, and she trembled. Bruce wasn't sure if it was because she was scared of him or simply needed a drink. He wished he hadn't finished off the vodka.

"Do you remember, Betty?" Bruce asked. "He drove a truck, dark, small. He took you back to the alley for sex, but something went wrong."

"So many men," Betty said, in a voice mixed with fear and humiliation. She sat up more and pushed away from Laurie. She rubbed her nose with the back of her hand, sniffling as she did so. "So many fucking men all wanting the same fucking thing. Suck me, fuck me, let me do what I want to do, bitch. Hands and fists always hurting, always hitting because they can, they can, they know they can," she cried, tears falling from both of her eyes. She reached up with one hand and gently touched her bruised eye. Snot dribbled from her nose. She wiped it away.

"It's okay, Betty," Laurie said, placing a hand on her shoulder.

"No," Betty whispered. "It's never okay, and it never will be," Betty said, glancing down into her lap.

"Betty, listen to me. This man, he tried to hurt you and you fell out of the passenger door. You ran and got away from him," Bruce said, dropping down to a knee so he was face to face with her.

Betty tipped her head to the side and nodded. "He wanted me to swallow and got mad when I spit. He called me something, maybe whore, slut, whatever, it didn't matter, nothing I hadn't been called before. His hand though, he hit me hard across my face. My head slammed back against the door, but I was smart." Betty smiled, revealing gaps in her mouth where teeth should be. "I didn't close the door all the way and it popped open, easy like. I was fucking smart that night."

"Can you describe him? Would you know him or his truck if you saw them again?" Bruce asked, writing in his notebook.

Betty rubbed her face with her left hand still clutching the glass in her right hand, the knuckles of her fingers turning white. "Maybe," she said softly, looking down at the glass. She closed her eye and let out a slow breath. "You got something better to drink than piss warm water?" she asked, looking at Bruce.

"I can get you something better," Bruce said. "I'll have Laurie run out and get it while you describe this asshole to me, and anything else you can remember." Betty nodded and Bruce handed Laurie two twenties. "A pint of vodka for me, the cheap shit is fine, and whatever she wants."

"Do you really think giving alcohol to her right now is the smartest thing?" Laurie asked.

"Just a little bit to grease the wheels," Bruce said, looking down at Betty.

"Since he's the one buying, make it Seagram's for me," Betty said, a high cackling laugh spilling from her mouth. Her feet hung over the edge of the mattress, the toes bent and crooked. Chipped polish covered the nails. She looked better now, more alert. Laurie frowned at her and Bruce but went out the door to buy the alcohol.

Chapter 19

Bruce woke up the next morning with a headache and a sore back. He had fallen asleep on the floor of Laurie's apartment leaning against the wall after listening to Betty tell her rambling story. An empty pint of vodka lay on the floor beside his left leg. It was a cheap brand that he had never heard of before, but after a few swallows it didn't really matter. The cap sat beside the bottle on top of his notebook, his pen beside that. Across from him Laurie slept on the mattress, spooning with Betty again. The wig she had been wearing the night before lay on top of a pile of discarded clothes. The hair that she had was cut short, close to her scalp. It was a bright red color straight from a box. An empty bottle of Seagram's sat on the floor beside the mattress, close to one of Betty's outstretched hands.

The light spilling into the apartment from the world outside was very bright and very painful. There were no curtains or blinds to stop it from coming inside. He could hear the sounds of traffic moving up and down the street just on the other side of the window. Everything beyond the thin glass seemed so close. It was as if the cars and the buses and the trucks were being driven just outside the window. Horns were blasting and people were shouting. The city of New York was awake and well. Bruce shook his head. *New York fucking sucks*, he thought, standing up and stretching his arms above his head. He stumbled his way to the bathroom and closed the door softly. The artificial glow from the light above the sink hurt his eyes and made his reflection in the mirror appear pale and sickly. He held a hand over his eyes and peed. The toilet flushed with a sick gurgling sound as the water slowly swirled around the bowl, disappearing somewhere three floors below.

Laurie was up when Bruce came out of the bathroom. She looked rough. It could not have been easy sleeping like that with Betty. The woman moaned and groaned while she slept, tossing and turning. Whatever dreams she dreamt must have been nightmares.

"Coffee," Bruce whispered, watching Laurie peel herself away from the other woman.

"Nothing here," Laurie whispered back, standing up and walking into the bathroom. She wore a t-shirt and light blue panties. Her legs were long and smooth looking. There was a tone to them that suggested years of being on her feet. She was still in decent shape. Bruce watched the bathroom door close. A moment later he heard the soft tinkling sound of her peeing in the toilet.

Betty sat up at the sound of the flushing toilet and looked around the room. Both of her eyes were open now. The black eye had an ugly yellow smudge along the edges that darkened to purple as it climbed toward her eye socket. Blotches of red swam around the whites of the eyes. Her neck was swollen, and Bruce was positive that someone had tried to choke her out the night before. She looked really bad and in need of medical care.

"Who the fuck are you?" Betty asked, trying to figure out where she was. The confusion was very evident in her eyes. She looked like a deer caught in the headlights of an oncoming car.

"I'm Bruce, a friend of Laurie's. We brought you here last night," he answered.

"I don't fucking know you," Betty said, sliding back on the mattress. She looked scared, ready to bolt. Laurie walked out of the bathroom right at that moment and Betty stopped.

"You're up," Laurie said, smiling softly. Betty relaxed just the tiniest bit at the sight of Laurie. She looked from the woman she knew to the stranger in the room.

"Where do I get coffee?" Bruce asked, walking along the far wall toward the door, afraid if he got too close to Betty she would run away or start screaming.

"When you get outside on the sidewalk turn right. There's a shop a couple of blocks down that sells donuts and coffee," Laurie answered. Bruce licked his lips and nodded. He checked his pants for money, his wallet, and his cellphone. He had everything he needed and headed out the door.

On the sidewalk, he turned right and began walking. He tried to ignore all the activity going on around him as he took his phone from his pocket. He called Shelby. He answered on the second ring.

"Special Agent Shelby," Shelby said.

"I found a girl who escaped from our guy," Bruce said.

"Where is she?" Shelby asked.

"She's with me right now but I'm not sure for how much longer. She's a bit jumpy, if you know what I mean," Bruce explained.

"She's a crackhead? That's just fucking great. They make such good witnesses," Shelby complained.

"I don't know if she smokes or not," Bruce said. "She drinks, but I'm not sure about drugs."

"A hooker, I suppose."

"Yeah, she works the street, how else would she have had a run in with this asshole," Bruce answered, beginning to feel a little pissed off.

"Fine, get her to me and I'll interview her," Shelby said.

"I'm not sure if that's possible at the moment. Can't you come to me? I'll get her set up at my place later this morning after I pump some coffee and donuts into her."

"Your place?" Shelby asked. "Where the fuck are you?"

"I'm staying in the warehouse district," Bruce answered.

"You better not be screwing around on my dime," Shelby growled into the phone.

"Fuck you," Bruce said and disconnected the call. A few minutes later he walked into the shop.

Bruce returned to the apartment with three cups of coffee and a half-dozen donuts. The three of them sat on the mattress and ate in silence. Laurie gathered up the trash and forced it down into an overflowing can in the kitchen.

"Look, I'd like you to tell an FBI agent what you told me last night," Bruce explained while Laurie took care of the trash. Betty's eyes went wide.

"Fuck that," Betty said, standing up and taking a step toward the door.

"I'm serious. He's the one investigating all of this and he's going to be the one who catches this asshole," Bruce said, standing up.

"Not interested," Betty said, her hand on the door. "I don't talk to cops and I sure as hell don't talk to no fucking FBI agents." The door opened.

"Betty, he's only trying to help," Laurie said.

"You know they don't give a shit about us. We're nothing to them but whores and sluts and holes they can stick their dicks into," Betty said, stepping into the hallway. "Good luck, Bruce Westman," she said, closing the door. Betty was gone. Bruce turned and looked at Laurie.

"I'll find her tonight and talk to her. Maybe she'll listen to me," Laurie said, shrugging her shoulders.

"I hope so, because she's the only witness we have right now."

"She'll listen to me," Laurie said, stepping into the bathroom again. Bruce heard the shower start a couple of minutes later.

"Fuck me," he muttered, looking around the tiny room. He left the apartment a few minutes later after leaving a note on top of the mattress for Laurie to call him. He placed several twenties on top of the note.

Chapter 20

It took Billy several tries before he had his routine down. He had to replace the passenger side window of his pickup twice. He even lost a girl once. She had fallen out the passenger side door and taken off before he could subdue her. He quickly realized that he needed to figure out something better. He needed a way to incapacitate them that was quick and efficient. The solution came to him during a delivery to a pharmacy in Brooklyn. He needed a drug. Something strong enough that it would knock them out but not so strong that he risked killing them before they served their purpose.

He finished his last delivery of the day and went back to his apartment in the city. That night he poured over articles on the internet, researching different drugs and methods for delivering them. In the end he settled on a drug called Fentanyl. Fentanyl was a strong narcotic used during surgeries and for controlling pain. It was also something that had become popular on the street so he shouldn't have a difficult time finding it for sale. A couple of nights later he found a dealer in Harlem who could get him what he needed.

The dealer explained that you needed to cook the drug up in a spoon just like you would heroin. The good thing was it only took a few grains of fentanyl and a tiny amount of water to produce a shot. The dealer, a tall skinny African American with pockmarked skin watched as Billy drew the liquid from the spoon into a syringe. He smiled at Billy. The smile revealed several missing teeth and two gold capped teeth. Billy grinned back at the man and held the syringe up in front of his face.

"You gonna use dat or what?" the dealer asked, licking his lips. "Just slide that bitch in your arm. It's all good shit." Billy's smile widened and he made as if he were going to do just what the dealer had said but at the last instant, he jabbed the needle into the dealer's leg.

"You first, nigger," Billy said, jumping back.

"Motherfucker," the dealer shouted, swinging for Billy. He managed to strike him across the jaw, but the blow was weak. The dealer fell back against the wall and slid to the ground, a trickle of blood running from his mouth where he bit his tongue. He tried to stand but he couldn't seem to control his feet. Billy watched his head fall back against the wall, a bit of pink spit running from the corner of his mouth. In seconds, he was out cold.

Billy looked back down the alley where the deal had gone down and saw no one. The alley was plenty dark, and he felt safe kneeling down in front of the dealer. "How about we try this again," Billy whispered, cooking up another shot in the spoon. The dealer's lips moved but no words came. His eyelids fluttered, but they didn't open. Billy ignored it all as he filled the syringe, slipping the pointy end into the man's neck. The plunger depressed slowly so he could watch the drug leave the clear tube.

After a few moments, the dealer slipped the rest of the way down the wall until his face lay in the trash tossed and forgotten in the alley. Billy prepared another shot and gave that one to the dealer. The man took a slow labored breath, and then stopped breathing. Billy waited a few minutes to see if he would start breathing again, but he didn't.

"Perfect," Billy whispered, gathering up everything the dealer had taken into the alley. In addition to the six tiny zip-loc baggies of fentanyl, Billy found three packets of a brown powder he suspected was heroin, and six rocks of crack cocaine. He took everything, including the cash the dealer had and placed it inside a black leather pouch he tucked inside the waistband of his pants. He left the dealer where he had died among the forgotten trash. He covered the body with plastic bags and discarded newspapers. He didn't really care if the man was found or not, he just wanted to get away before he was found.

That night Billy drove out to his land and practiced with the syringe on a watermelon until he had the delivery of the drug down. He didn't want another piece of potential art escaping before he had a chance to make something out of it for his wall. He set the watermelon on the end of a plunger that he had found in the basement of the old house. He set the plunger on a chair so the watermelon stuck up high enough that he could pretend it was a person's head. He even drew a face on the watermelon with bright red lipstick that he had picked up at a Walgreens. He had the lips puckered like a whore giving head.

He sat down in a second chair beside the first chair with the watermelon person on it and dropped his pants down around his ankles. It was sort of like sitting in the front seat of his pickup. He was positioned in the room so he could look out the window and pretend it was the windshield on his truck. The room was dark like an alley at night but not so dark that he couldn't see. For the sake of realism, he jerked off each time before practicing his move, so he felt the same way he did after the whores blew him. By the end of the weekend, he was spent and exhausted, but he had the move down to perfection. Over and over, he masturbated until his dick was raw and only a tiny dribble of cum came out. Over and over, he plunged the hypodermic needle into the watermelon, squeezing off a shot of water for the sake of realism. It all felt incredibly amazing.

In late October of that year, Billy went hunting for prey. His new kit was ready for action. The needle sat in a pouch stitched into the driver's side door where he could reach for it with very little effort. As he had with the watermelon, he practiced removing the needle from the pouch until slipping it out was as natural as peeing in a toilet. He was excited and nervous as he left his apartment that night. His dick was painfully hard by the time he pulled up to the curb to speak to one of the sluts working the Point.

The evening was cool, bordering on cold. The sky was dark with clouds and the traffic was light for a Thursday night. The whore that approached his passenger side window was nothing special, just another unworthy thing among a multitude of unworthy things. She wore tight shorts in spite of the cool weather that allowed her ass cheeks to hang out and a t-shirt knotted at the bottom that allowed a sliver of her stomach to show the top pink edge of her panties. Her hair was long, blonde, with streaks of hot red here and there. He noticed that she walked with a slight limp as she approached the truck. She looked young, but he wasn't sure just how young she was. He rolled the passenger side window down.

"Whatcha looking for, baby?" the slut asked, leaning down into the window so he could look straight down her shirt. Her breasts hung down so he could just make out the dark edges of her nipples. He could see the freckles covering the top of each breast. He felt himself cum just the tiniest bit inside his boxers. He swallowed hard, unable to speak. "Cat got your tongue, baby?" she purred, glancing into the back of the pickup.

"A blow job, that's all I want," Billy stammered, unable to say anything else.

"I can take care of that for you," she said, opening the passenger side door. Billy watched as she sat down and closed the door. The shorts rode up even more and he imagined that he could see the outer edges of her pussy lips. She set a hand on his thigh, one finger touching the hardness inside his pants. "Oh my, you are ready," she said, licking her lips. Her nostrils flared and Billy almost felt himself cum right there in his pants. The whore giggled and drew her hand back. "Just drive, baby," she purred. "I'll tell you where to go." Billy drove.

She had Billy park the car at one of the pocket parks in the Bronx, not too far from the warehouse district. It was well after midnight and the park was dark and well hidden from the street by the trees. The branches were full of bright reds and oranges. The leaves hadn't fallen yet but they were close. A fishy smell filled the air as a soft breeze that promised rain blew over the river. The few overhead lights in the park that he could see were out.

"This will do," she said, turning in her seat so she could face him. She placed both hands on Billy's lap, softly stroking his dick through the fabric of his pants. "Thirty-five, and I'll suck you off. Forty-five, if you want me to swallow," she whispered into his ear, stroking him harder. Billy squirmed in his seat. He was ready to explode.

"Swallow," Billy grunted, unbuttoning his pants and pulling down the zipper. She pulled his dick out of his pants and went to work. Billy came with a loud shout a minute later. He had a hand on the back of her head forcing her face all the way down into his lap as he emptied himself inside her mouth. She had tried to lift her head up, but he wouldn't allow her to until he finished.

Billy leaned back against the door when he was done, one hand fishing behind his back for the pouch. His fingers slipped inside the fabric, feeling the coldness of the needle that rested there. He looked across the seat as the whore dabbed at her mouth with a tissue. He felt his anger growing inside his head. His vision turning red. The time had come for him to do what he had come out there to do that night.

"Money," she said, forcing a smile, holding out the hand she had just used to dab at her mouth. Billy nodded twice before lifting his hand away from the pouch. It came up in a flash while his other hand pinned her head against the passenger side window. The needle pierced the soft flesh beneath her jawline. It sank in with ease.

"Motherfucker!" she screamed, her arms swinging wildly. Billy pulled back from her and watched as she fumbled for the door handle. A thin trickle of blood ran down the side of her throat. The door opened and she fell out, landing on the ground with a loud thump. She tried to rise but her body wouldn't obey. She fell back, muttering something over and over until she passed out.

Billy stepped out of the pickup whistling a tune from an oldies station. He walked casually around the other side of the truck and looked down at the woman. Drool ran from the corner of her mouth. Her head was tipped to one side. She looked so helpless.

"Fucking unworthy whore," he whispered, bending down to pick her up. He set her back inside the truck, making sure to fasten the seatbelt. Her head lolled to one side with her mouth hanging open. She looked like a drunk passed out or someone trying to catch some sleep on a long drive.

After that first time with the needle, everything always went according to plan. He picked them up, forced them to swallow, drugged them, brought them back to his workshop, made art out of them, and then displayed them so all could see what unworthy whores they really were. He felt no emotion for them, no guilt.

He wasn't even sure if he could even feel guilt. He enjoyed the hunt, and the act of creating something from nothing. It brought him purpose, a reason for living. It made the world come alive for just a moment, to become real, but that feeling never lasted.

I am a modern-day, Billy the fucking Kid, he thought as memories of his collection swam through his head. He wanted to get back to his house among the trees and sit in his studio. He wanted to enjoy his collection, but he couldn't right now because he had to drive around the city delivering his fucking packages. He looked out his windshield and smiled. *The world is my studio*, he thought. *Everyone is simply art waiting to happen.* He drove with the window open humming along with the music on the radio.

Chapter 21

Bruce's phone rang around four in the afternoon. He answered on the third ring, growling into the receiver. "What?"

"You have that girl who got away?" Shelby asked.

"No," Bruce answered, pushing aside the curtain and glancing out the window. Rain fell on the other side of the glass. Gray clouds drifted by overhead. It was a lousy late summer afternoon in the city. Everything had a dull dirty appearance outside the window. It was all washed-out grays, dirty whites, and blacks. Umbrellas marched along the sidewalks, clutched tightly by owners walking with heads down or faces buried in cellphone screens. It was all very depressing, so he stepped away from the window, allowing the curtain to fall back.

"What do you fucking mean, no you don't have her? I thought you said you were going to bring her to your place?" Shelby asked.

"No, I don't fucking have her," Bruce said, licking his lips, wishing he had a drink. "She wanted nothing to do with talking to you or anyone else in law enforcement," he explained. "I got my girl working on it though. She's going to talk to her tonight and see if she'll change her mind."

"Did you get her information?"

"Two Cups, Betty Two Cups," Bruce said, smiling. He knew that would drive Shelby nuts.

"Betty fucking Two Cups. What the fuck is that shit. I mean real name and date of birth. Social Security Number, shit like that, that we can use," Shelby shouted.

"Nope, private investigator, not a cop," Bruce said, hanging up the phone. The phone rang again a few minutes later. "What?" Bruce answered, squeezing the device so hard that he felt the casing shift in his grip.

"Don't you ever hang up on me again, asshole," Shelby shouted. Bruce hung up again and turned off his phone, tossing it onto the bed. He flipped his middle finger at the device before walking into the bathroom and turning on the shower. He sat on the toilet for a few minutes listening to the water splashing into the tub before running down the drain. It was almost relaxing.

Bruce walked out of the bathroom thirty minutes later feeling much better. He dressed, gathered a few items, and picked up his phone. He turned it back on and saw he had several missed messages from Agent Shelby and one missed message from his brother. He listened to his brother's message first.

"Hey asshole, call fucking Shelby back and stop being an immature dipshit," Jeffrey said. "And call your mother and let her know you're doing okay. How do you fucking leave town and not let her know?" Bruce deleted the message and listened to what Shelby had left.

Fucking asshole, Bruce thought as he deleted the last message from Shelby. He left the room and made his way down to the street. The air outside was thick with humidity and heavy with pollution as he stepped out onto the sidewalk. A light drizzle fell from a slate gray sky, just hard enough to be annoying. He quickly found his car still parked along the curb and got in, driving away slowly on the water-slicked streets. Traffic was rush hour heavy and inching along. *This fucking city never seemed to relax*, he thought. At a light, he called Shelby back. He answered on the third ring.

"Let's start over," Shelby said before Bruce had a chance to say anything.

"Fine," Bruce answered, rolling away from the light as pedestrians rushed through the intersection.

"If you talk to this person again, Betty whatever the fuck her name is, I need her information, or everything you get from her is no good to me. I need her real name and her date of birth. Everything else I need I can find out with that information."

"I'll find Laurie tonight and see what I can do," Bruce said.

"And we need to sit down and go over everything you have so far. Maybe over a bite, say around seven?"

"I'll try," Bruce said. Shelby let out a slow breath.

"Try to make it. Giovanni's on the Concourse. Food's good and I'm buying."

"Okay," Bruce replied, hanging up and tossing the phone onto the passenger seat. He drove until he found an open liquor store and ran inside. Music played softly from speakers as the door closed behind him. The interior of the liquor store was brightly lit so the patrons didn't have to struggle to find whatever they were looking for. Five quick minutes later Bruce walked out of the store with a bottle of vodka wrapped in a nondescript brown paper bag. Once he was seated back inside his car, he took a long pull off the bottle before setting it down in the cup holder and driving away from the curb.

For the next several hours Bruce drove his car around, watching the late afternoon activity of the Bronx. By the time it was time to start heading for Giovanni's, a third of the bottle was gone and he was feeling closer to what passed for normal, though his stomach was grumbling from the lack of food. Parking on a nearby street, he walked through the drizzle to the restaurant wishing he had an umbrella but knowing he'd probably never use it if he had one.

Even though he was early he saw that Shelby was already sitting inside at a table along a red brick accent wall in the back. He had a bottle of wine on the table and a plate of assorted cheeses and meats in front of him. A candle sat in the center of the table causing shadows to dance on the wall as wax ran down the sides.

"Glad you made it," Shelby said as Bruce sat down. Bruce poured a glass of wine and took a sip as he selected a slice of cheese from the plate.

"Figured since it was your treat, why the fuck not," Bruce said around a mouthful of cheese and Genoa salami. The waiter came up to the table a few minutes later and they ordered their meals.

"So, what have you got so far?" Shelby asked after the waiter walked away from the table. He took a sip of wine and a nibble of cheese while he waited for Bruce to answer.

"Nothing you don't already know," Bruce answered. "He's a white guy in his late twenties early thirties. I think he believes he's doing God's work or something like that. He's very organized. Everything he does is planned out. He's practiced this a lot, so he makes no mistakes. I get the feeling that he started this as a kid working his way up to people."

"Everyone fucks up," Shelby said, sipping more wine. "Bundy got found out on a simple traffic stop. BTK used the wrong computer disc. Everyone screws up."

"Well, he's good and he's getting better. He drives a small pickup. Ford Ranger, I think, dark color. He's picking these girls out because they're not real to him, you know what I mean?" Shelby nodded. "He thinks of them as being unworthy and he wants everyone to know that they are. That's why he leaves them the way he does. He's making a statement. It's also why he can do whatever it is that he's doing to them before he leaves his message for the world to see."

"What is it that he's doing?" Shelby asked.

"I don't know that yet. All I've seen is him taking the girls. I don't know where he goes or what he does when he gets there, or why he's doing it. If you give me more time, I'll figure it out."

"Take a guess," Shelby said, swirling a mound of spaghetti onto a fork.

Bruce sopped a slice of bread in some olive oil and oregano. He bit off a chunk and chewed before setting what was left on a small plate in front of him. Looking across the table, he sighed.

"Creating something. If I had to guess I'd say he's creating something with their skins." Shelby nodded. "After he has what he wants, he dumps them as a way of saying to the world that they're useless and unworthy now. That's what the message of rosary and the upside-down crosses mean. He displays them like they're praying for forgiveness, but he's making sure everyone knows they can't be forgiven."

"Who's forgiveness? Theirs, his, God?" Shelby asked, pointing up at the ceiling.

"Maybe all three," Bruce said as the waiter refilled their wine glasses because the bottle was empty.

"Three days. I can give you three more days before a shitload of agents descend on this city and the press begins to really roll with this. After that happens, I can't have you anywhere near this thing," Shelby explained. Bruce narrowed his eyes. "I get it, you're psychic, or something like that, but the agency wouldn't understand that shit. They're not as open minded as I am."

"Fuck them," Bruce said as the waiter set a plate of lasagna in front of him. Shelby laughed.

"Three days and then you're going to have to be scarce."

"As long as I get paid," Bruce said.

"You're a hard man to like, Bruce Westman," Shelby replied before digging into his lobster ravioli.

Bruce left the restaurant an hour later and made his way out toward the point. He drove by the strip club where he had met Laurie the night before and didn't see Laurie or Betty out front. He drove up and down the different streets around the club searching for the pickup or the girls and found nothing. The streets were busy though, with plenty of activity. It wasn't until around two in the morning that he came across Laurie walking along the sidewalk. A cigarette dangled from her mouth, the smoke curling above her head. He pulled to the curb and rolled down his window.

"Get in," he said. Laurie opened the door and slid into the car. She opened the glove box and took out the bottle of vodka and took a sip, licking her lips after she swallowed.

"Better than what I got ya last night," she said, screwing the cap back on.

"What happened to Betty?" Bruce asked.

"I don't know. I looked around but couldn't find her."

"Are you sure you looked around?" Bruce asked.

"What the fuck is that supposed to mean?" Laurie asked.

"Nothing," Bruce said, shaking his head. "Look, we got three days to figure something out and then the big boys are coming, and I have to disappear. That means you'll have to go back to sucking dick for a quick buck."

"Fuck you," Laurie said, taking another swig off the bottle. Bruce held out his hand for the bottle and finished off what was left. He tossed the bottle into the backseat where it joined others.

"Drive down along the water," Laurie said. "We might find her down there if she's had a good night. She'll go down there to pass out." Bruce drove.

They found Betty Two Cups leaning against a tree close to the river. Her head leaned to one side and her eyes were closed. Drool ran from the corner of her mouth.

"Son of a bitch," Bruce said. "She's fucking plastered again."

"If you had to do the things that she does every night to survive, you would be too," Laurie said, getting out of the car. Bruce followed her over to where Betty sat leaning against the tree. "Betty, it's Laurie and Bruce," Laurie said, kneeling in the grass.

Betty's head slowly straightened, and she opened her eyes. They were bloodshot but it was clear that she recognized the two of them. She smiled. "Fuck me," she slurred, spitting a wad of blood and phlegm into the grass. "Fucker mother fuck me with a pool stick," she mumbled, leaning her head back against the tree. "It hurt. It hurt so fucking bad," she sighed, sliding off the tree. Laurie caught her before she hit the ground.

"I'm so sorry," Laurie said, hugging the woman to her. "Why don't you come with Bruce and me and we'll bring you back to his place."

"A pool stick, he fucked me hard with a pool stick," Betty cried in one long breath before passing out. Bruce scooped her up in his arms and set her down in the backseat of his car. The odor coming off her body was almost enough to gag him. In the overhead light, he saw bruises on her face and arms and a dark stain on the back of her shorts. He wasn't sure if it was blood or shit, or both. Whatever had happened to her that night, had been bad.

"She needs a doctor," Bruce said, sitting inside the car.

"Maybe," Laurie said.

"And she needs to dry the fuck out before she kills herself or somebody finally kills her."

"She isn't the only one out here like this," Laurie said, closing the passenger side door.

"Fuck you," Bruce said, driving away. "We're taking her to my place and I'm calling Shelby to let him know I have her, and this time she's staying."

"She's not going to like that."

"I don't care. She's the only one who has seen this prick, and he needs to talk to her."

"Alright," Laurie said, looking doubtful. Bruce nodded and continued driving.

At the hotel where he was staying, Bruce and Laurie set Betty between them and guided her into the building. They carried her up the stairs and to his room. Laurie took her into the bathroom and cleaned her up while Bruce brewed a pot of coffee. He went down to the lobby while the shower ran and bought some snacks from a vending machine. Laurie and Betty sat on the bed when he came back into the room. A towel was wrapped around Betty's head, and another covered her body.

"Here," Bruce said, tossing a bag of tiny chocolate chip cookies onto the bed. Laurie grabbed the bag and opened it. Betty took a cookie and nibbled. Crumbs dribbled onto the towel. She looked like a mouse nibbling on cheese. The bruises on her face and arms had yellowed at the edges. Her eye was still swollen from the night before.

"How is she?" Bruce asked, pouring three cups of black coffee.

"Bad, but she'll survive," Laurie said.

"My asshole hurts and there was blood in my fucking underwear, that's how I am," Betty said, gulping the coffee Bruce gave her. "And stop talking to me like I'm a fucking child."

"Sorry," Bruce said. "Do you want to talk about it?" Bruce asked uncomfortably.

"Fuck you," Betty said.

"He's trying to help," Laurie said.

"Who the fuck asked him to," Betty said, holding out the cup for more coffee. Bruce poured.

"You got anything to add to it?" Betty asked, shaking the cup. Black coffee spilled down the side of the cup and ran over her hand. Bruce shook his head. Betty frowned and drank the coffee.

"Look, I need more information from you, and I can pay you," Bruce said, taking the empty cup and setting it beside the coffee maker. Betty looked over at Laurie and Laurie nodded.

"Help him, Betty, he cares, and his money spends just like anyone else's," Laurie explained. Betty eyed her suspiciously for a second before looking back at Bruce.

"What do you want to know?" Betty grunted, laying back on the bed, head on the pillow, hands underneath it. She crossed her right leg over the left and glared at Bruce and Laurie. She looked miserable. She looked like an abused Raggedy Ann doll.

"To start with, I need your real name and date of birth," Bruce said, taking out his notebook.

"Elizabeth, fucking Louise Carter. My folks were big jazz fans, so they called me Betty." Bruce wrote. "I was born April 14th, 1989, in Portland Maine. According to my moms, there was still snow on the ground when I was born." Laurie took Betty's hand and held on to it while she spoke. "I ran away from home when I was sixteen to be a star and to get away from my step daddy. He had roaming hands and I don't mean he was Italian either. As you can see, I'm still fucking working at it, trying to be a star and all," Betty said, laughing at her own joke or maybe her laughter was just her way of not crying over what her life had become. Bruce and Laurie didn't laugh.

"That's all I need for now, Betty. In the morning that FBI Agent I told you about the other night will be here and he's going to ask you more questions."

"I said I didn't want to talk to no fucking cops," Betty said, trying to sit up.

"Six girls have fucking died and who knows how many others and you're the only one that we know of who's seen this fucker," Bruce said, standing up, the anger obvious on his face. "So, you're going to talk to the fucking agent and tell him what the hell happened that night and anything else that he asks you." Betty fell back on the pillow unable to rise from the bed. "Now the two of you can sleep in the fucking bed and I'll take the chair."

"Fuck you, asshole," Betty mumbled weakly before passing back out.

"She'll talk to him," Laurie whispered, curling up against Betty. She wrapped one arm over the other woman's shoulder and closed her eyes. Bruce sighed and sat down in the chair. He watched the two of them sleep for a few minutes. Their breathing fell in rhythm with each other. It was relaxing to watch them like that. For a moment he could almost forget who they were or what they did. Taking out his cellphone, he sent a text message to Shelby letting him know he had Betty. By the time Shelby replied he was fast asleep.

Chapter 22

Betty woke up later that morning in terrible pain. Horrible cramps racked her body. The sheet she slept on was covered in blood and tears fell from her eyes. She looked worse than she had several hours ago when they had found her in the park. Sweat ran down her forehead and her hair hung in damp clumps along the sides of her head. Her breathing was shallow.

"She needs an ambulance," Laurie said, worried about her friend. "She's running a fever, and something has to be busted up inside her to keep bleeding like that."

"Fuck me," Bruce muttered, walking out the door so he could go down to the lobby to ask them to call an ambulance. When he walked back into the room, he heard Laurie and Betty in the bathroom. Betty cried on the other side of the bathroom door while the shower ran. They came out of the bathroom a few minutes later. "An ambulance is on the way," Bruce said as the two women sat back down on the bed. Betty wore one of Bruce's t-shirts and a pair of his boxers.

Someone knocked on the door a few minutes later and Bruce thought it was amazing that the ambulance had gotten there so quickly. He opened the door expecting to see paramedics but saw Agent Shelby instead. He stood in the hallway wearing a light blue dress shirt and dark slacks. He looked well rested.

"Fuck me," Bruce said, stepping aside so Shelby could walk into the room.

"Good morning to you too," Shelby said as he closed the door. "What the hell is wrong with her?" he asked, taking in the crying woman on the bed and the other woman hugging her.

"I think she was raped last night with a pool stick and needs to go to the hospital," Bruce explained in a low voice, pouring two cups of coffee.

"Did you get her information like I asked?" Shelby asked, taking one of the cups from Bruce.

"Yeah, and some background too. I have what she said the other night as well."

Shelby walked over to the bed and sat on the end. He looked at Laurie first and then at Betty. "I'm Special Agent Shelby with the FBI," Shelby said. "I'd like to ask you some questions before the ambulance gets here."

"Do you think you can talk?" Laurie asked, brushing hair off Betty's forehead. Betty grimaced, nodding and wiping away her tears with the back of her hand.

"I'm going to record this interview," Shelby explained, setting a recorder on the bed. Betty nodded. "What happened that night that you ran away from that man?" Shelby asked.

Betty took a shuttering breath and let it out slowly. "I was working the point. A pickup truck, a small one, pulled up and this guy asks for a blow job."

"Do you remember the color of the truck? Make, model?" Shelby asked. In the distance he heard the sound of sirens.

"Dark. Small, but I don't know nothing about makes or models of trucks," Betty answered, leaning more into Laurie as she spoke. Outside they could hear the siren as the ambulance drew closer. Laurie glanced at the window.

"I'll go downstairs and lead them up," Bruce said, slipping out the door.

"So, he picks you up. What did he say? What words did he use?" Shelby asked. Betty thought about her answer.

"He rolled the window down. It was one of those windows that you had to roll down by hand, so he had to lean across the seat. I asked him what he was looking for and he said kind of shy like, "a blow job." I got in and he drove away to this alley that I know. I was smart though, because something felt wrong. The light inside his truck was broke so I was able to keep him from knowing that I had the door open just a little bit." Betty smiled even as more tears rolled down her cheeks again. Outside the sirens had stopped.

"Go on, Betty," Shelby encouraged.

"He parks in the alley, and I tell him how much, and he agrees. So, I do what he's paying me to do. When he cums, I spit it out into his lap because he didn't say anything about swallowing, and he gets angry. He calls me a whore and I tells him to fucking pay me, but he comes at me instead, slamming me into the door. I fall right out of the truck. Fucking smart, right?"

"Fucking smart," Shelby agrees.

"Anyway, I run back down the alley and out onto the street, disappearing into one of the buildings nearby. I see his truck, and I can tell from where I'm hiding, he's looking for me."

The door to the room opens and three paramedics come into the room followed by Bruce. Two are carrying bags and monitors.

"Let them check you out, Betty," Laurie said, standing up and backing away from the bed. The paramedics begin to do their thing, checking her vitals and seeing where she's hurting.

"She needs to go, now," one of the paramedics said, turning around and helping the other paramedic work the gurney into the room.

"I don't need no fucking hospital," Betty cried, looking at Laurie.

"You do, sweetie. Do you want me to ride there with you?" Betty nodded and allowed the paramedics to help her onto the gurney.

Out on the street, Bruce watched Laurie and Betty drive away. Shelby stood beside him. They didn't speak until the ambulance disappeared around the corner.

"You did good, Westman," Shelby said.

"Whatever," Bruce said. "Do you know where they're taking her?"

"Yeah, one of the paramedics said, North Central on Kossuth."

"I'm going to head that way in case Laurie needs a ride back," Bruce said, starting back into the building.

"Call me later and let me know what's going on with her and try to get back out there tonight. I also need to know how to find that other one, Laurie, in case I don't have you around to help."

"Yes sir," Bruce said, flipping Shelby off. Shelby returned the salute, watching as Bruce walked back inside the building.

"Asshole," Shelby said, turning and walking down the sidewalk.

Bruce found Laurie at the hospital sitting in gray industrial chairs lined up along a gray and white wall. A television played across the room from where she sat, tuned into one of the twenty-four-hour news channels. A large aquarium filled with colorful fish gurgled against another wall, and there were several other people sitting in seats looking lost and worried. Laurie sat in one of those seats sleeping with her head tipped back against the wall. She slept with her mouth open, snoring softly. Bruce sat down beside her and started flipping through his cellphone while he waited for her to wake up.

"Hey, asshole," Laurie said softly twenty minutes later, stretching her arms above her head. Bruce smiled and put his cellphone away.

"You hungry?" Bruce asked.

"I could eat," Laurie said.

"She going to be okay?" Bruce asked.

"She's tough," Laurie said. "Doc said she'll need to spend the night but she's going to make it. They had to give blood and stitch her up."

"Good," Bruce said, looking down the hallway. "Do you know if they did a rape kit on her?" he asked, following the signs for the cafeteria.

"Yeah, and they gave her a million dollars for her troubles too," Laurie said.

"I mean it," Bruce replied. "How else are they going to catch the pricks that did her like that last night."

"For a smart guy you're so fucking stupid, Westman. No one cares about people like us. We're nothing but trash to be tossed in the gutter and forgotten. Cops don't care, our families don't care, no one cares, we're just fucking whores, and everyone knows you can't rape a whore."

"That's not true," Bruce said, turning a corner and walking into a cafeteria. The hospital cafeteria was a large stark white room with white tables and chairs scattered everywhere. Overhead fluorescent lights gave the room a sterile look that made one think they used hand sanitizer to clean every surface. At the front of the cafeteria was a half wall separating the food line from the sitting area. Several folks with trays stood on the other side of the half wall pointing at this, ordering that. Smells of food and grease filled the room.

"It is true, but it's sweet that you don't think so," Laurie said, picking up a tray and getting in line. Bruce followed her into the line shaking his head and wondering what had gone so wrong in her life to lead her to this place.

Betty Two Cups sat in a bed in a room with two other patients. An IV was hooked up to her and ran back to a pole and a bag of clear fluid. She appeared very pale and out of it. A white gown covered her body. Bruce thought in spite of everything, she looked better than the first two times he had found her out on the street.

"Betty," Laurie said as she walked up alongside the bed. Betty turned her head slightly and focused her eyes on Laurie.

"Fucking good shit," Betty said, giggling.

"I bet," Laurie said.

"Hey," Bruce said, walking up alongside Laurie. Betty's eyes moved slowly to Bruce and for a moment he was sure she had no idea who he was and then he saw the light of recognition go off inside her head. She smiled.

"Good shit," she whispered, licking her lips. "It don't hurt so much no more neither."

"Good, that's good," Bruce said.

"Betty, Bruce and I are going to take off. You listen to the doctors and do what they say. If the cops come by you answer their questions," Laurie said.

"Fuck da cops," Betty slurred, her eyes drooping.

"Come on," Bruce said, taking Laurie's arm and leading her out of the room. "We'll come back tomorrow."

Laurie followed Bruce out of the hospital. Outside the building, summer was still holding on. The afternoon was muggy and promising more rain later in the day. Gray clouds filled the sky, racing away to the west. Whatever was coming was coming from out over the water.

Bruce led Laurie to his car parked in temporary parking. She got in and rolled down the passenger side window before lighting a cigarette. Bruce paid the attendant and drove out onto the street. Laurie allowed her arm to hang out the window swimming through the air. She looked a thousand miles away puffing on her cigarette.

"She's tough," Bruce said at a light. Laurie took a moment and smiled around the cigarette tucked tightly in the corner of her mouth.

"Not really," she said, not bothering to look at Bruce. "We can act tough, but the truth is we're all soft on the inside. It sucks but its life." Bruce shook his head.

"I want to go back to that alley this afternoon and see what else I can find out," Bruce said, pulling away from the light, following the gaggle of cars in front of him. "I also want to check out St. Mary's Park. A body was found there not that long ago near the rocks beneath a tall tree beside the path."

"Sure, I can take you there," Laurie said, tossing the cigarette out the window. Bruce drove the car back into the Bronx. Overhead, the clouds grew darker, but the rain continued to hold off.

Chapter 23

St. Mary's Park was really nothing more than a small patch of green surrounded by concrete in the middle of the city. The traffic outside the park seemed to invade every corner even though the trees and the rocks prevented most from having to see any of it. St. Mary's was a place where the residents of the Bronx could get away to a green space and relax in the sun. There was even a pool where residents could swim and paths where they could walk. Large rock outcroppings were scattered around the park, perfect for sitting or sunning or simply somewhere to go to imagine you were anywhere else, that is if you could pretend to not hear the traffic just on the other side of the trees and rocks.

Bruce parked out on the street and he and Laurie walked into the park. From a distance they looked like friends or lovers enjoying each other's company. Laurie walked with her hands shoved into the pockets of her jeans. Bruce walked with his hands free. It was an easy afternoon stroll, or it seemed that way to the casual observer.

Bruce used the photos that Agent Shelby had provided to find the right tree. It was a tall oak with twisting branches that spread wide overhead. Green leaves covered most of the branches, so a wide oddly shaped circle of shade spread across the ground. The tree grew beside the asphalt path that circled the park at the bottom of a grassy hillside. Across from the tree was a stand of rocks. Several people were sitting on the rocks enjoying the afternoon even though the sun was hidden behind a sky of dark clouds. Bruce and Laurie ignored the people as they walked up to the tree.

"Can I see," Laurie asked, glancing down at the picture in Bruce's hand. Bruce held onto the photo for a moment before handing it over to her. He watched as she looked at it. Her face was expressionless.

Laurie held a photograph of a naked woman kneeling in front of the tree where they now stood. Even though this picture was taken from a distance she could see something sticking out from her back. She couldn't tell what it was, but it looked so wrong. To a casual observer, the naked woman appeared to be praying in front of the tree. If she hadn't been naked, and if her back hadn't been a raw, ripped-apart piece of meat, she would have thought the woman was just another forest freak praying to one of their forest gods. At a quick glance it almost appeared peaceful, except for that something sticking out of her back. Bruce handed her another photo.

This photo was taken closer up and taken from the front. Laurie could see the woman's face. The expression on her face was one of pure horror. She must have died in horrible pain. Her eyes were opened wide as they looked off into space. In spite of the twisted look of a painful death, the woman looked familiar. Laurie was positive that she had seen her on the street before. She was one of the younger ones, new to the neighborhood. Life and men hadn't erased that youthfulness completely from her face yet. Laurie handed the photos back to Bruce. She had seen enough.

"I don't need to see anymore," Laurie said, looking at the tree again. "I think I know her," she whispered. "One of the young ones new to the Point."

"I'll get you her information," Bruce said, walking up to the tree. He set a hand on the rough bark. It crumbled beneath his palm. He closed his eyes and allowed his breathing to slow. The sounds of the world slowly disappeared. He felt himself slipping away as the drift took hold of him. The drift was sudden and violent. It took him quickly to somewhere distant. He felt himself falling into nothingness, just simply drifting away.

Bruce found his body floating upon a rough sea of darkness. He was being tossed up and down and side to side as waves that he couldn't see had their way with him. All at once, everything came to a stop. He felt himself land on his knees. There was a taste of blood in his mouth, bright pain flared inside his brain. White light enveloped his world, stinging his eyes. He wanted to cry out, but he couldn't. He tried to speak but all he heard was a strangled gasp of breath.

The world that surrounded him was white and hot and filled with pain. It clouded his thoughts and prevented him from thinking. Bruce closed his eyes and reached out with his hand into the drift. He felt a cool breeze across his body. Goosebumps tingled over his skin. His eyes opened again, and he saw that he was naked now and the world was dark. Fear wormed its way through his mind. More goosebumps crawled over his skin. He tried to stand, but his legs were bound together. All he could see in front of him was the rough bark of an old oak tree. Giant black ants crawled through and over the valleys in the bark. He could see droplets of moisture as they dribbled down from the branches overhead.

Bruce tried twisting his body around to see where he was, but excruciating pain shot through his limbs. His back felt like it was on fire. Every nerve ending felt like the tip of a hot match was being held against it. Even though he was unable to speak, his mind screamed a thought-shattering scream that drowned out every other sound. Ribbons of snot blew out of his nose. Tears washed over his face. The pain in his back was so incredibly agonizing that all he wanted to do was crawl inside the tree and escape.

"In the name of the Father," a voice cried out behind him. "In the name of the Son. In the name of the Holy Ghost. I am his instrument that carries out his verdict, and you have been judged unworthy. An unfaithful servant. You cannot enter into the Master's rest."

Something cold and hard touched his back. It lingered there a moment, teasing the skin just enough that it lit fresh fires of intense pain across every exposed nerve ending. Bruce's mind screamed again as the pressure of that cold steel built and then everything went white as something split the very universe around him. He heard a scream tear through his lungs as something passed through his body, tearing and ripping away at his flesh and bone. He felt it explode out the other side, ripping through his abdomen. His whole body felt like it was on fire now. The very act of breathing sent waves of pain lashing against his brain. He couldn't move. He couldn't get free. There was no escape from this as it took hold of everything.

Laurie saw Bruce stagger and his body go rigid. She watched him fall to the ground beside the tree, crying out into the late afternoon as if someone were killing him in the most horrific way imaginable. She watched him writhe in the dirt at the base of the tree, tears running from his eyes, his hands clawing at his chest as if something were attacking him. His body twisted like it was trying to break itself apart in the throes of a massive seizure, and then everything stopped. With a hand to her mouth, Laurie stared as Bruce fell back, falling limp to the ground as if someone had pulled his plug or his battery had simply run out of juice. A soft whispered moan escaped from between his lips. It looked as if he had passed out.

Laurie rolled Bruce over, wondering if she should call 911. A pink colored drool ran from his mouth. His breathing was slow but steady. Sweat ran down his forehead. Another whispered moan rolled out from deep in his body. She sat there holding his head in her lap, wondering what she should do.

"Is he alright?" a woman asked from the path. Laurie looked and saw that the woman pushed a stroller. A baby cooed from the seat. Thankfully the woman was the only person around at the moment paying them any attention.

"Yeah, he has seizures. He'll be fine," Laurie explained. The woman looked doubtful but walked away, following the asphalt path out of the park.

The drift switched. Bruce felt as if he were riding a tilt-a-whirl at the carnival as the switching of the drift happened. His tortured body swung out wide into the darkness before being yanked roughly back toward the center, toward the light. One second, he was pinned to the ground like a butterfly on display beneath a pane of glass, and the next he was looking down at a naked woman dying at the base of the tree. A rosary dangled from her hands; the cross jammed between her held-together fingers. An upside-down Jesus looked back into her dying eyes. The plastic cross glowed green in the darkness making the upside-down Christ appear like one of those Roswell New Mexico aliens.

Standing just behind the woman, Bruce could see that her back was nothing more than raw exposed tissue. He could see where the killer had peeled away her skin from just below the shoulders to the top of her ass. A piece of rusted rebar stuck up from out of her back pointing back at him like an accusatory finger. Blood ran over her pale white ass in a twisted stream.

Bruce wanted to look away, but he couldn't make his body obey. His hands moved as if they had a mind of their own. He reached down and dropped his zipper. His fingers fumbled with the clasp of his jeans for a moment and then his pants were undone. He felt the fabric as they slid down his legs, followed by his underwear. He felt himself take his penis in his hand. He peed into the open wound of the woman's back. The urine splashed and ran in thin little pink streams over her flesh. He pulled his pants back up when he was done and walked away from the body.

Bruce walked away from the body without worry or fear, following the path back out of the park. Out on the street, he turned and walked two blocks away until he stopped beside a small pickup truck. It was a Ford Ranger. Several years old. Something out of the 90's maybe. In the reflection of the tinted window, he saw the killer looking back at him. He was young, but he knew this already. He was unshaven but didn't have a beard or mustache, just dark unshaven stubble. He wore round rimmed glasses and had a small overbite. He looked grungy, like he hadn't had a shower in a while. His hair was short and dark but hung over his forehead in greasy strands.

The killer opened the driver's side door. No overhead light came on inside the truck. The cab was a dark cave. The door closed and the engine started. The green glow of the instrument panel cast the cab in a surreal light that left Bruce feeling nauseous. The killer drove away from the curb, his headlights illuminating the road ahead. Bruce wished he knew where they were going. He tried to see the street signs but couldn't make anything out through the windshield. It was so dark outside, and any oncoming lights were simply blinding. The killer drove over a bridge. In the rearview mirror the city slowly disappeared behind them. The killer's eyes, blue with dark circles beneath them, appeared in the rearview mirror. At first, they simply looked normal, but they quickly filled with panic. The killer looked into the mirror as if he had seen a ghost.

"Get out! Get the fuck out!" the killer screamed at his reflection, slamming his open hand against the mirror. Bruce felt the slap as if the killer had somehow managed to strike him. The force of the blow was enough to drive him from the drift. He opened his eyes again and saw a worried Laurie looking back down at him. He tried to speak but only managed to turn his head away and throw up into the grass.

"I was getting ready to call 911," Laurie said after Bruce finished vomiting and lay back. She cradled his head once more in her lap. After several minutes he sat up slowly, wiping his mouth with the back of his hand. He looked around the park. A couple stared at them from across the path and up the hill.

"I'm okay," Bruce said, even though he felt very far away from being okay. He had never been seen inside a drift before. He hadn't known that someone could see him.

"You're an asshole, just so you know," Laurie whispered, standing up and brushing the dirt from the seat of her jeans. Bruce leaned against the tree and gathered himself together, wishing he had Father Murphy to talk to.

Chapter 24

Billy sat inside his city apartment on the end of his bed. He was worried, full of rage, and feeling violated. Sweat ran down the back of his neck and his breathing was rushed. He had never felt this way before because he had always been in control of the world. He believed he was special, set apart, holy. Now, he learned that he wasn't the only one who was special. A worried fearful expression creased his face. He kept glancing around the small apartment expecting to see the intruder again, but no one was there. Reaching back, he turned on his bedside lamp to chase away the hungry shadows creeping across the floor. The digital clock beside the lamp told him in tiny red numbers that it was after four in the afternoon. He shook his head trying to clear away the distractions, trying to remember his dream.

The dream had seemed so real. He dreamed that someone had been inside his head poking around. It took him back to an earlier recollection. He enjoyed reliving these experiences, feeling the power spread through his body as he left his displays for the world to see, except this time. In this dream, it felt like he had a hitchhiker inside his head. A spy taking notes. Someone seeing things through his eyes. It left him feeling violated.

"Drifting," Billy whispered into his empty room, not understanding the word, but knowing that it had importance somehow. That feeling inside his head, it felt like tiny spiders crawling around his brain. It had been a horrific violation of his soul that left him feeling exposed like a naked wire inside a wall.

Whatever it had been, whoever it had been, they were gone now. The spiders had left his brain and he was alone again. Billy stood and walked into the bathroom, looking into the mirror above the sink. He looked deeply into the mirror, wondering if he would see the hitchhiker looking back at him, but he only saw himself. It was his own eyes staring back at him. The hitchhiker was gone.

"Mirror, mirror, on the wall, who the fuck was inside my head, after all?" he said to his reflection. Snorts of laughter escaped his throat. A mist of spit sprayed against the mirror. He felt silly looking at himself, expecting the mirror to answer back like something from a Disney cartoon.

Billy walked out of the bathroom and dressed. He grabbed an apple from the mint green refrigerator beside the small stove. At the door to the apartment, he paused and twisted the doorknob to the right once, twice, and a third time, before opening the door and stepping out into the hallway. He looked to the left and to the right, gazing down the poorly lit hallway. It was empty. He closed his door, twisting the knob three times again before locking the deadbolt. In the garage, he found his pickup parked in its usual spot. He checked the top of the driver's side front tire for the piece of cardboard he left there to make sure the truck hadn't moved during the night. After sitting down inside the truck, he nervously looked up into the rearview mirror, again expecting to see something else, to see someone else staring back at him. He smiled at the sight of his own eyes in the reflection.

"Fucking-A-right,' he said to the image looking back at him before starting the truck. From his pocket, he removed a loaded syringe, dropping it into the pouch secured to the driver's side door. He adjusted his mirrors, tapped the top of the steering wheel three times, and backed out of his space.

"What should I do, what should I do," he sang as he turned out onto the street, falling into the flow of the traffic, driving away from the setting sun.

He found a girl to his liking around ten o'clock. The night was still young, but he was horny, and she was offering. The whore stood alone on a corner beneath the yellow glow of a streetlamp watching the traffic going here and there. She was an older girl, in her thirties, maybe early forties, but she could have just as easily been younger because life on the street wasn't easy on any of them.

The whore had a bit of weight to her and the thought of peeling her back, peeling away all that lovely skin, made him so hard. *So much lovely skin,* he thought, touching himself. He ached to bring his blade over her flesh. He longed to prepare it for display in his studio. *She will be such a nice addition,* he thought, slowing down at the curb. The whore walked up to his passenger side door, bending down so she could look inside the truck. He leaned across the seat and rolled the window down for her.

"You looking?" she asked, glancing up and down the street with weary eyes. Billy nodded. "You a cop?"

"No," Billy replied, his voice rough. He licked his lips.

"You're a fucking cop," she said and started walking away. Billy yanked his dick out of his pants and jerked on it.

"I'm not," he said. "I'm just looking for a little help with this."

She stood at the window watching him tug on himself through his open zipper. "Twenty-five and I can help you with that," she said, opening the door. Billy nodded and watched her sit down. He left his dick out and she started playing with it while he drove.

Billy found a spot to park. It wasn't perfect but if he took much longer, he would just cum all over her hand while he drove. She leaned down over him once he parked and began to suck. Her mouth was so hot, he came in less than a minute. Semen ran out of the corner of her mouth. She wiped it away with her hand. She turned and rolled down the window with that same hand and spit. Billy stabbed her in the back of the neck with his syringe while she was looking away. The steel shaft plunged easily into the soft flabby skin at the back of her neck.

"What the fuck!" she screamed, turning back around with that same hand now on the back of her neck. Billy smiled at her and watched as she fumbled with the door latch. She passed out before she could open the door. Billy seat-belted her in and fixed her so she appeared to be sleeping. Then he slowly drove away.

At the house, Billy strapped her to a red dolly because she weighed too much for him to carry her up the stairs to his workshop. He had bought the dolly months ago for just such an occasion. At the top of the stairs, he decided to leave her on the dolly instead of moving her to the wheel because she was starting to wake up. He stepped back to watch.

First her eyes opened, and she looked around. There was confusion on her face that slowly gave way to fear and then outright terror. Her mouth opened wide, and she screamed. Her screams filled the house and the woods outside. He didn't mind listening to her screams. They only made him hard again, and there was no one near to hear her scream other than him.

Billy took hold of the dolly again while the whore screamed and pleaded. He set it down in the middle of the workshop beside the wagon wheel. Trash crunched beneath its wheels. The screams died down into senseless blubbering now as he began cutting away her clothing. Her flesh hung over the sides of the dolly. Her skin was pasty white and flabby. Her large breasts hung down toward the floor. He pinched them and every time she cried out, they jiggled. There were rolls of flesh on her back that jiggled whenever he slapped them. Her buttock was large and cratered with pock marks and scabbed-over pimples. He was disgusted and disappointed by what he saw. His blade was going to have a difficult time working its way down her back. He wouldn't, he just couldn't, settle for inferior art.

An idea came to Billy sitting there in his workshop looking at the whore still strapped to the dolly. He stood up from his chair and dragged the dolly back out into the hallway to the top of the stairs. He set the dolly up, so all she had to stare at was the floor. The tires hung slightly over the top step. He tied weights around her ankles and a weight around her neck, so her head was pulled down over the handle. He shoved a stack of books under her fat, flabby, stomach until the weight of the weights and the books beneath her, forced her back to arch up into the air. The rolls of flesh on her back disappeared. Her skin tightened. She almost looked like a bitch in heat presenting herself for his pleasure. Her wide ass posed high in the air for his use and abuse.

"Be very still now," Billy whispered. She said nothing. Her face was bright red because most of her oxygen was being cut off by the handle. "This might hurt a bit," he whispered close to her ear, setting the blade just beneath her shoulders.

"Please," she begged in a strained rasping voice. Billy ignored her plea and sunk the blade. She screamed in spite of everything until there was nothing left inside her to form a scream. Billy giggled hysterically, working his blade deep into her flesh. She screamed so loud her face turned a shade of purple. Billy continued giggling, drawing the blade slowly down her back, rocking it back and forth, separating layers of skin from her body.

Billy held the flayed flesh in both of his hands when he finished. A tight smile filled his face. His tongue flicked out from between his lips. "It's magnificent," he whispered, ignoring the strained blubbering cries coming from below. He left her like that at the top of the stairs, streams of blood, bright and red running down the sides of her body.

Billy returned to the stairs a few hours later and found that the whore had died. "Bad ticker," he shouted, making sure to avoid the urine, the shit, and the blood covering the floor beneath the dolly. It ran down over the steps in thin streaks. He bent down close to her ear. "You're a fucking stupid whore. You should have held on so I could have presented you properly. You've ruined everything now."

Billy grasped the dolly's handle and lifted until he could gaze into her face. Her eyes were open, staring off into whatever hell waits for whores like her. Red squiggling lines twisted through the whites of her eyes. Her mouth was open, tongue and lips swollen. Streaks of blood and dried tears covered her cheeks. He spit into her open mouth. "Fucking whore," he whispered into her face before giving the dolly a shove.

The dolly fell end over end down the stairs, the sound slamming through the house. Halfway down the top half of the body came free. The books tumbled away, and her head banged into the wall. At the bottom of the steps, Billy heard the loud snap of bone as everything landed awkwardly. It sounded like branches snapping in a strong wind in the middle of the night during a thunderstorm. Billy jumped up and down at the top of the staircase, clapping his hands and laughing like a crazed clown. He ran down the stairs and started kicking the body. Blood sprayed everywhere but he kept kicking until the face was unrecognizable and the chest split open. Finally, out of breath and exhausted, he sat down on the bottom step, running his fingers through the blood, enjoying the tackiness.

Billy freed the corpse from the dolly after resting for a few minutes. He cut the body into manageable pieces and buried them in the front yard beneath a tall pine tree. He masturbated on top of the fresh grave, pissing into the disturbed dirt after he finished. An owl hooted somewhere in the distance drawing gooseflesh up his arms.

"Screw you," Billy whispered back at the owl, rubbing his hands up and down his arms to chase away the chill. Glancing up at the sky, he saw that sunrise wasn't that far away now. "Go away, Mr. Owl, before I find you and mount you on the wall with the rest of my art."

Billy stripped down and washed up in the kitchen where he kept gallon jugs of water for just such an occasion. He walked back upstairs, wet and naked, and went into his art studio. In the center of the room, he sat down in his chair, admiring his work in the glow of the lanterns. *It looks magnificent*, he thought. "Perfection under glass," he whispered into the soft yellow glow of the lanterns, watching the dancing shadows crawl across the walls as dawn began to settle on the land.

Billy slipped from his chair around five in the morning and curled up on the floor. The wood felt cold against his exposed skin, so he lay there in a tight ball, sleeping until the light of the new day filled the house. It was cool outside and cold in the house when he woke up. Autumn was finally here. The leaves would soon be changing color. His property looked incredible in the fall, the hills covered in bright reds and oranges. It was pure art on a grander scale than he was capable of creating.

Inside his workshop he dressed before making his way downstairs and back outside. At the driver's side door of his pickup, he paused and looked out at the trees where he had buried the body. As much as he enjoyed last night, he knew he was going to have to hunt again. He needed to finish the display after all. Halfway done was only halfway unfinished, and he couldn't have that. It was a good thing that there were so many unworthy things out there in the world. Billy slipped behind the wheel, started the pickup, and drove away from the house.

Chapter 25

Bruce woke up feeling like someone had worked him over with a sledgehammer. His body hurt all the way down to the center of his bones. Even his eyeballs felt like someone had gone over them with a strip of eighty grit sandpaper. Slowly, he rolled from his bed, listening to the snap crackle and pop of his joints, and limped his way across the floor to the bathroom. The shower ran hot, and steam quickly filled the tiny bathroom. He peed in the toilet and brushed his teeth before stepping into the shower and sitting on the floor. He sat with his head between his knees, letting the hot water wash over his body and work into his muscles. The spray was like thousands of tiny red-hot needles poking at his skin. It felt wonderful. He sat like that for twenty minutes enjoying the simple act of just being still before he began to scrub away the grime from the day before.

Bruce made his way down to the lobby of the hotel afterward and saw Laurie sitting in an overstuffed chair next to an empty fireplace. She wore torn jeans, black heeled boots, a dark blue t-shirt with an unbuttoned, orange-colored plaid shirt over it, and glasses. Bruce couldn't remember seeing her with glasses on before and wondered why she didn't wear them more often. They made her look smart and interesting.

"Hey," Bruce said, walking up to the chair. Laurie looked up from the magazine she had been reading and smiled. He couldn't get over how normal she looked with clean clothes on, her hair combed back, and those glasses.

"Hey," she said, setting the magazine down on the arm of the chair and standing. In the boots, she stood an inch taller than Bruce.

"How long have you been here?" Bruce asked, the two of them walking out of the hotel lobby together.

"An hour," Laurie answered, the door closing slowly behind her. She stood on the top step looking down at Bruce.

"Why didn't you just come up and wake me?" Bruce asked, stepping onto the sidewalk.

"I figured you needed to rest," she said, following him.

"Thanks, I did. But you could have woken me up," Bruce replied, standing beside his car with the passenger side door open. "You hungry?" he asked, wondering if they were really okay.

"I could eat something," Laurie said, taking a seat inside the car. Bruce closed the door and walked around to the driver's side. He sat down and pulled away from the curb.

"You look good by the way," he said, glancing into the rearview mirror.

"Thanks," Laurie said, looking out the passenger side window. Bruce saw she was embarrassed and wished he had kept silent. She cracked the window and lit a cigarette. They didn't speak again until they reached their destination.

They stopped at Liebman's Deli. Bruce ran inside while Laurie waited in the car. He paid for two bologna omelets, fried potatoes, coleslaw, no pickles, and two black coffees with cream and sugar on the side. He passed the food through the passenger side window. Laurie held the two bags in her lap while Bruce drove. The odor made her mouth water.

Bruce parked the car at Ewen Park and the two of them walked out into the grass and sat down on the hillside. They ate in silence, enjoying the food and the quietness of the park. Clouds hung in the sky, but the day was warm. For a moment as they sat there, the sounds and sights and horrors of the city disappeared. For just that moment, it felt as if the two of them had been transported to an island in the middle of the ocean. It was so peaceful and relaxing while they ate. They pretty much had the park to themselves.

"About yesterday," Bruce began, gathering up the trash. "I just want to say that I'm glad you were there for me. I know I didn't prepare you for what happened."

"What the fuck was that?" Laurie asked, sipping coffee from her cup while a cigarette burned in her other hand.

"So, I can kind of do this something where, I can get into people's heads. Sometimes the bad guys, sometimes the victims, but it's always just been me."

"I think you called it drifting."

"Yeah, that's the name I came up with for whatever it is that I'm doing. I don't really understand it, but I think it has something to do with me getting blown up in Iraq. The roadside bomb kind of jiggled my brain or something," Bruce explained. Laurie nodded though she didn't really understand.

"So, I guess it's like your superpower or something?"

"Not really. I mean it does some good, but it sucks too. It's like they're living inside my head, and I can feel what they're feeling and sometimes, God help me, I like it," he said, pausing. "If they're scared, then so am I, and if they're excited, then so am I. It's like I'm being forced to experience whatever they're experiencing. Pleasure, pain, fear."

"Do you feel everything they feel? I mean like if they're doing it, do you feel like you're doing it?" Laurie asked.

"Yeah, I do, and if they're dying, I feel that too."

"Fuck," Laurie said, drawing the word out before taking a deep drag off her cigarette. Bruce nodded and stood.

"Come on, there's a spot in this park that I want to check out. A body was found there back in July." Laurie nodded and stood. She followed Bruce to the bottom of the hill where children played in the winter on their sleds. She followed him to a stand of several trees just off a dirt path and watched him kneel in front of one of the trees. He set the palms of his hands in the dirt, digging his fingers into the ground. She stood to the side watching as he closed his eyes and slowly drifted away.

It fits, she thought, standing there looking on. *He looks like he's drifting away on a breeze or something.*

Bruce found himself being swept away on a dark tide in the middle of a black ocean. The drift pushed him along until he found himself standing several feet away from a tree inside a small park. It was dark outside. Long shadows crawled across the ground, twisting their way between the trees like so many hungry snakes. Though everything felt strange he knew where he was just the same. At night, well beyond midnight, the park felt dangerous. Above, clouds filled the sky, splitting and dividing the moon into uneven pie slices and hiding whole galaxies of stars.

In front of him, a naked woman kneeled before a tree whose shadows covered her like a blanket. A length of rebar stuck out of her back like a lightning rod, though no lightning fell from the sky. It was obvious to Bruce that the woman was dead. Her head lolled to one side and her eyes were expressionless. Her exposed back was nothing more than a ravaged and torn piece of exposed flesh.

Beside Bruce the killer stood, their shadows mingling together like conjoined twins. He was taller than Bruce and younger. The individual whiskers along his jaw and chin stood out in the weak moonlight that managed to look down upon the world from between the clouds. The killer turned slowly beside him until they faced each other.

"They are the unworthy," the killer whispered in a sleepy sing song voice, his eyes flashing like overhead lights. Alarm bells went off inside Bruce's head. He felt suddenly very exposed and vulnerable. Something he had never felt before while drifting. "They must see the unworthiness of their lives before the Lord."

"Who is this they?" Bruce asked, trying to step back and free his shadow from the killer's before he was infected with whatever sickness this man carried around inside his head, but try as he might he was unable to move.

"They are the shadow walkers that fill this world. The creatures who inhabit the daylight, who suck all the life from creation," the killer answered, sweeping his hand out toward the edges of the park and the city beyond.

"Who made you the judge?" Bruce asked, fighting against whatever force was holding him in place. He thought if he could just move, he could somehow stop this monster from killing again.

"I am the instrument, the executioner of God. I am his chosen judge," the killer said, raising his arms above his head.

"No, you're just some sick fuck who gets his jollies off killing women, and I am going to stop you," Bruce said with an effort of will that finally allowed him to move enough to reach out. He grabbed for the killer with numb hands, but they only ran through the body as if the killer were nothing more than a ghost. Laughter filled the shadows that surrounded him. It was a high cackling laugh that seemed to roll through the air like summer thunder.

"I am unstoppable, and you are nothing but an insect beneath the sole of my shoe," the killer growled.

Bruce took a step back even though his feet felt like they were mired in quicksand. "I am inevitable!" the killer shouted, causing Bruce to stop and cower like a scared little child trying to hide from the monster in the closet. A hand covered his face as he looked back at the killer through splayed fingers.

Somehow the man standing before him seemed taller and more substantial now. The killer loomed over him, his shadow expanding, his physical stature continuing to grow until he stood above the tops of the trees like a Manhattan skyscraper. It was a terrifying thing to witness. The sky disappeared. Shadows were swallowed whole. The killer's foot rose into the air like a giant rubber stamp. On the sole of the shoe was a mountain range of patterns crawling across the sole. Bruce shrank back as the shoe descended toward him with such force, ready to squash him like a bug on the kitchen floor.

"Fuck!" Bruce shouted, falling back against the tree with his hands in the air as if something were attacking him. Laurie reached out but missed his shoulder. Bruce tumbled to the ground, squirming about like he was trying to escape from something. "Son of a fucking bitch," Bruce shouted, dirt and leaves kicking up into the air at the base of the tree. He stopped and retched several times but managed to hold back the vomit.

"What the fuck was that all about?" Laurie shouted at him, bending down to help him up. Bruce brushed away her hand and stood.

"He fucking knows," Bruce said, brushing dirt from his pants. "He knows I can see him. He drifts just like me, or maybe better than me, I don't know, but he can see me and talk to me."

"Well, that fucking sucks," Laurie said, standing next to Bruce. She set a hand on the tree and then quickly drew it back remembering that someone had died there. A scowl spread across her face, and she rubbed her hands together.

"Come on," Bruce said. "I need to call Shelby." Laurie followed him back to the car, lighting a cigarette along the way.

Billy sat up in the bedroom of his small city apartment. It was late morning and he had only been asleep for a couple of hours. He looked around the room with wild eyes as if he expected someone to be there, but there wasn't anyone. Sighing, he sat up in his bed, the sheets pooling around his thighs. He wore gray boxers and a white wife-beater t-shirt, stained and tattered. His eyes swept the room once more, making sure that he was alone. No one was there except for the shadows crawling along the walls. He let out a breath that he had been holding, feeling safe for the moment.

"Itsy bitsy spider crawling around my brain," Billy whispered into the shadow filled darkness inside his apartment. White light leaked around the edges of the blackout curtain hung over the one window that looked out onto the world. "Bad, bad, boy," he mumbled, getting to his feet. The floor was cold and hard. His toes curled and goosebumps crawled up his naked legs.

Billy walked across the floor and into the bathroom. He came back out a few minutes later scratching himself. "How do you catch a spider?" he asked the gloom filling his apartment. At the window, he paused and pulled back the curtain so he could look outside. What he saw caused a shiver to creep through his flesh. The shadow people were everywhere outside his window. How he hated them for populating his world, for corrupting all of creation. The curtain fell back, and he smiled. "How indeed," he whispered, twirling around in a circle like a ballerina. "Why, you squish them like a fucking bug!" he shouted into the darkness before laughter spewed from between his lips. Gales of laughter filled the apartment now and he pressed his fingers over his mouth trying to contain it, but the laughter still came. Someone to his left began to bang on the wall and Billy finally managed to stop. Tears fell from his eyes, and he wiped them away. Soft giggles rolled out from between his lips. Drool ran down over his chin. He felt giddy.

"Can't disturb the roaches," he whispered, looking at the wall.

Billy dressed in his deliveryman's uniform before leaving his apartment. He drove his truck around the city, leaving packages here and picking up packages there. He tried to forget about the trespassing spider inside his head, but he couldn't, no matter how hard he tried. Every time he looked up into the mirror he was reminded of the trespasser. At the end of the day, he left his delivery truck in the parking lot and drove home so he could dress properly for the hunt.

Smash the spider, he thought later that night, driving around in his pickup truck, searching the city for the unworthy. Rage and anger filled his mind as he crawled up and down the streets looking for someone to be transformed into art. He hated the other, the one who could see him. He hated him so much because like him he was real among so many unreal things.

Billy gave up his search around three in the morning. He saw plenty of potential out there, but the Lord didn't speak to him. None of them called out to him. *Maybe tomorrow,* he thought, heading back to his small smelly apartment, missing his perfectly clean art studio. "So many pictures on the walls. So many stories to tell. And best of all, no spiders allowed," he whispered, turning down his street.

Billy crawled out from his truck and took the graffiti-splattered elevator to the third floor of his apartment complex. The hallway outside the elevator was dark and dank and smelled of urine. The cold tile echoed loudly with each footfall as he made his way to the door. It took two keys to undo the locks and three twists of the doorknob to right to open the door. He stepped into his apartment, surveying the shadows, and closed the door, making sure to twist the knob three more times to the right before securing the locks. He placed the keys in a bowl by the door, kicked off his shoes, and allowed his pants to drop down around his ankles. He stepped out of the pants and took off his work shirt and the undershirt beneath. A stark white belly that hadn't seen sun in a very long time hung over the band of his yellow stained underwear. Black hairs stood out against the white skin surrounding his belly button and climbing up to cover his chest and shoulders. He rubbed a hand over his belly, jiggling the gut just the tiniest bit.

He crossed the small room without turning on any lights, coming to a stop in front of his bed. Instead of sitting down on the bed he dropped to the cold tiled floor, crossing one leg over the other. The dirt and dust bit into the naked skin of his butt, but he ignored it, closing his mind off to everything. He set his hands, palms up, the tips of the middle fingers and the tip of each thumb touching each other. Except for his junk hanging out between his legs and his balls resting on the floor, he looked like someone practicing Eastern Meditation. Each breath was slow and steady. One breath in, one breath out. A soft hum filled the silence of the apartment. With his eyes closed, the world slipped away, and the slide was upon him. Everything else dissolved and disappeared into nothingness.

Billy called what he did the big slide because that was how it felt to him. It was like being on one of those slides at a carnival where you ride a rough strip of burlap to the bottom. The first time he had experienced the big slide was shortly after the accident while he was still in the hospital. That feeling, that sense of being elsewhere, left him breathless and frightened. He had been making his way around the halls of the hospital on his gimpy injured legs. The hateful nurses that watched over him said he had to walk if he wanted to go home, and how he wanted to go home. He wanted to be anywhere else besides where he was. The hospital was like a prison, and he wanted to escape it so badly.

The hour had been late, well past visiting hours and well past anyone caring where he was or what he was doing. Darkness filled the long empty hallways while the glittering lights of the city winked and blinked beyond the glass windows. It was all a bit surreal at night being inside the hospital, when the hallways were empty, and the sick and injured people slept. Only a few nurses and cleaning personnel populated the building. Some chatted outside doorways or huddled behind the protective walls of nursing stations. They all ignored him as he made his way around, taking slow unsteady steps.

On the night of that first slide, he had come around a corner and slipped. His body fell down to the green and white industrial tiled floor as if it moved in slow motion. Stars, brighter than the lights of the city, lit up brightly in his eyes. Blood flooded his mouth as he bit down on his tongue. He reached out for the cart in front of him to steady himself and as his fingers curled around the cold white plastic, he felt himself sliding down an invisible hill. The sensation was disturbing. It curdled whatever flowed inside his stomach. There was no breeze to mark his passage, but he knew just the same that he was flying down a hillside as if he were an out-of-control comet while somewhere in the distance someone screamed. The scream echoed out into the onrushing darkness as he flew along that invisible hill until he came to a sudden, bone-jarring stop. The darkness that surrounded him dissolved, replaced by a bright white light that stung his eyes and caused tears to fall.

At the bottom of the hill where the darkness had given way to light, he found himself inside a room. He was still in the hospital, this much he could tell, but the room he was in wasn't his own room. The walls were the same powdered gray color and the lights set in the ceiling were still sickly fluorescent lights that left him feeling like he was being doused with radiation. There was a bed in the room with a nurse standing beside it in her white outfit and white rubber-soled shoes. She wore white nylons that clung tightly to her muscled legs. Monitors beeped and hummed beside the bed, and fluids ran through clear tubes that dangled from bags hanging from poles. Numbers flashed on the monitors and there was the wheezing labored sound of someone struggling to breathe.

Believing that he had to be dreaming, Billy approached the bed, fully expecting to see himself lying there hooked up to all sorts of equipment, but it hadn't been him. He stood beside the nurse, a young white woman in her late twenties, early thirties. She was tall and big breasted. Her uniform was tight against her tits, and he wished he could have reached out and touched them. In the bed, he saw an old black man. His skin was sort of gray. The man looked withered and wasted, just a poor creature grasping at the remaining threads of life. He had thin snow colored hair clinging to the sides of his head, thick white eyebrows, and a cheesy mustache that was just as white as the little bit of hair that he had left on his head. A ribbed tube came out of his mouth and ran out to a machine beside the bed. The tube was taped to one side of the old man's mouth. Drool leaked out along the edges of the tube.

Billy glanced over at the nurse, and she appeared nervous. Her eyes darted back and forth making sure she was all alone. She kept glancing over her shoulder at the door as if she expected to see someone walk into the room at any moment. Her long boney fingers twitched and scratched at her legs.

The nurse was totally unaware that Billy stood right there beside her observing her. He knew what she wanted to do. He could taste it as she gazed down at the old man, and Billy wondered if he had simply died out there in that hallway. Was he a ghost now, trapped inside the hospital for all eternity?

The nurse glanced at the door once more and her eyes seemed to relax. Without thought or worry now, she reached down and detached the tube that fed oxygen to the old man. She held it away from the piece that still extended from the old man's mouth. With her free hand, she pinched his nose between her fingers. The old man began to cough around the tube still inside his mouth and lodged deep in his throat. His eyes opened wide and were filled with fear and panic. He fought feebly for life, for the ability to breathe. A weak hand snaked out from beneath the covers reaching for the nurse's hand, but it fell back before he could even touch her. The panic faded from his eyes. A single tear ran down his face. His body relaxed.

All at once, alarms sounded inside the room. They weren't loud. They sounded like they came from somewhere down a long tunnel. A flat red line ran across the heart monitor. Numbers quickly fell. The nurse put the breathing tube back together and struck a red button behind the bed. More alarms sounded and people came running into the room. Everyone worked to save the old man, even the nurse that had killed him, but it was all for nothing. She had done a good job. He wasn't coming back from that.

Billy watched as everyone left the room one by one until only the nurse was left. She glanced at the closed door again before turning back to the old man. Gently, she brushed the side of his face with her hand. It was a tender motion that left Billy confused. The nurse turned away from the bed and pushed the crash cart from the room. She left it in the hallway beside the door and walked away.

Billy followed the nurse down the hallway to a bathroom. He followed her inside the bathroom and watched her lock the stall door. He watched her sit down on the toilet, hiking her dress up, peeling down her nylons, and dropping a pair of black silk panties. He watched the nurse slip a finger inside herself and masturbate. She touched herself until her eyes rolled up into the back of her head and all he saw were the whites. The nurse came hard with a muffled grunt and a stretched out leg that slipped beneath the stall door. Billy felt himself cum right along with her.

After the nurse finished, she stood and walked over to the sink, looking into the mirror, smiling at her reflection. She took out a small white notebook from her uniform pocket and opened it to a blank page. She wrote the date and time on the page, and beneath the date, the number twelve. She flipped back over the other pages in the notebook and Billy saw more dates and times and numbers. On the first page in the notebook was a date and time along with the number one and Billy quickly realized that the old man had been the nurse's twelfth victim. The thought was enough to make him cum again.

"She's just like me," Billy thought, breathless. He watched the nurse fix herself up in the mirror and walk out of the bathroom, headed back to the nurse's station. As he watched her walk away, he thought he could perhaps love her, but then the world shifted, sliding sideways with a jarring jolt. Everything was dark again and he felt like he was drowning. He reached for the surface wherever that might be and found himself on the floor again beside the cart.

"*Is this the same cart? The same room,* he wondered. The cold white plastic didn't give any answers, but he supposed it was the cart that the nurse had rolled out into the hallway after killing the old black man. He looked down at himself now and saw a spreading wet stain at the front of his hospital gown.

It had taken Billy several minutes that night before he managed to make it back on his feet, and it took even more time before he managed to make it back to his room. He went into the restroom and closed the door. The overhead light came on and he opened his gown. His underwear was a sticky mess. He took them off and tossed them into the trash. For good measure, he balled up several paper towels and tossed them on top of the discarded underwear. He wet another paper towel and cleaned himself off in front of the sink.

"That really happened," he whispered into the bathroom mirror when he finished. Back in the room, he dressed into another gown before he made his way back to the bed. He didn't understand what had happened that night, but it had been something amazing, something incredible. It had been a gift from God. He was like Spiderman or something. He had a superpower.

The next day during another walk he saw the nurse from his dream the night before, or whatever it had been. She stood behind a desk writing notes in a chart. He wondered if she still had the notebook with her, tucked inside her pocket. He wondered if she still masturbated in the restroom. He felt himself growing hard at the thought and turned toward the wall to hide himself.

Billy wanted to talk to the nurse that night, but he couldn't bring himself to say anything to her. All he could do was make his way back to his room, hiding the fact that he was so excited from anyone that might notice. Back inside his room, he went into the bathroom and masturbated quickly into the sink.

Several more times before his discharge, he saw the nurse. She was always dressed in white, always looking so prim and proper, but he knew her secret. Every time he saw her, he wondered if she had added any more dates and numbers to her notebook. The thought always caused him to grow hard. It was so dirty, so nasty. He wanted the nurse so badly because they were like siblings, the two of them. Kindred spirits on a special journey through life. He wanted to share himself with her as she had unknowingly shared herself with him. He felt honored that he had been allowed to see her as she was because that meant he wasn't alone in a world full of mindless shadows. He had company.

Chapter 26

"You're done, Westman," Shelby said over a plate of roast beef and mashed potatoes. Brown gravy ran over the side of the plate dripping onto the tabletop as he smashed a roll into the potatoes.

Bruce looked across the table at Shelby wanting to lash out, but he had known this was coming. The fact that it had arrived didn't take the sting out it happening to him. What he wanted to tell Shelby was to go fuck himself and the political organization that he worked for, but he held back. Maybe he was growing up, becoming an adult. *Jeffrey would be proud of me,* Bruce thought, watching Shelby stuff a roll soaked in gravy and mashed potatoes into his mouth, followed by a forkful of beef. Brown gravy ran down his chin, dripping back into the plate. He followed all that with another slice of roast beef. *Fucking pig,* Bruce thought, shoving his plate away and standing up. Stepping back from the table without a word, he dropped his napkin onto his plate.

"Finish your food," Shelby mumbled around a mouthful.

"No, I got to go," Bruce said. "I got to find Laurie and let her know what's happened and pay her for helping me out. Shelby pulled an envelope from his pocket and dropped it on the table.

"Take it," he said. "I know that this sucks, but I told you when the big boys came, I'd have to let you go. They wouldn't understand this shit that you do. If someone found out, I'd find myself working in the South Dakota field office investigating cattle theft or something on national park lands. Can you see me, a big black city boy investigating cattle theft?"

"Yeah, I get it," Bruce said, scooping up the cash in the envelope and walking out of the restaurant. Out on the sidewalk he headed to where he had parked his car. He paid the lot attendant and drove off in the direction of Laurie's apartment. At a light, he opened the glovebox and took out a small bottle of vodka. He set it between his legs, unscrewed the cap, and took a swallow of the hot liquid. He followed that with two more swallows before the light changed.

Bruce parked down the street from Laurie's apartment along the curb. He locked his door and casually made his way back up the half a block. A wino sat beside the stoop outside her rundown four story building. He looked like he was seventy or eighty but probably was only forty or fifty. The wino had his hand out and Bruce dropped a five into the open hand before heading up the three steps to the entrance.

The lobby of the building was dark, and it stunk of day-old trash mingled with just a touch of shit and piss. A single bulb covered in grime cast its meager light over the lobby from a smoke-stained ceiling. The light did little to drive away the shadows crawling along the walls and living in the corners of the lobby like the stoned-out ghosts of Christmas past. Someone lay passed out on a threadbare couch off to one side. Bruce couldn't tell if they were male or female and he didn't really care as he mounted the stairs to the second floor. The hallway at the top of the stairs was long and dark. He walked down the center until he reached Laurie's door. Standing there in the dark hallway left him feeling claustrophobic, like he was trapped in a cave beneath a mountain of rock and dirt. Sweat ran down the back of his shirt. As quick as he could, he knocked twice on the door and waited. Thankfully, she answered right away.

"Hey, I thought we might patrol the streets around the strip club tonight," she said, stepping back from the door with a smile on her face. "We might come up with something since he hasn't done anything for a while. He might be out and about looking for someone," she added, stepping around the mattress on the floor.

Bruce watched her as she moved about the small room. She looked so much better than she had that first time he had met her. A cigarette dangled from the corner of her mouth, the smoke leaving a path along the ceiling as she paused at the bathroom door. Her hair was swept back away from her face and her makeup was applied with subtleness. She cleaned up well, and her clothing was more conservative than what he had seen her wearing before. She didn't look anything like a prostitute anymore. That exhausted, used-up look was gone from her eyes. She even looked attractive, not that she was ugly before, but now she looked like someone you could date.

"Here," Bruce said, stepping into the apartment. He held out fifteen hundred dollars, cash. She took the money from him and raised a questioning eyebrow. Bruce took a deep breath.

"We've been fired by that fuck, haven't we?" she asked, squeezing the cash in her hand. She looked as if she were ready to cry.

"Yeah, we've been fired. Can't have the riffraff mucking shit up, you know," Bruce said, feeling like a shit.

"So that's it then, I just go back to sucking cock for thirty dollars and getting fucked in the ass for a hundred?" Laurie shouted, throwing the money in his face. Twenties flew all around him, but he made no attempt to grab for them.

"You could keep working for me," Bruce said without thinking.

"How? I thought we were fired."

"You could come back with me to Connecticut and really work for me. Taxes and all, no health insurance," Bruce said, smiling.

"Fuck you and fuck your charity. I've made it this far without you," she shouted, really crying now. Bruce felt horrible.

"I mean it, Laurie. Think about it and call me," he said. "You really have a knack for this stuff."

"Fuck you!" she screamed, running into the bathroom and slamming the door. Bruce turned and walked out of the apartment. Outside on the street, he paused and took a swig from the bottle he had tucked away in his back pocket. The alcohol warmed his insides and took away a bit of the sting of what had just happened. He started down the sidewalk toward his car. The wino on the stoop watched him go.

Back at the car, Bruce unlocked the door, noting that the day was chilly and promised rain. He wondered if summer was finally over as he sat down in the seat without closing the door. Looking out the windshield he sighed deeply, closed the door, and started the engine. The car ran like that, parked at the curb for several minutes. At some point, the bottle found its way into his hand, and he drank until it was empty, tossing it into the backseat. A moment later, he drove away from the curb feeling like a failure.

Chapter 27

The slide came upon Billy as it always did. It simply overtook him and swept him away from the world. At the bottom of his imaginary hill, he opened his eyes and entered into somewhere else. The world that sat before him was a drab one-room apartment. It didn't look much different than his own one-room apartment except that he was looking at a woman standing just inside a doorway. Her hair was tied back and pulled tight against her head. She wore little makeup, jeans and a blue baggy sweatshirt, but he knew her for what she was. He knew she was one of the whores that sold themselves to men for money. She could try to hide it. She could try to pretend she wasn't one of them, but it was obvious to him that she was one of the unworthy ones, and God had shown him that He needed to collect her.

Billy watched her lips move, and he heard the words she spoke, but they came to him like a distant whisper. He paid no attention to what she was saying. It was all so much like a movie on a large screen. Just mindless noise. He could tell she was angry and hurt. Tears lined her face. They fell in slow motion to the thin, almost nonexistent carpet that she stood on. She threw a handful of money in his direction, but he made no attempt to catch it. The money flew like so many fluttering butterflies. He watched it fall slowly to the floor like feathers caught on a breeze. Looking up again, he saw she was speaking, yelling at him, in fact, before going into the bathroom. A moment later he left the apartment.

Outside the apartment, he followed a long dark hallway to a flight of stairs that he took down to the ground floor. At the door he caught a reflection in the glass and saw that he was the man who had been snooping inside his head, and he knew that the man was just like him. He could slide too, but he didn't like it like he did. This man felt cursed by what he could do. *What a fool*, Billy thought.

Billy closed his eyes and tried to imagine being completely inside this man's head, and then he just was. He was the snooping man now. It was him that took a drink from a bottle of alcohol at the bottom of three steps. He saw the wino sitting there watching the world pass by in his drunken stupor. The man turned and he turned with him. They walked down the sidewalk. Billy saw the city through the snooping man's eyes. It was all like nothing he had ever seen before. He was seeing the world through the snooping man's eyes, eyes that could see things the way he saw them and yet saw them differently at the same time. He knew the snooping man's name was Bruce. He wondered if Bruce knew his name.

Billy dove deeper into Bruce's head and saw that the inside was full of dark places. There was so much damage in there, so many broken things strewn all about. It felt like being beneath an ocean in the middle of a storm. He was drowning in the darkness there. He couldn't breathe. All he knew was that he had to get out of there or risk being trapped forever. Billy squeezed his eyes shut, and suddenly he was free of Bruce's mind.

Bruce, Bruce, Bruce, you look like such a moose, he thought, walking down the sidewalk alongside his host. They walked together until they stopped in front of an old blue car parked along the curb. There was rust in the paint and damage to the rear fender. The door opened with a loud creek, and they sat down inside, staring out the windshield and drinking from the bottle again. They drank until the bottle was empty. Bruce the Moose started the engine. The car didn't really roar to life, just coughed reluctantly. Billy sat there with Bruce looking out through his eyes again at the world beyond. It felt so good sitting there with that mind-numbing warmth spreading through his body. It felt like a comfortable blanket or a favorite pillow. Billy himself had never drunk any alcohol before, but if this was how alcohol felt he might just have to try it in real life.

The car pulled away from the curb with a jerk and a wave of unsteadiness swept over Billy. The world felt like it was spinning out of control and Billy tried to hold on, but he felt his mind slipping, sliding again. He wondered if this was how it felt to be drunk. Cars and buildings drifted by with a dizzying effect. Everything felt out of balance and out of control, and suddenly, Billy felt very scared. He wanted out of that darkness.

Bruce felt a twinge of something as he rolled through a red light. Horns blared but he didn't notice them. Something pointed was twisting around inside his head and he had to stop it. Squeezing his eyes shut he tried to focus. Horns, and shouts of people, shrieked all around him. They were what was real, he told himself. Then he opened his eyes. His car sat stopped in the middle of an intersection. Traffic was stalled all around him. Angry drivers yelled and threatened him. He was scared, but not of the people. Something else had him feeling scared.

"Drive that fucking thing, asshole," a driver shouted as he drove around the car. Bruce threw up the middle finger, glancing up into his rearview mirror at his reflection.

"What the fuck," he whispered to himself, easing off the brake and driving the rest of the way through the intersection. He pulled over to the curb and stopped. His head felt like it was on fire. His brain felt like there were a million ants crawling around inside. Something was there that didn't belong there.

"You can feel me," Billy whispered.

Bruce looked over his shoulder. "What the fuck," he cried, realizing he wasn't really alone in the car, even though there was no one else in the car. "Get the fuck out of my head, get out, get out, get out!" Bruce screamed into his rearview mirror.

Billy's eyes flew open. He was no longer sliding. He looked frantically around his one room apartment expecting to see that he wasn't alone anymore, but there was no one there. The room was empty. His breathing slowed and he uncrossed his legs. He stood. His knees hurt and he rubbed them until the pain eased. He dressed and went to the bathroom sink to splash cold water on his face.

Bruce remained at the curb for several minutes, wishing he had another bottle. The alcohol from earlier was wasted now. He was totally sober. "He can fucking drift," Bruce said to his reflection in the rearview mirror, making sure it was himself that he saw there looking back. His eyes looked scared. His head hurt, and he felt violated. He wondered if that was how it felt to others when he drifted into their lives. *They're fucking killers*, he thought, easing whatever guilt he felt. Leaning across the seat, he opened the passenger side door and vomited into the gutter. He sat back up when he finished, wiping his mouth on the back of his hand. He was afraid to look in the rearview mirror again. He was afraid of what he might see staring back at him.

Billy left his apartment later that evening, wondering how he could use all this new information to his advantage. *I need to stop this asshole, this snooper*, he thought. *He'll ruin everything if I don't.*

Billy drove his pickup out of the parking garage, heading for the Bronx. The need to hunt burned inside his mind now. He had to find another so he could show the shadow people how unworthy they all were. The drive to create art was simply too much for him to resist. Like the alcohol, it burned deep inside him.

"So much work to be done," he said to his reflection in the rearview mirror. "Can't let myself be distracted. No, no, no," he whispered. Billy drove down the street heading toward Hunts Point. As he drove a plan began to form inside his head about how to deal with his new friend, Bruce the Moose.

Chapter 28

Laurie stood in front of the bathroom mirror looking at her reflection. She looked so strange standing there dressed like a normal person. "Fuck you," she whispered at herself as she lifted the shirt she was wearing over her head. She changed quickly out of her clothes and into what she considered her real work clothes. Once she finished, she stood there in front of the mirror wearing short shorts that let her ass hang out. She wore a tight purple t-shirt with the sleeves cut off that allowed people to see her tits whenever she lifted her arms. The shirt was knotted in the front to expose her belly button and the top frilly edge of her pink little girl panties. A wig of bright red hair covered her head and hid her much shorter-cut hair style. The fake hair ran down her back in tight curls. Heavy makeup made her eyes stand out and her lips appear fuller. A cigarette rested behind her ear while a lit cigarette hung from the corner of her mouth. She was ready to hit the streets.

"Fuck him," she said into the bathroom mirror, applying a bit more lipstick. "I'll catch this asshole all by myself."

Laurie left her apartment building, walking down the sidewalk in her red stripper shoes. She turned right after several blocks and kept walking until she was a block away from the Hunts Point strip where the rest of the girls hung out most nights. As early as it was, there were already a few other girls stationed at various spots along the strip. Men prowled up and down the street picking up girls or dropping them off. For a Monday night it looked like it might be a busy one. Laurie ignored most of it. Her eyes were focused on the vehicles driving up to talk to the girls and the men driving them. She had an idea what she was looking for so if they drove in a car, she just ignored them. If they tried to pick her up, she turned away like she wasn't interested.

It was well after midnight when she saw the small pickup, just like the one Bruce had described, driving slowly up the street. The truck crept along the curb; the driver eyeing the girls standing beneath the pools of light gathered beneath the streetlamps. Laurie stepped up to the curb so that the driver could get a good look at her. She brushed the fake hair away from her face and smiled a bright red lipstick-filled smile. The truck stopped and the passenger side window rolled down. Even in the dim glow thrown by the streetlight inside the cab, Laurie saw that the driver looked just like the man Bruce had described. She felt a chill crawl along her skin. Goosebumps rose along the back of her neck. *It's him,* she thought.

The driver was young, clean shaven. He had dark hair and a tiny mole on the side of his face. He appeared shy and unsure of himself, refusing to make eye contact with her. He looked like a little boy, lost and afraid, out for his first blow job. The man behind the wheel wore dark tan Dickies like the UPS men wear when they're out making their deliveries and a black t-shirt. His hair hung over his forehead in tight curls that she might have found cute if she hadn't been so scared.

"You looking for company?" Laurie asked, bending down so she was looking right into the cab of the pickup, and he could look right up her shirt. She knew her breasts were her best feature, and she knew how to use them to attract men or women.

"Yeah," Billy said softly, feeling himself beginning to stir inside his pants. From where he sat, he could see the tops of her dark nipples.

"You a cop? You have to tell me if you are," Laurie said, knowing that he wasn't, but still playing the game. He felt too right. She wished she could call Bruce. She had the cellphone he had given her tucked in the back pocket of her shorts, but it might have been sitting on her mattress for all the good it was doing her right now. She placed a hand on the windowsill and flexed her fingers, so her nails stood out. She detected the odor of fried foods but saw no evidence of any inside the cab of the pickup.

"I ain't no cop," Billy whined, realizing that the whore that stood before him was the same one he had seen during the slide. She looked different but also the same. *It's a wig*, he thought. "I want a blow job," he stammered, feeling like he was about to explode right there inside his pants. He squirmed a bit in his seat trying to ease the pressure.

"Well, let me see your shit and maybe we can work something out," Laurie said, keeping eye contact with the man.

Billy looked out of the windshield. He saw a few other girls along the curb or back on the sidewalk. None seemed to be paying either of them any attention. He drew in a deep breath and let his zipper down, pulling his dick out. It was as stiff as a board, pointing up at the ceiling. Laurie looked at it and licked her lips.

"I guess we have a deal then," Laurie said, opening the door. The dome light didn't come on. She sat down in the passenger seat and Billy drove away. He left his dick out while he drove. It felt much better that way.

"Turn here," Laurie said. "Now go down that alley there," she said, pointing to the right. Billy did as she said, turning down the dark alley. It was the same alley where that one whore had gotten away from him in the beginning.

Laurie felt nervous now as the man parked the truck. He left the engine running but turned off the lights. She wasn't sure what to do next. She hadn't thought this far ahead. Again, she wished she could call Bruce.

"Aren't you going to suck it?" Billy asked, his voice husky. Laurie looked down and saw that he was yanking on himself, so his dick pointed at her. She looked up and his mouth was open, his breathing hard, and his face flushed. She thought he was ready to cum right there.

"Why are you in such a rush, big boy?" Laurie asked, setting the tip of her finger on the tip of his dick. "Why don't you tell me your name so I can call you something." Billy closed his eyes and swallowed hard as she slid her finger along the underside of his shaft.

"Billy, Billy the fucking Kid," Billy moaned. He came all over Laurie's hand in a rush of hot fluid that spilled all over the front seat of his pickup truck. Panicked, ashamed, he reached out and caught Laurie behind the head.

"Suck it, bitch, suck it," Billy growled, shoving her head down with one hand as he reached behind himself for the pouch on the door.

Laurie tried to pull away. She tried to resist, but he was simply too strong. Her face slammed into his softening dick. She felt it flop against her cheek, his pubic hairs scratching her face. She could hardly breathe. Something sharp suddenly jabbed into the back of her neck and pain exploded inside her head. She screamed into his thigh as he jammed her face down into the seat between his legs. The vinyl was stiff and split, slicing into her face.

"You, fucking whore. You fucking stupid whore. I told you to suck it, I told you to. You should have obeyed my will. I am inevitable, I am the light that stalks the shadows. I am His instrument of judgement."

Laurie felt the world slipping away as she struggled to breathe. The words being spoken above her didn't feel real any longer. Everything seemed to exist outside of herself. The hand that held her down felt so far away now, the pressure slowly fading like a dream. For a moment she wondered if she were lost at sea, sinking beneath the waves as they crashed on top of her. Sinking into the darkness beneath the earth and sky where the creatures of the ocean hunted. She tried to force her way back up toward the surface, but her body felt like it weighed a thousand pounds. The world slowly slipped away until it became nothing but darkness.

Bruce stood outside Laurie's apartment. The door loomed large and gray in front of him. He wanted to knock on the door but couldn't bring himself to do so. He felt horrible for how he had left things with her. All he wanted to do was help and he made a fucking mess of everything. *I'm not some fucking knight in shining armor*, he thought, finally bringing himself to knock. The echo on the other side of the door sounded empty, like there was no one at home.

"Laurie, its Bruce," Bruce said, leaning into the door. "Come on, answer the door. I just want to talk." Bruce tried the knob and the door simply opened. The fact that the door wasn't locked wasn't so strange, she didn't have much for someone to steal. The small room was as dark. The only light he could see came in through the window. "Laurie, it's me," Bruce said, walking into the apartment. He left the door ajar and looked around the small room. He didn't see her. He went over to the bathroom and opened the door. She wasn't in there either. The clothes she had been wearing earlier sat on the floor. He stepped into the bathroom and stood at the sink.

"Fuck," he said, looking at his reflection in the bathroom mirror. He looked so exhausted. There were bags beneath his eyes and dark circles. He looked years older than he should have. He reached out to touch the mirror.

The drift came upon him suddenly. He hadn't been ready for it and slumped against the wall between the sink and the door. He slid down along the wall until he thumped to the floor, but he noticed none of that because he was inside the drift now.

Inside the drift, he saw Laurie as she had been earlier that evening before she left the apartment. She wore heavy makeup and hooker clothes now. She looked ready to work the streets, like she had that first night when they had met. A redheaded wig adorned her head and made her appear younger and sluttier. She didn't look any better than she did when she was herself, just easier.

"Son of a bitch," Bruce shouted, his eyes flying open. "She's going after the killer." Bruce stood and ran from the apartment. In his car, he called Shelby but got his voicemail. He left a message. "Hey dickhead, Laurie is going after the killer on her own. Call me back when you get this message, or I'll call you back if I find out something more." Bruce disconnected the call and drove away from the depressing building. As he did so he tried to recall what he had seen inside the drift. *She wore a t-shirt and tight shorts. There was something sticking out of one of the pockets as she left the bathroom and walked across the apartment,* he thought as the blast of a horn snapped him out of the memory.

"Fuck you, dickhead," Bruce shouted out his window before driving through the intersection.

Around two thirty in the morning, Bruce found Betty Two Cups leaning against a telephone pole. She was shirtless and braless. Her tits sagged down to her belly button. A pool of chunky vomit sat in her lap. She looked horrible but at least no one had beaten her this time. He got out of his car and walked up to her.

"Betty," Bruce said, leaning close to the woman. The smell was awful but somehow, he forced himself to ignore it. Betty's eyes opened to thin slits as she gazed drunkenly at him. It took her a moment to figure out who he was and then a light went off somewhere inside her fogged head.

"Bru," she slurred, spitting a wad of phlegm on the sidewalk beside her, almost hitting his right foot.

"Yes, I'm Bruce, Laurie's friend," Bruce said, shaking Betty's shoulder just the tiniest bit. Her eyes opened wider, and she looked down into her lap.

"Motherfucker, I puked on myself again," she said sadly. "And I think I pissed myself too." Tears slid from her eyes. Bruce stood and went back to his car. He took the windbreaker from the backseat and laid it over Betty, so she wasn't exposed anymore.

"Betty, have you seen Laurie?" Bruce asked.

"Laurie, she's nice," Betty said, trying to push herself up off the ground. She didn't get very far. Bruce caught her before she fell over.

"Betty, focus. Laurie, have you seen her?"

"No," Betty snapped, yanking her arm away from Bruce's hand.

"She might be in trouble, Betty. Can you keep an eye out for her? Have her call me if you see her," Bruce explained. "It's very important."

Betty sat up a bit straighter. Her eyes focused a bit more. She nodded her head slowly. "I can do that," she said, feeling behind the telephone pole for her shirt. It wasn't there. Bruce didn't see it anywhere.

"I put my jacket over you, Betty," Bruce said, and Betty looked down, noticing the windbreaker for the first time. Bruce slipped a couple of twenties in one of the pockets of the windbreaker. "I also put some money in the pocket of the windbreaker. Don't go drinking or taking anything. I need you to look out for Laurie like she's looked out for you."

"I will," Betty said, looking a bit more sober now. She turned the windbreaker around and zipped it up. Bruce stood and started to walk back to his car. "Hey, check the alley," Betty called after him. "If she's working, she might be down there, you know, doing her thing."

Bruce looked back at Betty and smiled. "That's good," he said. "Now keep an eye out for her and have her call me if you see her," Bruce said.

"I can do that," Betty said, leaning back against the telephone pole. She looked up into the light beaming down from the streetlamp. Bruce sat down in his car and drove away.

Chapter 29

Billy drove through the darkness of Upstate New York toward his house and his wonderfully amazing studio of art. Tall dark trees reached out along the roadway like the hungry shadows of ancient warriors awaiting the bloody battle. Their limbs were bent and twisted and crooked, creatures drawn from the worst imaginations. The headlights of his pickup stabbed through the darkness like a lighthouse upon a hill warning wary ships of danger ahead. At this early hour of the night, his were the only lights revealing the long, lonely roadway in front of him.

Occasionally an eighteen-wheeler would scream by heading south toward the city, but mostly it was just him and the whore, and the darkness that surrounded them. Thankfully, the shadow people were all still tucked safely inside their fake homes waiting to begin their fake lives. Oh, he knew he had to be careful of them because if they ever noticed him, if he ever gave them the chance, they could hurt him. The shadow people weren't without teeth, after all, and sometimes they had very sharp teeth. They had their laws and their rules to hide behind, and they expected him to live by those laws and rules, but he knew how to get around all that happy crappy shit. They would never imprison him again.

Billy glanced across his seat at the woman sleeping there. She was strapped into the seatbelt so she wouldn't slide over or slip down to the floorboard. She looked pretty in the slight light of the instrument panel. She even looked just the tiniest bit innocent, but he knew her for the whore that she was, even if she pretended that she wasn't sometimes. His mother had taught him well. She taught him how to pick out the whores from the sheep.

"Sleep," he whispered at the woman, brushing a finger along the side of her bare leg. The skin felt cool to his touch. Smooth beneath the tip of his finger. She was so smooth, so tempting. *She should make a fine addition to the gallery*, he thought, allowing his fingernail to press deep into her leg. The skin puckered as the tip sank. She moaned and fidgeted in her sleep, but she didn't wake up. The fentanyl was too good for that. She should sleep deeply until he was home, and she was secured in the workshop.

He reached up under her shirt and felt the skin of her back. It was just as smooth as her leg. His nostrils flared and he giggled. A bit of spittle ran from the corner of his mouth. His tongue darted out and caught it before it had a chance to run down his chin. The whore snorted and grunted. She sounded like a cartoon mouse racing through a cartoon maze searching for a prize that wasn't there. He giggled again at the image of her running through a maze before pulling his hand back.

"Some sharp cheese for the little mouse," he whispered, jabbing the tip of one finger into her left breast through the shirt she wore. His dick grew stiff. He withdrew his finger slowly. The whore moaned again. He grinned at her and thought, *it will be our time soon enough.* He placed his hand back on the wheel and continued to drive northbound into the early empty hours of the morning.

Bruce drove his car slowly down a dark alley just off the strip where the girls worked the streets. It was the same alley where Laurie had taken him. Where he had discovered Betty's escape from the killer. The lights of his car showed an array of trash shove up against the sides of the two brick buildings he drove between. A great deal of it still spilled out along the path he drove down. Graffiti adorned the walls, placed there by street artists and gang bangers bent on making names for themselves. Rats, the size of large cats, darted through the trash, unafraid of his presence and undisturbed by the glare of his lights. Their tiny red eyes glowed sickly bright above twitching black noses and wiry whiskers. They looked alien and hungry and full of disease, and worst of all they reminded him of his time in Iraq. He felt that twitch of nerves and fear as images he wished he could forget flooded his brain. His car came to a stop.

Bruce and his squad patrolled the streets of Bagdad, half the time during the day and half the time at night. It was during the nighttime patrols that things were the worst. At night even the shadows became threats. Every sound was someone out to kill them. Most times, they rode through the city together in Humvees, but sometimes they had to patrol on foot. These foot patrols were done as four-man teams with an Iraqi interpreter. Up and down the streets they went shining their flashlights, revealing whatever horrors lay hidden in the shadows, never knowing if at that very moment their number was going to be punched by some Allah-screeching fanatic with a bomb strapped to his chest or a gun in his hand. It was the most stressful time of his life, but also the only time in his life that he truly felt alive. Fear and adrenaline had a way of doing that to a person, and he craved it like a junkie.

The men he had served with in Iraq were his brothers in a way that Jeffrey could never be. They counted on him as their squad leader, and he counted on them to watch over his ass. He had their backs, and they had his. Some of the interpreters even became part of the family, graphited into the unit, but not always. Sometimes the interpreters were just as bad as the fanatics. Trust was a hard thing to come by out there in the sand and heat.

On the best of the worst nights, when everything was quiet, he and his fellow soldiers shared the streets with the stray dogs and the fat rats while everyone else was safely tucked away in their beds. He was grateful and honored to serve with these men. It was on a quiet night while they patrolled on foot when he came across two of the meanest and nastiest rats he had ever seen. They were fighting over something in a pile of trash. Tearing into each other, neither willing to back off or back down. Curiosity got the better of him and he went into the alley to investigate, figuring they were fighting over a bit of meat or bone.

In Iraq, the rats were not afraid of people. They didn't run away just because someone approached, and sometimes they even held their ground as if they were ready to fight over whatever it was that they were gnawing at. These rats that fought each other that night weren't any different. They didn't run away as he approached. One of them even reared up on its hind legs and bared its teeth at him. The other rat just continued to try and drag whatever it was that he had away.

Bruce swung his rifle at the rat standing up like a man ready to fight and fired a round. The small body exploded in a shower of blood. The other rat forgot what it had and scurried off into the trash. Bruce turned his flashlight to see what the rats had been fighting over and saw that it was a human skull. Skin and gristle still clung to the bone. Bits of long dark hair ran thinly from the scalp in brittle strands. Something white and juicy sat back in one of the eye sockets leaking viscous liquid out the side. What was left of the nose gaped out at the world like something from a zombie movie.

The odor of gunpowder mingled with the smell of trash. The combination nauseated him. Another soldier walked into the alley, his weapon ready, his eyes wide and searching for threats. Bruce glanced his way and then back at the skull. In the light of his flashlight, he saw that the skull was just a little bigger than a softball. He groaned, realizing that it belonged to a child.

A little girl, he thought, feeling his stomach twist and turn. He swallowed hard. His weapon hung by its sling in front of him, dangling at his waist. His hands clenched into fists. He tried to swallow again but vomited on top of his boots instead. He vomited again and again until he couldn't throw anything else up. The other soldier in the alley looked away.

Like most things in the Middle East, the child went unidentified and unnoticed by anyone. No one had come to report a missing child, and no one had seen anything. It was all so unfair and so horrifying. Life meant nothing out there. Not his life, not the lives of the men and women he served with, and most especially not the lives of the little children who only existed on the fringes of what passed for society out there. It was all so fucked up and useless. They had been fighting each other for thousands of years and probably would continue fighting each other for a thousand more, and in the end, him being there wouldn't make any difference.

Bruce pushed the memory of that night away from his thoughts. It was just one of the many nightmares he had to live with every day. He forced the memory back inside its box, and then he placed the box up on the shelf inside his head among many, many other boxes of horrible, terrifying memories that he wished to forget. A shrink at the VA had taught him that trick along with several others for dealing with his PTSD. It usually worked most of the time, but sometimes the boxes spilled off the shelves and broke open. Sometimes, when this happened, everything had a chance of sliding off the rails. Self-medication worked most of the time, but God help him when it failed.

Bruce lifted his foot off the break and drove the rest of the way down the alley. He parked his car at the end and stepped out. Even though it was close to being cold outside, the alley felt warm and sticky like on a humid August evening. It stunk like spoiled food and week-old shit mingled with piss. It was a horrible combination of odors that assaulted his senses and twisted his stomach into knots. He tried not to breathe through his nose as he walked around to the front of the car. He wished he had a bottle in his hand. He wished he was back home in his tiny apartment in East Hartford three quarters of the way toward being passed out drunk.

Bruce walked into the white glare of his headlights, studying the ground in front of the car at the end of the alley. He had no idea how many hookers had been using the alley that night, but he guessed it was quite a few. He saw tire tracks on top of tire tracks left behind in a large spill of yellow greasy sludge. It looked like old lard left in a coffee can beside a stovetop. He squatted and set the palm of his hand in the sludge. It felt warm and slick. It felt like butter that had melted and then cooled again as his fingers pushed through. He wanted to pull his hand back, but he kept it there and closed his eyes. The drift thankfully came quickly.

There was no slow drift upon the ocean this time. What he saw was a parade of cars driving up and down the alley. It was a never-ending stream of blow jobs, hand jobs, fucking, and anything else one human could do to another human short of killing them. He saw women and men and children being used as things instead of as people. He saw abuse of the vilest kind that someone could do to another person. It was all so overwhelming, so punishing. He wanted to leave the drift, but he forced himself to watch and wait.

Somewhere within the drift came a small pickup truck. It drove into the alley and proceeded to the end, just like the others except, this time Bruce knew it was him. The pickup was the same late model Ford Ranger he had seen before. It was the right color and the right age. Through the windshield he saw the killer sitting in the driver's seat and Laurie sitting on the passenger side.

Bruce came around to the passenger side window and pressed his face up against the glass. He could see the killer clearly sitting across from Laurie with his dick out, his hand wrapped around it. From his vantage point it looked as if the dick was pointing at him, accusing him of failing to protect Laurie.

The drift shifted and suddenly Bruce found himself sitting in the truck with the killer. The tip of his finger was touching the killer's dick. He wanted to pull it away, but he couldn't. He was Laurie and this is what she must have done, and now that he was her inside the drift, he was being forced to do the same.

The killer groaned and Bruce looked up from what he was doing and saw that the killer had cum all over his hand and all over the seat. He tried to pull his hand away from the mess but all at once his world turned upside down. His face was shoved down into the killer's lap, pressed up against the flesh of his thigh. Somewhere above him he heard the killer screaming but he couldn't make out what the sick son of a bitch was saying. He couldn't breathe, his face was being pushed down into the slick vinyl seat between the killer's legs. He struggled to get away, but the killer was too strong. Something sharp jabbed into the back of his neck. The pain of whatever it was broke through for just a moment and then everything began to slip away on a cloud. It felt like he was drowning, like he was somewhere beneath the ocean as waves pounded above. He tried to focus his thoughts, but he couldn't. The world turned from shadowed light to the purest, darkest black he had ever experienced.

Bruce fell back hard. The ground was filthy, but thankfully he fell well outside the patch of greasy nastiness where he had had his hand. His eyes flew open as he thumped down and bit his tongue. Looking up, he saw that he was sitting in the whitewash of his own headlights. The palm of his left hand was covered in a disgusting yellow goo that smelt like burnt ass. He wiped the hand off and frowned at the stain he left on his pants as he stood. The world swam as he gained his feet and he had to hold out his hands to steady himself. He spit out a mouthful of blood from biting his tongue and looked at his car.

He has Laurie, he thought. That much he knew for sure, and he knew that her time was short. The killer wasn't going to wait long to get to work on her once they arrived at the "killing point". Bruce staggered over to his car and called Shelby. The phone went straight to voicemail. He punched the hood.

"Motherfucker, you better call me back," he shouted into the phone after the beep as he dropped into his car. "The ass fuck has Laurie now. Fucking call me!"

Bruce hung up and tossed the phone onto his seat. He dropped his head against the steering wheel and took several deep breaths. The hard plastic dug uncomfortably into his forehead. His left hand smelled like fried food. He wiped the hand on his pants again. "She's still alive," he whispered through the steering wheel and into the darkness below where his feet rested. "I'm going to save her."

Bruce drove the car back up the alley and out onto the street. The traffic was light. He paused in the mouth of the alley unsure which way he should go. Nothing within the drift had told him where the killer went. He didn't even know if she was in the city still or even in the state of New York. He had no clues.

Sighing deeply, Bruce turned right and started down the street. He didn't really know why he turned right but it felt like the way to go. At a light, he hesitated before deciding to head back to Laurie's apartment. He parked out front along the curb and ran inside, not caring if some cop came along and put a parking ticket on his windshield.

The door to Laurie's apartment was still unlocked so he walked right inside. He was there to find something that belonged to her, something special that might connect him with her. He picked up a shirt next to the mattress and felt nothing. He tossed the shirt down and picked up a ballcap on the floor next to the mattress. It was a New York Yankee's ballcap. He hated the Yankees but set it on his head anyway.

Nothing happened. He turned the ballcap around, so the bill faced backwards, and the drift came upon him at once. This time the drift was no gentle trip but a wild rush through space that ended with him standing beside a much younger Laurie. She had to be no more the seven or eight. The ballcap he found sat on the head of a man that looked similar to her. *A brother? Her father?* he wondered. The man wore the cap backwards. A cigarette was planted at the corner of his mouth, the smoke rising above his head. Laurie was looking at him with a bright smile on her face. There was awe and wonder in her eyes. She looked so happy and innocent.

The drift shifted and Bruce was standing in front of a casket now. Laurie stood beside the casket, tears falling from her eyes. A woman with dark hair lay inside the casket. Flowers were clasped in her hands upon her chest. *She had to be Laurie's mother,* Bruce thought. The man who earlier wore the ball cap stood beside Laurie, holding her hand. Tears fell from his eyes as well. A stern looking woman stood beside the man. She resembled him in the face and the eyes. As Bruce studied her, he saw that there was anger and hate in her eyes. Bruce wondered if it was for the woman in the casket or for Laurie. A wave of sadness swept over him, and he suddenly felt himself falling away.

Bruce's eyes flew open and he tripped over the mattress on the floor. A mini sandstorm of dust leapt from the floor. The ballcap stayed on his head. He jumped up and ran out of the apartment, leaving the door open. He had what he needed. In the hallway, an old woman watched him take the steps two at a time. She waited until she heard the front door open and close. She waited until she was sure he was gone before she made her way down the hall and peered inside the open door to Laurie's apartment. A frown creased her face. There was nothing there to take. She closed the door and went back to her own apartment.

Billy parked his pickup in front of his old, dilapidated house. There was no driveway to speak of, so he simply parked in the grass across from the doorway. It was dark outside and darker still after he turned his lights off. He let himself out of the truck and went around to the passenger side door. The door opened with a loud squeak that echoed into the silence of the forest that surrounded his property. He let out a slow breath that puffed in front of him in a thin gray cloud. There was a sharp chill to the air.

Laurie sat motionless in the front seat of the truck. The only sign of life was the slow steady rise and fall of her chest. To anyone, she would have looked like she was sleeping. Her body was seat belted tightly, so she sat upright with her head simply tipped to one side so she looked like she could have just fallen asleep like that while her husband, or maybe her boyfriend, drove the two of them home.

Billy released the seatbelt with a click and Laurie slumped sideways, almost falling out of the truck. Billy caught her before she fell, scooping her up into his arms and carrying her unconscious body into the house. He paused at the bottom of the stairs to catch his breath before starting his climb. At the top of the stairs, he set Laurie down on the floor and dragged her body the rest of the way into his workshop. Once through the door, he left her sprawled out on the floor while he went about gathering the necessary tools for what came next.

Once Billy had everything set out that he would need, he used a pair of sharp scissors to cut away her clothing until she was completely naked. He threw the clothes into a trashcan beside the door. He would burn all of it all later, after he was finished creating his art.

Billy sat down beside Laurie's naked body after he finished, looking at her pale skin. He noticed that one of her breasts was slightly smaller than the other. Even the areolas were different sizes. He giggled at this and set a finger on the tip of one nipple, pressing down until she moaned from somewhere deep in her drug induced sleep. He grinned, watching the nipple pop back up, hard and stiff like a teeny tiny prick. He rolled the body over just enough to look at her back side. He grew stiff, just like the nipple had at his touch. The skin back there was so soft and smooth. He touched it gently, caressing it with the tips of his fingers. He longed to do more to the whore, would have done more, but before he had the chance, something unexpected happened. Billy slid down the slide.

Billy went for a ride through the darkness to the bottom of the slide. He hadn't been ready for the ride. It hadn't happened like this for a long, long time but he went with it just the same. Everything around him was swallowed up into the darkness until he reached the bottom of the big slide, and then suddenly he was thrust into the front seat of a strange car. Right away, Billy knew the car belonged to the other, to the stranger who could see inside his head sometimes.

In front of the car, Billy saw a street lit up by streetlights. It was the world on the other side of the windshield and the world was dark. A few cars drove by, and as they did, Billy realized he was back in the city. It was early morning. No later than three or four. Trucks and delivery persons drove through the neighborhoods making their early morning rounds.

The car came to stop at a light. The surroundings didn't look familiar, but it was the city. Through the windshield the traffic light looked like a tiny red moon of some far-off distant planet. Beside him, fingers drummed. Billy turned his head enough so he could look at the other. He giggled into his hands.

"I have your whore," he whispered at the other, looking into the rearview mirror at a set of strange blue eyes. The eyes, belonging to the other. They gazed back hard at him. They were opened wide, clouded by confusion and a bit of shock. *He sees me now*, Billy thought, amazed at the idea that they could share the same space. He waved at the reflection in the mirror. The other did not wave back.

Bruce sat at a light waiting for it to turn green. Beside him sat his silent cellphone. He wanted to scream at it again because Shelby hadn't called back yet, but he didn't. He looked out the windshield while drumming on the steering wheel. *Where the fuck are you?* he thought, scared and worried about Laurie, feeling helpless and out of control.

Bruce reached for the phone again, ready to call Shelby, but something interrupted him. He felt a presence inside his head. He heard a faraway voice from somewhere distant whispering something that he couldn't make out. Slowly, he glanced up into the rearview mirror, half expecting to see a ghost in the backseat, but there was no one there. His eyes looked panicked in the reflection from the mirror. He looked away and drove through the intersection, pulling over to a free space along the curb. After putting the car in park, he leaned his head back against the headrest, and closed his eyes, forcing everything from his mind. The sounds of his automobile, the sounds of passing cars. Everything was cleared away, every thought, every worry, every concern. He pushed it all away until there was nothing but him.

The drift came over him like a punch in the gut. It was sudden and painful. He heard himself screaming into a darkness where he couldn't even see his hands in front of his face, and even worse, he knew he wasn't alone there.

"Where is she?" Bruce shouted into the darkness. A shadowy figure appeared before him. He couldn't see anything else in the dark, but he could see the figure as if it existed outside the darkness. It was the killer. He had no face, no real shape, but it was him just the same. It was like he could feel his essence polluting the world where only the two of them existed at the moment.

"Why is this one so important?" the shadowy figure asked, his voice very nasal. "She is nothing but unworthy trash to be disposed of and displayed as an example to the shadow people. They must know that I alone execute the judgment of God upon the worthless sinners of this world."

"Who are you?" Bruce asked, trying to move closer but the distance didn't change.

"I Am," the killer replied. "When they ask who sent you, say that I Am has sent you," the killer said. Gray smoke appeared, swirling around him in a whirlwind.

"You're no God," Bruce said. "You're not the God of the Old Testament or the New. In fact, you're nothing but a sick psycho killer that I'm going to stop."

"You cannot stop me," the killer shouted, and Bruce felt his world shift as if the killer's words had enough shape and form to drive him away. "I have your whore and soon she will be nothing but a reminder to the shadow people of this world that everyone is worthless and unworthy before me."

Bruce lurched for the figure, and something gave way between them but when he looked up, he came away with nothing but wisps of smoke. Shrieks of laughter echoed all around him like physical blows to the body.

"You're going to have to do better than that," the killer teased from somewhere in the darkness, his voice rising an octave. Bruce screamed, feeling himself being drawn away. The drift shifted.

When things came back into focus, Bruce found himself standing outside somewhere. It was dark but he saw trees and shadows crawling across the ground. In fact, he saw lots of trees surrounding an open field, and in the middle of that field was a rundown house. He was outside the city somewhere, just not sure where. He took a step toward the house. The ground was soft beneath his feet. The air was cold, colder than it was in the city. He took another step toward the house, and another, and another until he could make out the faded white paint, chipped and peeling away. The house felt abandoned. He took a step toward the front door of the house and his eyes flew open.

Light traffic drove by on the street outside his car. A man was walking his dog on the sidewalk. The man glanced sideways into Bruce's car while the dog hiked his leg on the back tire of the car in front of him. Bruce watched the dog walker continue down the sidewalk, disappearing around the corner.

Bruce closed his eyes and counted to ten before opening them again. He took a slow steadying breath and let it out as he removed the ballcap from his head, clutching it tightly between his hands, hugging it to his body. The only thoughts running through his mind were about Laurie and the danger she was in. He had an image of her in his mind from earlier that day. A slight smile crossed his face and he held onto that image, forcing away all thoughts of the killer, the house he had seen, or the other women that had died by the killer's hands. The only thoughts he allowed were of about Laurie until a thought came out of the darkness where he drifted. This new thought came to him like an animal caught in a trap, clawing its way to freedom. The thought dropped from his brain and rolled along his tongue waiting to be born. Over his lips, the thought emerged and formed into the world as a single spoken word.

"North," Bruce whispered into the stillness of his car. His voice had a thin quality to it as he spoke the word into existence. "I have to head north of the city," he whispered, putting the car into drive and pulling away from the curb.

Bruce allowed nothing else to cloud his mind as he drove down the street. He didn't think or consider where he should go, he just simply went. Left here, right there. He followed his instincts and the silent whispers from somewhere deep inside his mind. All he did was drive down one street, up another, over a bridge, and out of the city. The feeling he felt was like having an internal GPS running in the background of his brain. He was just an instrument being used by whatever force was controlling this thing that he could do. This gift from God as Father Murphy called it. Bruce prayed if it was in fact a gift from God, then he prayed it would lead him to wherever Laurie was before it was too late.

Releasing himself to whatever force or power that was leading him, Bruce eventually found himself driving down the darkened roads of Upstate New York. It had been over two hours since he left the bright lights of the city well behind and he had no idea where he was, but that didn't bother him because he wasn't the one in control right now. This drift-enabled GPS was in control, and it funneled all the directions from somewhere beyond his understanding, and he was okay with that. God, Buddha, or Ronald MacDonald, whatever it was, was in charge, and he was only along for the ride right now.

As he continued to drive, he noticed that the sunrise wasn't all that far away now. The sky off to the east had that soft glow that only came with the coming of dawn. Trees towered all around him on either side of the roadway. They hovered over the asphalt, forming a canopy of branches overhead that threw fleeing shadows before the lights of his car. If he hadn't been so worried about Laurie, he might have enjoyed this drive into the countryside. It reminded him of summertime trips with his brother and his mother. His mom loved taking drives through the countryside, exploring far off locations, discovering new adventures for the two of them to experience, and sometimes turning blindly down a dirt road and following it to wherever it led. This was nothing out of the ordinary for them. Even at such a young age these trips he took with his brother and his mother had made such an impact on the man Bruce would become one day.

All at once the directions stopped filtering into his mind. One moment he knew where to go, and the next there was nothing. In the slight glow of dawn, Bruce looked around and he saw what looked like a narrow dirt driveway some twenty feet behind him. He eyed the driveway in his rearview mirror for a minute, waiting to see if anything else was going to come to him, but nothing did.

The road he was stopped on was empty and dark beneath the overhead branches. He hadn't seen another car for a while now. Dark shadows drifted through the trees along the roadside in the glow of his headlights. He pulled further to the side of the road and tossed the car into park. Opening the door allowed a chilled draft of air into the car that caused goosebumps to crawl up his arms. He could see his breath as he exhaled. The shadows filling the gaps between the trees felt as if they were creeping toward him now that the lights of his car had been extinguished. He snatched up his phone from the seat and saw there was no cell reception. Sighing, hoping Shelby got his messages, he stood and walked back to the driveway, leaving his car parked on the side of the road. Leaves crinkled beneath his feet as he walked along the side of the road. At the driveway, which was really no more than an overgrown dirt track, he peered into the deeper shadows that hid everything beyond. "Fuck," he whispered, shivering some as he shoved the cellphone into his pocket.

Bruce walked back to his car and opened the trunk. A dim light came on from beneath the lid, revealing what lay there among the trash and a spare tire. Moving some of the trash aside, He grabbed a flashlight, a notepad, and extra bullets for his gun. After checking to make sure the weapon was loaded, he shoved the gun into the back of his pants. It felt like it weighed a thousand pounds back there digging into the skin of his back. He could feel its deadly presence, the coldness of the blued steel. He reached up to close the trunk but paused and removed a blue fanny pack from a crate. It was a homemade first aid kit. He strapped the fanny pack to his waist, making sure the hand drawn red cross on the front stood out so if someone found him injured, they would know what to do.

Bruce walked around to the front of the car and scrawled a note on a sheet of paper from the notepad he took from the trunk of his car. He placed the note under a windshield wiper. "Call Federal Agent Jerrod Shelby of the FBI if you find this note and I haven't returned to my car by eight o'clock in the morning. Tell Agent Shelby where you found my car and let him know that Bruce Westman left this note." Bruce made sure the note was secured and walked back to the driveway.

Looking into the shadows again, Bruce thought he could see a little bit further down the overgrown dirt track. Sighing, he started down the driveway without using his flashlight. It was still dark enough outside that the shadows hid him as he walked, but that darkness was slowly beginning to lighten. He wanted to keep his approach a secret for as long as possible. He was ready to dive into the trees if a vehicle should approach. Above him, birds began to twitter in the trees.

A hundred feet in, he stopped and looked over his shoulder. He couldn't see the roadway from where he stood. He turned on his flashlight, cupping his hand over the end, and shined it down at the dirt driveway. There were fresh tire tracks in the overgrown weeds. Someone had been this way, and it hadn't been all that long ago. He turned the flashlight off again and shoved it into one of his pockets. A hundred feet further on, he stopped again. A rust covered chain hung across the driveway between two faded white poles. Padlocks held the chain in place. A no trespassing sign hung down from the center of the chain. The sign was old, but the words were still very legible. "Trespassers will be prosecuted." Bruce ignored the warning and stepped over the chain, continuing down the driveway. An owl hooted in the distance as if offended that he had ignored the warning. The sound the owl made in the quietness of the early morning caused more goosebumps to populate his arms.

Some outdoorsmen you are, he thought to himself. The owl hooted again as if laughing at him after reading his thoughts. Bruce flipped his middle finger up in the direction of the hoot and continued walking.

A quarter of a mile in the driveway opened up to an overgrown field. A rundown farmhouse stood in the middle of the field. In the dusky light of early dawn, the house looked gray and foreboding. All the windows were dark and empty. Everything about the house felt lifeless and abandoned, haunted. A dark blue Ford Ranger pickup sat parked in front of the house. Bruce felt for his gun in the small of his back, reassuring himself that it was still there. He slipped his phone from his pocket and looked down at the screen. There was still no signal. A thought occurred to him, and he tried to find a phone application, hoping it might let him know if Laurie was there or not. The tiny circle just spun and spun. Sighing, he shoved the cellphone back into his pocket and stepped in among the shadows of the trees at the edge of the field, studying the house.

Chapter 30

Billy was inside his workshop. Laurie lay face down on top of his wagon wheel. Her legs were spread wide apart, and her arms were spread up over her head. Billy had just finished securing her feet to the wheel and was ready to do the same to her legs when she began to stir. The fentanyl was finally beginning to wear off, but he didn't mind now. He knew from experience that it would still be some time before she was awake enough to do anything like fighting back, and he enjoyed it when they screamed and begged. It always made him hard and added to the experience. He licked his lips and smiled in anticipation.

"Wakey wakey, eggs and bakey," Billy whispered beside the whore's head. His tongue flicked out and drilled into her ear. Her eyes blinked several times, and she twisted her head to the side, away from his probing tongue. Billy grinned and prepared to secure her left leg to the wagon wheel. They were always so much fun when they were like this, drifting somewhere between wakefulness and drugged sleep. They belonged to him completely.

The slide that came upon him now was a total surprise. It was something that he hadn't prepared for so when it hit him like a sledgehammer his naked body simply fell on top of Laurie's naked body. A whoosh of oxygen raced out from between her lips as his full weight fell upon her. The shock of the killer's weight helped her revive from the fentanyl much quicker than she normally would have. Her eyes flew open in a terrified panic.

While Laurie woke up, Billy slid through the darkness until he reached the bottom of his slide. It was there at the bottom as the world came into focus that he saw the other one. The other was hiding among a stand of trees covered by shadows and darkness, but he was there just the same. Overhead the sky was beginning to lighten. The day was just beginning to take shape. Billy tried to see what the other was looking at and saw it was an overgrown field with a house somewhere in the middle of the field.

"No!" Billy shouted, realizing that the other was hiding inside the trees that hid his property from the roadway. "Motherfucker, I'll kill your trespassing ass!" Billy screamed, trying to claw his way back up his slide before the other noticed him ease dropping.

"Go for it, shitbag," Bruce whispered, flipping his middle finger at Billy's retreating image. The shock of his discovery was enough to push him free of his slide.

Billy came back from the slide all at once and sat up quickly, forgetting all about the whore beneath him. He ran from his workshop, gathering up his clothing as he went. In the hallway he dressed quickly before racing down the stairs, the slap of his footsteps following him as he went.

Laurie felt the weight of her abductor lift off of her, but she held her breath just the same. She kept quiet, listening to the sounds of her kidnapper as he ran down the stairs. She didn't know what had happened, but she was thankful he wasn't in the room with her any longer. She kept still until she was sure the man wasn't inside the house with her any longer.

Laurie opened her eyes slowly to the stillness that surrounded her now, twisting her head as much as she could in each direction to look around the room. Even though she had heard him run down the stairs and out the door, she was scared it had all been a trick. As she looked around, she was sure he would be standing right there ready to attack her.

"Thank God," she whispered at the floor only inches from her face when she saw she was alone in the room. She tried to twist her body around, but she couldn't move. Taking a breath, she tried pushing herself up but that only made the room spin and all she could manage was a few inches before the ropes that held her stopped her. Giving up, she settled back down. *Smaller efforts*, she thought, twisting her feet at the ankles. Her left foot came free after a few minutes, followed by her right foot. Kicking her right foot out, she created enough slack that her leg came free, and her knee dropped to the floor between the spokes. She followed this with her left leg. Now, with both knees free and on the floor, she pushed up with everything she had inside of herself and the ropes around her arms loosened enough that she was suddenly and painfully free.

Looking beneath her, Laurie saw that she had been tied to an old chipped and rusted wagon wheel that looked like it had come off a stagecoach a hundred years ago. She searched the room quickly for her clothes, but they were nowhere to be seen. She stood on stiff legs and walked barefoot through the trash on the floor to the door. The old wood floor beneath her feet was cold. Goosebumps covered her body. She hugged herself tightly.

Laurie stood in the doorway looking down a short hallway. She half expected to find the man standing out there, but he wasn't. What she saw was a flight of stairs to her right and three closed doors to her left. Cautiously, she stepped out into the hallway. All she wanted to do was run down the stairs and escape, but she knew that wasn't the smartest thing to do right now. *There could be others,* she thought.

Laurie stepped to the left and opened the first closed door. In the dim light of early dawn, she saw this first room was a filthy bathroom. A large claw-footed tub sat against the far wall. The enamel was chipped and stained with rust and other gross things. The tub was full of liquid gore that was nothing but a disgusting swirl of red, yellow, and white. Broken pieces of bone and strands of hair floated inside this swirling mess. Beside the tub there were old, rusted buckets, caked in dried blood and human waste. Much of what was inside the buckets had spilled out onto the bathroom floor. Flies buzzed everywhere and the odor was so overwhelming that she gagged. She covered her mouth and nose with one hand to keep from vomiting and closed the bathroom door.

Standing outside the bathroom, Laurie took several steadying breaths before going further down the hallway. At the next door, she twisted the knob and the door opened up to a room she never expected to see inside the house after the bathroom and the room she had been held in. This room was so clean it was spotless. After what she had seen in the bathroom, this room seemed like it existed on another planet. The only piece of furniture in the room was a simple wooden chair that sat in the middle of the room. The walls were adorned with pictures hung perfectly aligned, side by side. Laurie stepped into the room for a better look and saw right away that there was something wrong with all those pictures on the walls. The frames didn't contain photos or drawings. Instead, they held what looked like tanned leather hides. She thought of all the women killed with patches of skin missing from their backs and realized what it was pinned beneath glass inside the frames. *So, so many frames displayed on the walls.* She thought.

"Holy shit," Laurie whispered, and vomited all over the floor. Snot ran over her upper lip, but she hardly noticed as another wave of vomit exploded from her mouth. "This is what this sick fuck has been doing," she groaned, wiping at her mouth with the back of her hand. *This is what he had been planning to do with me,* she thought as she took another step inside the room and dropped to her knees. Tears ran from her eyes. When she was able, Laurie stood and looked out into the hallway. Her eyes were wide with fear.

Where the fuck did he go? she wondered, hurrying out of the room, not bothering to close the door. Cautiously, she made her way down the stairs, peering over the railing, making sure he wasn't waiting there in the dark somewhere. On the first-floor landing, she paused, listening to the sounds of the house. It felt empty. She crept to the front door and opened it, looking outside, across a field of tall grass. She saw something at the far end of the field, saw someone.

"Bruce?" she whispered. She saw Bruce in the early morning light stepping out from the trees. He stopped and waved his arms at her before going into a jog through the high grass. He didn't move quickly because the grass was hindering him, but he was closing the gap between them. Laurie felt her spirits rise. She stepped outside and crossed the small front porch, waving back at Bruce. In her excitement she almost failed to see another figure stepping out from the trees behind Bruce. *It's him,* her mind screamed. *It's the sick fuck who drugged me and dragged me out here.*

Laurie took a breath to shout a warning to Bruce, but a gunshot shattered the silence. The gun sounded so incredibly loud as its boom echoed across the field. The sound hit her like a fist, but she kept her eyes on Bruce as he fell into the grass and disappeared as if swallowed up by something unseen from beneath the earth. Laurie screamed. The killer ran out into the field.

Billy had left the house through the back door, crawling through the grass, making sure to keep out of sight until he reached the trees. Once safely hidden among the shadows, he worked his way around until he was behind the other. As he prepared to attack, he saw the whore at the front door, standing on the porch waving her arms and knew he had to act quickly before the other reached her and ruined everything.

Billy crept closer as this other began to make his way through the field toward his whore. The tall grass kept him from running across the field, but he was moving quickly. *Fucker, fucker, fucker,* Billy thought, hating this man more than he had ever hated any other living thing.

Billy left the safety of the trees, stopping several feet in front of them. He drew a small, .38 caliber revolver from his pocket and pointed the gun at the other. Over the hard metal sights, he saw the whore getting ready to shout a warning. He pulled the trigger. The other fell, disappearing into the grass. The whore screamed. Billy grinned and started running as best he could toward where he had seen the other fall.

One moment, Bruce was picking his way across the overgrown field. He saw Laurie on the other side of that field and knew he had to get to her. For some reason, she was standing there naked in front of the rundown farmhouse waving her arms at him. *She's alive,* he thought. He didn't know where the killer was, but he was determined to get Laurie to safety and worry about him later. As he lifted his leg, a shot rang out. He heard it thunder toward him, and while at the same instant feeling something hotter than the sun tear through his shoulder. The force of that something knocked him to the ground like the hardest punch he had ever felt. All the air exploded from his body. He heard himself gasping for breath. Cold wet dirt filled his mouth. He couldn't move his left arm and it was then that he knew that he had just been shot. "Fuck me," he grunted, holding his left arm tightly to his body. Blood quickly soaked through his shirt and ran down his back. "Get moving," he whispered through clinched teeth.

I've been motherfucking shot, Bruce thought, low-crawling through the grass, working his way toward Laurie and the house. The bones in his shoulder grated against each other. He wanted to scream but used that pain to focus everything on moving forward. In the distance he heard someone screaming, and behind him he heard someone running through the field. The person running was much closer than the person screaming. Bruce rolled over onto his back, ignoring the lightning of hot pain slamming through his body. He drew his gun, pointing it up through the grass, and waited. A figure appeared from out of the shadows. Without bothering to aim, Bruce pulled the trigger four times. Shell casings flew through the air. The figure that appeared disappeared. He didn't know if he had shot the bastard or not.

Ignoring how much pain he was in, Bruce managed to stand and run away from the house to the trees. He didn't see the killer, but he didn't want to take the time to search for him either. If he was still out there somewhere, alive, he wanted to lead him away from Laurie. Another shot rang out. He heard the round crash through the branches just above his head. He cut to the left and ran as fast as he could, each step sending a tidal wave of pain through his shoulder. Branches and leaves slashed at his face, but he didn't feel any of the damage they were causing as he ran through the woods. Behind him, he couldn't hear the killer, but he knew he was out there somewhere. Cutting to the left, he leapt over a small stream at the bottom of a slight hill. Another shot rang out, followed by another. Bruce slipped and fell, slamming his forehead into a stone. Bright white stars flashed in his head. The pain in his shoulder leapt to a whole new level. He fought to remain conscious.

Billy ran after the other, firing at him every chance he had. The man was quick, much quicker than he was, but he knew the area better. He smiled when he saw the other fall after jumping across the stream. He didn't know if he had shot him again or he had fallen on his own, but he slowed just the same, cautiously approaching the water. Holding the gun in front of him, Billy pointed it at the other from the edge of the stream. He really felt like Billy the Kid as he stood there looking down at the other.

Billy had no idea how many bullets he had left in his gun, and he didn't want to take the time to look. His shoes were soaked. The water was cold. The other lay on the upward slope of a small hill going away from the stream. He was still. He might even be dead. Billy smiled. *I got you now,* he thought.

From the front yard of the farmhouse, Laurie watched Bruce and the killer run into the woods. She heard more gunshots and cringed with each one. She ran across the small yard and out into the field, ignoring the fact that she was completely naked. She ran through the tall grass only thinking about Bruce and how he had risked his life for her. She ran into the woods, following the sounds of the two men running somewhere in front of her. She moved quickly on her bare feet, feeling no pain as she went. She heard a shot and in the shadowed light, saw Bruce fall. Her heart stopped. From where she stood, she watched the killer cross a stream, pointing his gun at Bruce.

Laurie took two steps and stopped, picking up a stone the size of a softball from the ground. She hefted the stone in her hand and slowly made her way toward the killer. At the water's edge, she didn't even hesitate. She walked into the frigid water, hardly noticing it at all. Her eyes, her whole being, was focused on the killer. She wondered how he couldn't hear the sound of her heart beating like a jackhammer inside her chest as she snuck up behind him.

"I told you I couldn't be stopped," Billy shouted at Bruce's motionless body. "I told you that I was the final judgement."

Bruce heard the words, but they didn't make any sense to him. They were just words being spoken from out of the darkness. They seemed to come from so far away that they held no power over him. His head hurt. His shoulder hurt. These things had power, but the voice speaking these words from somewhere on the other side of the darkness, didn't. He tried to move enough so he could see, but for some reason it was just too dark outside, and then he realized his eyes were closed. He opened one eye slowly and the most horrible pain shot through his body. It felt like someone had stuck a flaming torch into his shoulder.

You've been shot, dumbass, he thought to himself, swallowing hard. There was something else hurting. Not as much as his shoulder, but enough to make itself known. *I'm so fucked,* he thought.

The voice continued speaking from somewhere, but he couldn't make sense of what the voice was saying. It just wasn't important at the moment. Bruce tried to sit up again, but something was jabbing at his stomach. He focused on that instead of the voice and realized whatever it was, was held in his hand. At this realization a thought took shape in his clogged mind, and a hard smile crossed his face. *I have a fucking gun*, he thought to himself, rolling over onto his back.

Billy stopped shouting when he saw the other begin to move. He fired his gun and watched as the bullet punched a hole into the other's hip. Blood exploded from the wound. Billy giggled, jumping up and down and then his world went completely sideways as something blasted into the side of his head. He fell to his knee, the gun slipping from his hand. Stars filled his vision as he tried to shake off whatever it had been that crashed into his head.

Laurie stood behind the killer as he screamed at Bruce's motionless body. She was right behind the killer when he shot Bruce again. She swung the stone as hard as she could, enjoying the satisfying crack as it smashed into the killer's head. The killer fell to a knee. Blood ran from the side of his head. Laurie dropped the stone and ran past him. She ran to Bruce's side. Blood was pouring from his hip and his shoulder. He didn't look good at all. The color was quickly draining away from his face. She cradled him in her arms.

"You fucking cunt!" Billy bellowed as he slowly gained his feet again. He wobbled and the world spun but he stood there just the same. "I will fucking rip your fucking soul from your fucking body."

Laurie heard the killer speaking but ignored the words he was saying. He was just one of so many men who had said so many hurtful things to her over the years that none of it mattered any more. Her eyes were focused on the gun lying in the dirt beside Bruce. The firearm sat on top of decaying leaves and fallen twigs. The grip was covered in Bruce's blood. The firearm called to her.

Without looking over her shoulder at the killer, Laurie threw her body over Bruce's as if to shield him. She heard the high-pitched laughter behind her as her hand snaked around Bruce's body, her fingers clawing through the scattered leaves and twigs until they felt the cool smooth metal of the gun. She grasped the weapon and rolled off of Bruce, coming up into a two-handed grip, pointing the gun at the killer.

"Die, asshole!" she screamed, pulling the trigger over and over until the slide locked back.

Billy never saw the whore roll off the other's body. He didn't see her until he heard her speak, but by then it was too late. White hot pain crashed into his chest, into his stomach, and again into his chest. He fell back after the third shot, tumbling into the stream. The water felt so good against his skin as it crawled up and around him. All he could do was lie there looking up through the trees as the light of the morning sun began to poke through the canopy. Shafts of light stabbed at the forest, sparkling off the dew clinging to the leaves.

Billy sighed as he watched the new day dawn. His head sank beneath the water and his vision blurred. He tried to bring his face back above the surface of the stream, but he didn't have the strength to do it. He felt himself begin to slide and wondered if it would be Heaven or Hell that he saw at the bottom this time.

Chapter 31

Laurie pressed her hands over the gunshot wound to Bruce's hip because it bled worse than the gunshot to his shoulder. Her hands were covered in his blood, but she forced herself to ignore it. The way the wound was bleeding she thought the bullet might have hit an artery or something, but what did she know, she was just a whore.

Bruce lay unconscious just uphill from the stream. His breathing was labored. Laurie thought he was dying. She thought he was going to die right there with her hands pressed against his hip. Tears fell freely from her eyes. Snot ran from her nose. She ignored all of it and focused on Bruce.

"Don't you fucking die on me," she cried, pressing harder. Her arms began to shake.

Laurie heard something in the distance. It made a chop, chop, chop sound that grew louder as whatever it was drew closer. She looked up through the trees and saw a helicopter flying low overhead. It flew just above the tops of the trees circling slowly. She lifted a hand and waved. Several minutes later, a tall black man cut his way through the trees. He had a gun in one hand and his cellphone in the other. It was Agent Shelby. Laurie screamed. Agent Shelby ran toward her. She saw others running behind him.

"Hang in there, Bruce," Laurie cried. "The cavalry has arrived."

Chapter 32

Bruce opened his eyes and knew immediately that he was in a hospital. After his time in Iraq, he considered himself very familiar with their smells and sights. They all had that lingering death odor and the same industrial white walls. The beeps and dings also gave it away. Sighing, he turned and saw Laurie sleeping in a chair beside his bed. Behind her, sunlight filtered through drawn blinds causing creepy shadows to crawl over the walls. Swallowing, he forced his eyes away from the shadows and their hidden threats.

An IV pole stood beside his bed with tubes running back toward his right arm. Wires snaked out from his body like so many strings controlling a marionette. Lights on monitors blinked and blipped. A crooked green line marked each beat of his heart. Thankfully, he felt nothing. No pain, no worries, no cares. He wasn't even sure that he was alive. *I could be seeing all of this from above,* he thought. *Maybe that's why I feel no pain.* He licked his lips and tried to speak, but before he could form any words, he fell back to sleep.

Bruce woke again several hours later. The room was darker, but light still peeked around the blinds. The shadows around the window had melted away or maybe they were simply absorbed by the walls. Laurie was gone, her chair empty. Three balloons floated up above his bed, tied to one corner of the bed. The balloons bounced up and down from the overhead vent in the ceiling.

There were words printed on the balloons, but he couldn't make out what they said. He looked past the end of his bed and saw Jeffrey standing by the door, talking quietly into his cellphone. He looked exhausted.

"Hey," Bruce rasped, feeling the pain of his words. His throat felt like someone had used a Brillo Pad on it. Jeffrey turned and smiled. The phone fell away from his face.

"Hey asshole," Jeffrey said, but Bruce failed to hear him speak because he drifted back asleep.

Bruce woke again sometime later, and this time he felt pain and the world felt very real. There was so much pain attacking his body that he lay there wishing he hadn't woken up. Laurie sat in her chair again and Jeffrey stood by the window. He swallowed. His throat felt like it was on fire.

"He's awake," Laurie said, smiling down at him. She stood and leaned over the bed.

"Something, for the pain," Bruce groaned. Laurie pressed the call button, and a nurse came into the room.

"Mr. Westman," the nurse said. "It's so good to see you awake." The nurse shot something into his IV. She wrote something on a chart. "That should help. Call if you need anything." She left the room.

The pain eased after several minutes, and he could focus. For the first time he noticed that his left shoulder was bandaged and strapped down to his body. He remembered being shot in the woods. He closed his eyes and tried to remember the rest of what happened but couldn't. "The killer?" he asked, licking cracked lips and looking at Laurie.

"Dead," Jeffrey said. "This little lady here killed him deader than shit." Laurie blushed and looked away. Bruce nodded slightly.

"Thank you," Bruce said. "Can you sit the bed up, please?"

Laurie set the bed up a bit and Bruce sipped some water and crunched a few ice chips. He thought it was the best thing he had ever had in his entire life. It was even better than vodka. He saw another large bandage around his hip. The pain there was a five right now on a one to ten scale. He sort of remembered being shot a second time, but everything was still foggy. "What happened?" he asked, closing his eyes and swallowing hard.

"Well for starters, someone found that note you left on the car. They called Shelby and Shelby sent in the troops. He got there just in time to save your life. You owe him, big time," Jeffrey explained.

"What else?" Bruce asked.

"Later," Jeffrey said. "You need to rest and recover. I'll let Shelby fill you in on what they found at the farm." Bruce wanted to argue but he didn't have the strength, so he nodded. His head fell back against the pillow, and his eyes slipped closed. He slept for the rest of the night. Laurie stayed by his side all night long.

Agent Shelby walked through the door to Bruce's room the next morning. Laurie stood, yawned, and stretched. "I'm going out front for a smoke," she said, leaving Bruce and Shelby in the room together.

It was nine o'clock in the morning. A bowl of tasteless oatmeal and lightly toasted bread sat on a tray along with a small glass of orange juice. Bruce had barely touched any of it.

"Hospital food," Shelby said, pointing at the tray.

"Tastes like shit," Bruce groaned, pushing the tray out of his way. Shelby stood beside the bed. There was a thin grin on his face as he looked down at Bruce. Bruce didn't return the grin.

"Sorry about the phone," Shelby said. "I was on a date with my wife and off the clock for the night. I never gave you any of the other numbers to the unit if you had to reach me. Totally my fault."

"Fuck you," Bruce said. He squirmed around in the bed until he felt comfortable enough.

"Okay, fuck me," Shelby replied, pausing until Bruce settled back down. "My balls are big enough. I can take it. Besides, you caught the asshole, so there is that." Bruce flipped Shelby the bird with his good hand. "They dug up six bodies buried on that old farm to go along with the six that he left in the parks in the city. He was a very busy boy. The docs say that the oldest corpse has been out there for over three years, and the newest addition, less than a week. The press is calling him the Rosary Killer, but he called himself Billy the Kid or some dumb shit like that. There was a notebook in his art studio where he left times and dates. If each entry corresponds with a death, then he was probably responsible for more than thirty deaths."

"Art studio?" Bruce asked.

"Yeah, that's what they're calling the room where he kept his collected pelts. It was like something out of Doctor Demento's lab. Some real fucking sick shit"

"Thirty victims," Bruce said, amazed at the number.

"No one is really sure how many he might have killed over the years, and we'll probably never know. He started peeping at a young age. He had a juvie record for B and E and peeping at girls," Shelby explained.

"What about an accident or something. Head trauma maybe?" Bruce asked.

"Yeah, how did you know?" Shelby asked. Bruce didn't answer. Shelby continued. "In his twenties he was in a really bad accident with an eighteen-wheeler. He almost died." Bruce nodded. Shelby waited to see if he would say something more. He didn't. "Anyway, you did good, Westman. I really mean it. I have you listed as an official consultant now with the Bureau, so if you want to work with me again, I don't need to hide you, I just wouldn't recommend working with someone else. They wouldn't understand that voodoo shit that you do."

"Fuck you," Bruce said, sounding exhausted. "What about Laurie?"

"She's been here every day watching over you, driving the nurses crazy. You sure you haven't been hitting that?"

"No," Bruce sighed. "She's with me though. From here on out, we're a team, a package deal. If I ever work with you again, she's along for the ride." Shelby nodded.

"When you're ready, I'm going to need a statement from you," Shelby explained, stepping away from the bed. "Laurie has already filled me in on what happened out there, but I need something from you. You can leave the vision shit out of it, but I need something." Bruce nodded and flipped him off again. "It's good to see that your sense of humor didn't get shot off."

Bruce sat up in the bed. "I can do the fucking statement now," he said. "I'd rather get it over with so I can go home."

Shelby took out a recorder and set it on the tray table beside his bowl of oatmeal. Bruce took a deep breath and began to speak. In the end they decided to say that Bruce followed the signal from the find the phone application to the farm.

Chapter 33

Bruce was discharged from the hospital two days later. After being wheeled outside he had to use crutches to make his way over to Jeffrey's car. They drove over to the place where he had stayed in the Bronx to get his things. Laurie was standing outside the building with a brown paper bag in her hand and a cigarette dangling from her mouth. She stood on the top step, just outside the door looking badass in a maroon leather jacket, black jeans, and a white t-shirt. A thin cloud of gray smoke drifted just above her head like some satanic halo.

Laurie dropped the cigarette and smashed it beneath the toe of her foot before descending the steps. She met Jeffrey on the sidewalk and helped him get Bruce up the steps and up to his room. Bruce packed his stuff. Laurie made sure he didn't forget anything. She even checked under the bed before the three of them went back downstairs to the lobby. Bruce turned his key in at the desk. The clerk thanked him and asked him to leave a review on Google.

Outside the day was sunny but cool. Autumn had finally arrived for good in the northeast. The leaves were beginning to change colors, the days were growing shorter. Halloween was just around the corner. Jeffery and Laurie helped Bruce into his car. Laurie stood at the open door looking down at Bruce as he tried to make himself comfortable in the driver's seat.

"Did you mean what you said to me the other day?" Laurie asked, standing in the open door. Bruce nodded.

"Very much so," Bruce said.

"You ride with him," Jeffrey said. "Make sure he doesn't push it."

"I will," Laurie said, tucking the paper bag under one arm and walking around to the passenger side of Bruce's car. She opened the door and sat down.

"Is that all you have?" Bruce asked, eyeing the bag.

"Yeah, I didn't have much to begin with that I wanted to take with me. I gave most of my things to Betty." Bruce smiled.

"How's she doing?" Bruce asked, starting his car.

"She's okay. She's going to crash at my apartment for a while. I know it's not much, but it's better than sleeping on the street."

"Is she going to be, okay?" Bruce asked.

"She'll probably drink herself into an early grave, but yeah, she'll be okay," Laurie said.

Jeffrey pulled away from the curb and Bruce followed. They made their way through the city to the freeway, heading east toward Connecticut. Laurie lit a cigarette and blew the smoke out the window. Bruce smiled and drove. He didn't mind the cigarette at all.

Epilogue
Chapter 1

Bruce walked through the vestibule and into the sanctuary of Saint Christopher's Catholic Church. The shadows of long deceased saints crawled along the walls whispering their prayers into the rafters. The air was stale. Motes of dust floated through thin shafts of light filtering through the stained-glass windows. The silence inside the church felt heavy and lonely, full of lost sins confessed and hopeless prayers made to long dead saints. Father Murphy sat in the front pew with his head turned up to the large wooden cross and the crucified Christ looking down from it at the pews. Bruce sat down beside the old priest, setting his cane against the pew.

"Forgive me Father for I have sinned," Bruce said, setting a hand on the priest.

"You're forgiven my son," Father Murphy said. "Now learn how to forgive yourself." Bruce smiled and followed the priest back to his office. They sat down across from each other and shared coffee and donuts. Neither spoke while they drank and ate. The silence was comfortable, familiar.

"So how have you been?" Father Murphy asked, tossing his trash into a can beside his desk.

"Good," Bruce said. "I'm healing. My hip hurts all the time, worse when the weather is about to change. I hate having to walk with a cane, but I'd fall over if I didn't."

"It sucks getting old," Father Murphy said.

"Yeah, well some of us are aging a lot faster than others," Bruce said. Father Murphy laughed. Bruce laughed with him.

"How is Laurie?"

"She's settling in," Bruce said. "I'm going to have to find a bigger place for us though. Sleeping on an air mattress has to suck. I've offered her the bed, but she won't take it."

"I bet it does suck," Father Murphy said. "But I think it's about time you moved into something nicer anyway."

"Yeah, maybe something in Manchester or Hartford," Bruce said.

"Matthew and his sister are doing much better now that school is well under way," Father Murphy said. "They come once a week now and Mary has even started to attend mass on Sundays. I think the two of them are going to be just fine."

"That's good," Bruce said, feeling a twinge of pain in his hip. He shifted in the chair and the pain eased.

"So, tell me how you're really doing," Father Murphy asked, leaning back in his chair to listen. Bruce nodded and began to speak.

Chapter 2

The girl was dressed in a schoolgirl's outfit. She wore a short plaid skirt, a tight white blouse with the top three buttons undone so that her cleavage was showing. Her hair was pulled back in twin ponytails on either side of her head. She wore white silk panties that clung to her ass and showed just the tiniest bit beneath the hem of her skirt. The client liked it that way. He always had them dress that way for him. He paid extra for the young ones.

The client arrived at the appointed time like he always did. He knocked on the hotel room door and she opened the door. He entered the room with long purposeful strides like he owned the place. She made sure not to meet his eyes. She always made sure to keep her head down because he liked it like that. He liked his girls young and submissive.

The client was a tall man, tanned, in his thirties. He was in excellent shape. He wore dark framed glasses with large round lenses that reflected the lights in the room. He liked all of the lights on inside the room. She wasn't sure if it was because he wanted to see all of her or because he wanted to see himself with her.

She didn't know the man's name. He never used one when he came to play. He always called her Beverly, though that wasn't her name, but she didn't mind. She wondered if Beverly had been an old high school girlfriend, or maybe the name of his daughter. The sickos loved to fantasize like that. It got their dicks hard to think that they were fucking their daughters or their stepdaughters.

"Beverly," the client said, closing the door and twisting the deadbolt. The click of the lock echoed loudly in the room. A shiver twisted its way down her spine. She was familiar with that tone of voice and what it meant. "I think we need to punish you tonight," the client said, his nose flaring.

"Yes master," Beverly said, walking over to the bed. She stood there, obediently, with her head down, eyes focused on the floor. The client sat down on the edge of the bed and patted his leg. She hiked up her skirt and lay across his legs, so her ass stuck up in the air.

The first smack across her buttocks felt like fire, but the pain faded with each smack that followed. When he finished, her ass was numb. The client tore off her white panties. He shoved a finger up her ass and stood. She remained bent over so he could guide her onto the bed like that. He fucked her hard from behind, crying out as he came inside her. She stayed bent over the end of the bed until he slipped out of her. He wiped himself off on her ass, smacking her one more time and pinching one of her nipples until she cried out, but she never looked at him. The client left her there like that and went into the bathroom. She didn't move, not even when some of his semen ran down her leg.

The client came out of the bathroom a few minutes later. He dropped down beside her on his knees and began to cry. She listened to him as he shed his fake tears without moving. This was something he always did as well. He fucked her again a short time later, this time pulling out and shooting his load all over her ass. It ran down between her crack, but she didn't do a thing about it. She just remained bent over the bed in case he wanted to do something else. The client liked it that way.

The client left a thousand dollars on the nightstand after he showered. He smacked her ass several more times and shoved a twenty into her pussy before walking out of the room. She waited for several minutes before getting up from the bed. She collected the money from the nightstand, and from inside her vagina before walking into the bathroom. She turned the shower on, letting it run while she stood in front of the bathroom mirror looking at her image in the reflection.

"Your name is not Beverly. You are not that sick fuck's daughter." She heard her words but had a hard time believing them. She stepped into the shower and scrubbed her body. Later, she walked out of the room and went down to the lobby. She paid the man at the front desk two twenties, one of which had come from inside her vagina. The man at the desk sniffed the bills and smiled. She flipped him off and walked out the door.

She got into the passenger door of a late model Buick. An African American male sat behind the wheel. He smiled at her with gold teeth and held out his hand. She handed him everything the client had paid her. He didn't bother counting the money, because he knew she would never cheat him. She didn't look into his eyes either. She knew better. Years of service to him had taught her the things she needed to do to survive.

Twenty minutes later they arrived at another hotel. He parked at the back of the lot.

"You go to the third floor, room 307. This guy likes them young and playful, if you know what I mean. Act shy but fuck him good."

"I will Reggie."

"If he asks your name, tell him Amy or something sweet like that. Play it all innocent and we'll make another thousand." She nodded and opened the door to the Buick. Reggie was already on his cellphone as she closed the door.

The desk clerk watched her go to the elevator and push the up button. She glared at him while she waited, and he flicked his tongue between two fingers spread apart. She flipped him off and got into the elevator. The doors opened on the third floor, and she walked down the hall. At room 307 she stopped and knocked lightly. The door opened right away. A man grabbed her arm and yanked her into the room.

"Hi, I'm Amy," she said. "And I've been a naughty girl." The man smiled and let go of her arm. She reached out and loosened the belt from his pants. The client's smile grew even wider because he liked it this way.

Acknowledgments

I want to thank John Fitts who read this story with a red pen in hand slicing and dicing all of my mistakes. If there are any mistakes left to be found, they are completely my fault. I want to thank my Dad who never had a chance to see me publish a book. Even though you are gone, Dad, I can still hear you telling everyone around you, "That's my boy, the author." In my head you sound just like Tim Allen waving a power tool over his head, grunts and all.

About the Author

C.L. Thomas grew up in Southern New England in the 70's playing outside every chance he could, and one of his favorite games was playing cops and robbers. Little did he know that as an adult, in the United Sates Army, and later for the City of Houston, he would get to play cops and robbers for real. On several occasions he would come home from work and tell his wife, "I would have done this for free." For eight years, C.L. Thomas was a member of a tactical unit in one of the worst parts of the city. Working alongside five highly trained and dedicated officers, C.L. Thomas put his life on the line every day for the citizens of Houston.

C.L. Thomas has been writing stories since he was a sophomore in high school growing up in East Hartford, Connecticut. He brings his gritty work world reality to the pages of *The Hollow*, painting a picture of the world that very few people ever get to see.